# ROCK 'N ROLL
# MAYHEM 1970

## Also by this author

*Three Faces of Sex*
*Sensual Sorcery: Natural Beauty and Health Recipes*
*Chakra Psychology: The World Within*
*Sex As The New Religion*

# ROCK 'N ROLL MAYHEM 1970

## *A Maui Wowie Rock 'N Roll Rave about Music, Love and Life on the Road*

Stella Ralfini

Copyright © 2020 Stella Ralfini

**_Book covers: George Pazalos_**

ISBN: 978-0-244-55767-6

PublishNation
www.publishnation.co.uk

# ROCK N ROLL MAYHEM 1970

www.rocknrollmayhem.com

## A Maui Wowie Rock 'N Roll Rave about Music, Complicated Love, and Life on the Road

It is 1970. **Laura**, a music lover, fashionista and sex enthusiastic, feeds heavy metal band '**Streetcrash**,' a pack of lies about her experience in the music biz and is taken on as their manager for a trial period.

She hates her day job and tyrannous boss but can't leave until money comes in from Streetcrash. Her nights are spent frantically trying to get them signed to a record label. Her guesswork and bluff techniques go against her. A landslide of spectacular events lead to a black eye, being sacked from her day job and rendered penniless.

Love complications, infatuations, betrayals pile up as Laura kicks on doors until Streetcrash are signed. Plunged into more unknown territory, she must organize a UK tour and take on role of psychiatrist to stop Monster (Streetcrash lead guitarist), jump from his window after hearing news of Jimi Hendrix's death.

On tour, while the gigs go from strength to strength, on the tour bus Laura comes close to insanity as she tries to discipline heavy metal delinquents, pranksters and divas.

There is a happy ending. With a surprise.

What I truly hope is that you enjoy the journey. Whilst Rock N Roll Mayhem is a work of fiction, I have woven facts and major happenings from 1970 throughout. The fiction is fast paced and brings to life the psychedelic, hippy love, flower power years I remember with such fondness, and would love to bring back.

# GLOSSARY OF ENGLISH SLANG WORDS USED IN ROCK 'N ROLL MAYHEM 1970

## JOIN THE PARTY AT: www.rocknrollmayhem.com

| | |
|---|---|
| Bugger | oh shit |
| Con | cheat |
| Cops | police |
| Cobblers | nonsense |
| Colly Wobbles | out of balance |
| Coming on like a heat rash | brazen |
| Have your guts for garters | give you a real thrashing |
| Keep your hair on | stay calm |
| On the pull | hoping the law of attraction works in your favour |
| Nutter | mad person |
| Piss off mate | get away from me |
| Prat | awkward person |
| Randy | horny |
| Rile | infuriate |
| Shagger | fond of sex |

| | |
|---|---|
| Slapper | not fussy who she beds |
| Slut | without morals |
| Sod's law | fate |
| Take a leak | urinate |
| Tea leaves | thieves |
| Turf | throw out |

# ONE

Scream rising from my throat to my mouth, I thumped my fists against the sink. *Damn the stallholder in Chapel Street Market who conned me into buying his pathetic ensemble!*

Some might have laughed it off. For me it was a nightmare come to life. I could see the stallholder's smarmy smile as he tugged on the leggings to assure me that they were as indestructible as a cockroach. I could hear his smarmy voice. *'You'll knock everyone dead in this Parisian leopard print ensemble. It's got class. Like you. And at the price I'm selling, it's peanuts.'*

Burning with rage, I glanced down at my bare expanse of thighs. A minute before, I was a proud fashionista, meticulously put together from backcombed beehive to winkle pickers that matched my leopard print outfit. Without leggings, the dress looked as short as a T shirt, showed off my unshaved legs and the worst part was that I couldn't lift a muscle without looking obscene. Why did it have to happen to me *that* night when I planned to go backstage after the gig and chat up the lead singer of Streetcrash? Looking like a slut, who would spend the evening fingers on hem to ensure she didn't reveal her private parts, that meeting was out of the question.

I tentatively raised my arms, hoping against hope, the view I'd seen before had mysteriously disappeared. I was in that standing position when a girl with brassy pink hair sauntered into the washroom. I gave my hemline a ladylike tug and watched as, teasing the ends of her hair into a blur of candyfloss, she rolled gum around her teeth and gave my hem a

1

sniff of contempt. 'If you're on the pull, you can go back where you came from.'

Fashion and image were my highest priorities along with being selective about who I shagged so I was outraged. Not only because she thought I was in her tatty league due to my fashion disaster but assumed I opened my legs for all and sundry. I raised my chin, sneered at her fluorescent plastic earrings, pink lurex mini then gave her scuffed heels a grunt of dismissal. 'I have absolutely no interest in any of the men who frequent your pub. Here you go. All yours.'

Brassy jutted out her chest 'I don't like the way you said that.'

'Look, Brassy. I won't be responsible for my actions if you keep going 'cos I'm *not* in a good mood. I waved her off. 'Leave it.'

Brassy rolled her fists on the verge of retaliating but noting the growl in my eyes, wiggled off defiantly.

'Honestly, Laura!' Debs announced as she marched in from wherever she disappeared to ten minutes earlier. 'You'll never believe what that so-called pub manager said.' She grimaced at the sink which had stale water floating around the plughole and poked me in the arm. 'When I asked why no-one cleaned the obscenities off the walls in the toilets, he said there was no point because they'd be covered in graffiti again before he scrubbed the old graffiti off.' Debs retrieved a travel size bottle from the hip purse she carried for emergencies and tipped disinfectant into her palms. 'Then, when I told him about the sanitary towel I found on the floor, he said women shouldn't behave like pigs and pointed to a sign behind the counter which said, "We have a five star award", to which I said, 'Who gave you that, the department of filthy sanitary towels?' Eyes in irate slits, Debs wiped her hands on her jeans. 'I don't know why you dragged me to this dump when I was happy sitting at home watching *Top of the Pops*. You know I hate heavy metal

2

music but on and on you went about how Streetcrash had been treated like criminals by the press and...' Debs stopped waving her arms and watched me tug furiously at my hem. 'You can't wear *that* without leggings. Do you know how *rude* it looks?'

'It's taken you three minutes of monologue about the pub manager, hygiene and Streetcrash to notice your supposed best friend is having a break down? Stop thinking of you. Think about me!' I waved my fake nails which were pointed like talons to match my leopard theme. 'I snagged my leggings on these and they disintegrated to nothing. It was like watching snakes catch fire as ladder after ladder ran up my legs from ankle to thigh. I've never seen anything like it.' Rocking with frustration I covered my eyes. 'Why didn't I wear knickers?'

Debs slapped my arms down to my sides. 'Because fashion means more to you than being sensible. Now look what you've got yourself into.' She sank to her knees to tease down my hem at snail pace as though a slower approach might reap better results. 'If you didn't have humungous breasts and such a big bum it wouldn't look so short. If I was wearing this, it would be down to my knees.' She glanced up my dress, then stood up and patted my arm. 'Stand with your arms pinned to your sides. Think owl or penguin.' I tutted at the air. 'My other suggestion,' Debs said. 'Is that we go home but since *you* wouldn't want that, you'll have to get used to looking like...' She flicked a finger at my thighs. 'A leopard with hairy legs.'

I wanted to rattle her skinny shoulders. Not only was she suggesting I stood like a stuffed owl, she had no idea how humiliating my fall to shame was. Debs might not care if *she* ended up looking like half a leopard with hairy legs because she had no sense of fashion in the first place. You only had to look at the clunky army boots she wore, designed for trudging through snake infested swamps and her *Ban the Bomb T-shirt* to know that.

'Why, tonight?' I asked. 'I wanted to go backstage and...'

'Let's see if you can get through the next hour – and stop tugging on your hem. What if that starts laddering?' Debs plastered her nose with her hand. 'The stink in these toilets is giving me migraine. Let's get some air until Streetcrash come on.'

That's how we ended up in the backyard of the Rat, which was deserted except for us and a pigeon perched on a washing line above our heads that couldn't decide which way to turn its bum. The yard was an untidy crate dump with little place to stand other than a meagre patch by the back wall. Still feeling sorry for myself, I leaned against it listening to the sound of constipated water fight its way through rusty pipes.

'Stop tugging on your hem and tell me about Djerba,' Debs said. She tipped disinfectant down a drain that was giving off the smell of sweaty boiling socks.

'I told you other night when I got back home.' I mumbled.

'You got as far as telling me about free bathrobes and passed out. I've hardly seen you since then.' She tilted her chin up to look up at me, which was normal when we went out since I wore stilettos and she wore flip-flops or army boots. Debs gazed at me, her eager eyes framed by a bobbed haircut that made me think of floppy Spaniel's ears. 'Tell me more about the hotel in Djerba? What did you write for the travel blurb?'

'This 4 star hotel has been built to look like a Tunisian palace,' I said without interest. 'The marble entrance hall has a fountain and Tunisian themed lounge area. Terrace bungalows are situated on our private stretch of silver sand. Each has its own spa bath and a love tent on the beach. The—"'

'Love tent? On the beach?' Debs excitedly grabbed my arm. 'That's *definitely* going on my honeymoon list.' She dug me in the ribs. 'So who did you shag in Djerba? Come on. Spill the beans.'

I'd stopped spilling the beans to Debs months before because I was sick of her lectures about me being a sex addict, usually accompanied by the telephone number of a psychiatrist. 'Too much work,' I lied. 'But yesterday, I bumped into a guy in Selfridges called Chris. He stopped me at the men's cologne counter to ask if I preferred Eau Savage or Brut.' I thought better of mentioning our quickie in Selfridges Hotel in case that set her off on a holy grail of motherly advice.

Debs attention was on the drain, which she covered with a layer of tissues to stop the stink attaching itself to her skin. 'Are you seeing him again?'

I nodded. 'On Sunday.'

Debs waved her engagement ring under my nose. 'Ooh that means you'll have seen him twice. Maybe this Chris will prove the one? You'll be thirty in seven years. Your penchant for penis needs to come to an end before all the good men are snapped up.'

'Listen virgin, as you say I'm a sex addict so each to their own.'

While Debs stood there looking wounded, I turned my attention to the music coming out from the jukebox. After ten minutes of suffering Engelbert Humperdinck and Lonnie Donegan, someone in the midst of heathens put on Respect by Aretha Franklyn. Just like that, my mood shifted. 'We love Aretha. We love this song. Let's do the routine we do at home'

Debs gleefully hopped on the spot, probably because I smiled for the first time in an hour. Stepping right then left we did hitchhike thumbs for the *Re Re Re* bit of the song then window wash arms for the *Just a little bit* part. As the song went along, arms above my head, I added exaggerated bum wobbles. 'HAHAPHWA.' Debs waved a finger. 'I can see your pubes'. Laugh fading from her face, she lunged at my hem. 'Make yourself decent. Someone's coming!'

I turned to see Monster, the lead singer of Streetcrash. With the raunchy raw gait of a cowboy, he swaggered towards us and nodded. 'How's it going?' he drawled.

I couldn't believe my luck. Monster wasn't just a phenomenal musician, singer and lyricist, he was number three on my 'must shag' list and who I wanted to chat up after the gig. I swayed my hips with a touch of class. 'Great'.

'Meet Laura your greatest fan.' Debs poked me as though Monster couldn't see me. 'Laura never stops raving about your music.'

Monster was so distracted he couldn't see me. I was nowhere on his radar screen. 'Yeah, shame more people don't know about you.' I gave him my seductive smile. He stared through me, glanced about to see who was watching and lit a cigar-sized spliff.

While he stood there puffing, his hooded, broody eyes scanning the sky, I had the chance to take a better look. His wild mane of shaggy blonde hair, parted in the middle and way past his shoulders, framed his chiselled chin and full lips. I could see in the light that he had acne under his stage make-up, but it didn't make him less shaggable. Far from it. He emphasized his hazel eyes by wearing smudgy green eyeshadow and either had a huge dick or something stuffed down his underpants. The way it strained against his black leather trousers held me mesmerised.

'Wanna hit?' Monster turned to face me again and vaguely waved his spliff.

As I took it, I slid my nails seductively over the back of his hand to make my feelings clearer. Monster's response was to shake his hand as if he had ants crawling through his fingers. It was obvious that losing my leopard legs had affected my sex appeal which wasn't coming across as normal. I had a few puffs of the spliff to loosen up. It hit my brain like a firecracker. Monster's weed was strong enough to get an elephant high and definitely not for lightweights like me and Debs. As I went to pass it back to Monster, she snatched it.

'This is Gooood!' Debs gushed, puffing on it like it was oxygen and the world had run out of air. 'Is it Moroccan?'

'Maui Wowie.' Monster waved his fingers to let Debs know he wanted it back.

*Bugger! Mauie Wowie was strong enough to get a herd of elephants off their trunks.* I jogged Deb's arm to try to make her hand it over but Debs held on, no intention of parting with her prize because to her Monster wasn't a heavy metal icon to be revered, but her passport to stoners' land. Her smile positioned itself on one side of her mouth. I knew that smile. We were in dangerous territory. Stoned Debs got wrecked, threw up, made a nuisance of herself and started inane conversations with anyone who would listen, although most victims found excuses to make quick getaways. I knew the only reason Debs had a captive audience in Monster was because she had his spliff. Twice he plunged at her; twice I kicked her in the shin, but Debs, chattering faster than a ferret on coke, ignored us. At one point, Monster wrestled Debs' arm in an attempt to retrieve his joint while I, embarrassed she was showing me up, stamped on her boot. Debs held on ferociously and rattled on about moon risings and which horoscope signs Monster should avoid, her bobbed haircut swinging as she nodded, eyes glassy as runny honey. 'Tell Monster how much I know about astrology,' she said to me. 'Or haven't you been listening?'

'You were telling Monster why he should stay away from Capricorns.' I said it with venom in my eyes so she'd get the hint she was ruining my big chance with him. Waste of time. Debs grinned. I pushed her upright because she was lolling into me, gave her hair a tug hoping the shock would bring her back from outer space, then snatched the spliff and handed it back to Monster, at the same time pushing his head aside to avert a bombs-away delivery of pigeon poo. Too bewildered to understand what was going on, it plopped unnoticed at his feet. 'Take no notice of Debs. She's not used to Mauie.'

Monster took a few long draws on the spliff then, hiding it behind his back, glared at her. 'You,' he said, 'are a greedy cow, on top of which, you know zilch about astrology because I get on *very* well with Capricorn women.

'Leave him in peace,' I hissed.

Debs reeled around and threw her arm across Monster's shoulders. 'He's my mate. My mate Monster from Streetcrash and one day he'll see I'm right and say, "my friend Debs told me that."

I felt like dragging Debs away but knew in her state she'd struggle, which meant I'd have to raise my arms and Monster would get a bird's eye view of my private parts, which I wanted to save for somewhere better than the backyard of the Rat. Manoeuvring himself away from Deb's arm, Monster glanced at his watch. Bugger! He was leaving and because of Debs and having to stand like a stuffed owl, I'd allowed myself to fade into the brickwork. 'I'm sorry we didn't get a chance to talk.' I smiled beguilingly. 'I had loads I wanted to ask about your music. Streetcrash really is one of my favourite heavy metal bands.'

Monster stopping drawing on his spliff, the furrows on his forehead softened and he licked his lips as though I was a doll that had just come to life. He was on the verge of saying something when Debs piped up. 'OK,' she said, 'I shall now be the bearer of good news.'

'Someone's going to tape your mouth shut?' Monster said, hopefully.

'No. News that will make you glad you met me.'

Monster had the last toke of his spliff then squashed the roach under his foot. 'Haven't got time for more of your bullshit.'

Debs tugged his T-shirt to stop him leaving. 'The good news is that the eighth house is now moving into your fifth house of fame, which means you can expect *amazing* success with your career.'

'You're starting to be *really* annoying Debs,' I muttered.

'You have to make a wish,' Debs said. 'If you don't, your prophecy won't come true.' She stared foggily into Monster's eyes, willing him to respond. 'Go on, make a wish?'

'OK,' Monster said, giving Debs a poke in the chest. 'Even though everything you say is bollocks, *you* have chewed my ears off since the minute I came out to relax so I *am* gonna make a wish.' He looked up at a star in the sky. 'I wish some fucking record label could see our potential and sign us!'

'Laura knows loads about music,' Debs squeaked excitedly. She flapped her hands at her face, which got redder by the second. 'She even knows about…' Her skin turned egg yolk yellow. She made a gurgling sound then clutching her stomach, staggered off mumbling something about going to the toilet at the Red Lion down the road.

'Bit of peace at last,' Monster said once she disappeared from sight. His shoulders relaxed. 'Sorry I've been a prick,' His lips relaxed into a smile. 'Always feel anxious before a show – even in a dump like this.' He looked at me the way I wanted to be looked at and stroked my arm. 'So how come you know so much about music?'

'Music's been a passion since I was a kid, then I started hanging out with bikers at eleven and got into heavy metal.'

A cheeky twinkle appeared in his eyes. 'Bet you looked *very* tasty in black leather.' Grinning, Monster glanced up at my hair. 'Nice hairdo. Big and bold the way I like my women. Apart from the fact your hair's black, you could be Marilyn Monroe's sister.' Back to the Laura I knew best, I flirtily fluttered my false eyelashes. Monster smiled mischievously. 'Turn around and let me see if you've got the same arse as Marilyn.' Holding down my hem, I turned, wiggled it and turned back to see his reaction. He smiled in amusement then looked at his watch. 'I think you and me can have a lot of fun,' he winked. 'Let's have a drink after the gig and get to know each other.'

# TWO

The inside of the Rat and Parrot, reminded me of a bizarre version of an old western saloon. The walls proudly displayed worn leather saddles, moth-eaten cowboy hats, stuffed Moose heads, pistols, rifles and guns. The fleur di lie wallpaper, probably an orange colour in years gone by, had taken such a pummeling from dampness and cigarette smoke, it hung off the corners of the room in sickly yellow tongues. My eyes travelled to the worn, splintered stage which had a Bingo board on one side with a sign that said 'Tuesday 11.am – 13.00 pm Pensioner's Bingo. Big prizes.

It was tragic that Streetcrash chose such a gutter of mediocrity for their comeback performance after fifteen months of silence. What made it worse was that the Rat was a roost for skinheads who listened to Ska and Reggae and weren't known for their love of metalheads.

The skinheads sat on the far side of the pub at long wooden benches, as hacked at as butcher's blocks, sinking down pint glasses of lager in a couple of gulps. Their uniform look consisted of cropped or shaved heads, Ben Sherman shirts, Doc Marten or steel tipped boots and trouser braces. They were so rowdy, their voices carried across the pub to the bar where I stood, back against the wall to prevent anyone trying to put a crafty hand up my mini.

The straw hewn floor space in the middle of the pub overflowed with hardcore metalheads who had come from far and wide to watch Streetcrash perform. They were wearing their customary Skull and Cross bone T-shirts, black jeans, combat boots and studded bracelets with long hair either left trailing down, or tied back in ponytails.

I could taste the gnawing tension in the air as dirty looks passed back and forth between the clans, so wasn't surprised when six skinheads, already the worse for drink, swaggered over thumbs in braces and circled two metalheads. One of the skinheads spat on the ground. 'Yo, what you looking at?' he slurred. 'Take your greasy haired mates and get out of our pub!'

The taller of the two metalheads took a step closer. His fist came out. My heart sank. If it turned into a fight, the Streetcrash gig would be cancelled. Fortunately, the metalhead's friend stopped him by tugging back his arm. 'That skinnyfuck isn't worth it.' They moved off to get closer to the stage, followed by most of the other metalheads who for the same reason as me didn't want trouble.

There was no ventilation in the Rat so the air was a haze of smoke that smelled of stale beer and felt like a hundred degrees in the tropics. I could feel the scorch in my beehive and sensed it droop but with Streetcrash coming on any minute there was no way I would leave my prized position at the bar. Apart from which, when Debs came back from the Red lion, having undoubtedly accosted a new victim with her random topics, I'd be able to see her. An advantage of adding 5" heels to my 5' 5" height.

Apart from a bunch of builders in paint splattered overalls, the bar area seemed to be the territory of what I called the 'Shiny Suit Mob.' They were wannabe Krays with criminal backgrounds who dressed in expensive silk suits, handmade Italian stitched shoes, wore heavy signet rings and smoked Cuban cigars. They considered themselves 'large,' and splashed money about as if it was tissue paper which accounted for the number of peroxide dyed blondes who descended on them like bees to honey valley.

Sod's law sent Brassy to sit two stools away. Her back was turned, claws dug into a shiny to secure her prey.

When the stage lights came on, my heart started beating double time. Eyes transfixed, I watched Charlie hopscotch to the drums and hit the cymbals to introduce Tate who strolled on, bass guitar slung over his shoulder. Causing pandemonium as cheering fans pressed against the stage, Monster swaggered on, picked up his electric guitar, gave the crowd a nod of acknowledgment and started to play.

Within minutes, my joy turned to annoyance as squabbles and skirmishes broke out between the skinheads and metalheads. Most people around the bar were engaged in petty conversations about bank robberies and football instead of showering Streetcrash with the adulation they deserved. The words of the song they sang kept going in and out in the wave of noise.

I watched Brassy who'd been pushed back in the crowd and stood in front of me, cup her hands around her mouth and scream 'BOO. GER OFF.'

I jabbed her in the ribs. 'I'm trying to listen to them.'

Giving me a smirk, Brassy cupped her hands around her mouth again and shouted 'BOOOOO. GER OFF. YOU'RE GIVIN' ME AN EAR ACHE.'

I jabbed her harder. 'Last warning.'

'Piss off,' she said. Facing stage again, I watched her raise her hands to her mouth. Without further ado, I curled my foot round the front of her ankle and yanked. Balance lost, Brassy crashed into a robust girl who was holding a glass of cherry coloured liquid. SPLOOSH. Next second her lacy dress was splattered with red puddles. 'You clumsy cow,' Robost screeched, glaring down at her ruination. 'You just fuckin' covered me in Campari!'

Face mauve with rage, Campari dripping off her chin, Brassy pointed me out. 'That slapper tripped me up. She's…'

I played an innocent bystander spurring Streetcrash on. I was shouting so loud I drowned out the end of Brassy's sentence but from the corner of my eye saw Robost grab her elbow. 'Stop lying you cow. 'Give me two quid to buy a new dress before you get a feel of this.' She said, raising a chunky knuckle.

Inwardly I smiled until Brassy retaliated by pushing Robust into a skinhead dart player who was about to throw a dart. The dart bounced off the metal rim, diverted course and stabbed a metalhead in the neck. The metalhead swung a punch at the skinhead. Robost grabbed Brassy's hair and pulled until Brassy screamed in pain. Unable to hear one word of the song Monster sang through the swearing, screams and thumps, I ducked a stray fist and pushed through the mass to see Debs throw her arms about as she headbanged to the music. Her skinny drainpipes weren't only covered in mud, they had holes in the knees where she'd fallen over somewhere. Spotting me, she screamed 'Heavy metal rocks,' and vanished into the swell.

The hardcore metalheads were in trance mode and shook their arms expressing liberty, which didn't sit well with the skinheads whose glasses kept getting bumped. Winding my way through, a dancer's arm slammed into my beehive. Poking him in the back with a few choice words, I squashed through with a shoulder and forced a space in the front row.

Mesmerized, I watched Charlie crisscross his arms in a tangled weave and deliver blow after blow to all five drums. Charlie, an eccentric character known to do crazy stuff like set fire to himself on stage, was probably one of the fastest drummers in the world. As usual, he was lifting drum rolls into places they weren't meant to be, then letting them fall back into melodic driving tempo. Drumming with one hand, Charlie used the other to catch a glass someone hurled, span it on his fingertip and placed it beside him on the floor. Grinning throughout, he kick-snared, then using both sticks again, rained hard on the drums and went into sledgehammer mode.

Tapping his foot to the beat, one knee going in and out in the jerky style of Buddy Holly, Tate fingerpicked the strings of his bass guitar at dizzying speed to keep pace.

Monster, oozing sex and rough stuff, strutted across stage gyrating his hips, tossed his mane and spat out lyrics like a lion on heat. Placing his fingers on his electric guitar, he closed his eyes and strummed. The currents coming from the wire pick up chords produced long whiney sounds that were pure Hendrix. I could feel their vibration under the floorboards, in the head bangers' thumping feet and rattle of windows.

That turned out to be a defining moment in my life.

Not sure how it happened but one second I was sucked into Streetcrash's performance and the next decided I wanted to be their manager. Did Monster not say in the yard that he wished a record company would sign them? My 'prestigious' job in travel was going nowhere. I hated my boss with a vengeance. I was tough enough to knock on doors and bluff my way through until I got the hang of things, and how different could promoting travel packages be to promoting a heavy metal band? All I had to do was change my attitude so Monster forgot about our shag and convince him I was their missing link to stardom.

My thoughts faded in the cacophony as Streetcrash played their long song Everyone's a Mother Fucker. Even the skinheads and builders in overalls shook fists screaming, '*If you don't take what you want, some other fucker will,*' each time the chorus came around.

When Charlie ran around the drums hitting out at everything in reach, those of us in the know, knew it was instrumental time. Some of the skinheads kept up their racket but I'd attuned my mind so wasn't bothered. The head bangers fell into a lull as Monster and Tate took back-to-back positions and started playing duel rifts. How to describe the way Monster's soaring electric notes folded into Tate's deep, dirty strums as they touched heads like magnets drawn to the same sun. In real life Tate was known as the quiet one. On stage he was a dynamo who knew Monster so well he molded into his persona as though they were the same throbbing unit of flesh. I was aware of every strike of the drum, every twang, growl and zing of the guitars as Monster, sweat running off his T shirt, sank to his knees and threw his torso back to play guitar.

Streetcrash left the stage to roaring applause, having won over at least half the skinheads. I felt such pride at their victory under such dire circumstances I wanted to work for them even more. All I had to do was locate Debs, see what state she was in and decide what to do with her. I found her slumped on the floor with her head in her knees. She asked if it would look OK if she crawled out of the pub on all fours. Cradling her in my arms, I walked her outside and paid a taxi driver to take her home.

# THREE

The dressing room Monster sent me to while him, Tate and Charlie packed up their gear on stage, was as depressing as the rest of the pub. The walls were unpainted grey slabs of cement. The barred windows gave it the feel of a prison cell and the boxes of stacked peanuts, crisps and pork scratchings on either side of the door took up most of the floor space.

That was bad enough but as I walked the four steps to the plastic mirror above a cheap plastic table that sufficed as Monster's makeup table, I almost convinced myself that the witch gasping back was a trick of the light. It was *me* - not only unsuitably dressed for the most important business meeting of my life but looking like I'd had a rough night of sex. Red lipstick was smeared over my chin. The black kohl under my eyes had smudged so I looked like a panda. My beehive had collapsed into a donut and my gold eyeliner that I tilted at the corners to look like leopard's eyes leaked down my cheeks as though the cowardly leopard had bawled its eyes out. I listened to the tick of the clock that seemed to have sped up, as had the pound of my heart. Mind racing with opening lines to grab Streetcrash's attention, I got to work pushing hair clips into the base of my hive to resurrect it, dabbed away the smudged kohl, swept my fringe to one side, applied fresh lipstick and drew a thicker line of gold eyeliner to restore the leopard's courage.

I glanced at the clock again. Two minutes had passed. Streetcrash could appear at any moment and I still didn't have a clue what my first sentence should be to win them over. Shifting Monster's stage make up and a bottle of Jack Daniels to one side of the table, I stood palm pressed against the lid to remind myself that on no account was there to be any waving of arms throughout my sales pitch talk. Perhaps I could say I saw Streetcrash on par with Led Zeppelin and that with me on board, they were assured of superstar status?

I picked up Monster's harmonica and stared at it for inspiration, still no further on when Charlie bounced through the door with a drumstick behind each ear. Snorting, he took a packet of crisps out of an open box, ripped the bag apart and crunched noisily. 'Want one?'

'No thanks, Charlie.'

'Sit down if you like,' Charlie rattled the crisp bag at the two excuses for chairs in the room. 'Take your pick. Monster will be here in a mo.' I looked at him thinking how much like Keith Moon of the Who he was with his owly eyes, chubby cheeks and dark floppy hair – apart from the fact Charlie had purple streaks in his. Eyes transfixed to a wall, Charlie crumpled the crisp bag, lay it on the floor, whipped the drumsticks from behind his ears and smashed a cobweb to bits. A spider tumbled to the floor. Charlie, who wore a brown and yellow striped T-shirt that made him look like a giant bumblebee, threatened it with his sticks as it ran for cover and hid under a mop. 'I used to like spiders,' he said, helping himself to a packet of peanuts. 'Then I read Metamorphosis by Frank Kafka. Do you know it?' I shrugged because I didn't. Charlie, round black eyes full of suspense did something with his arms that looked like he was pretending to be an insect caught in a net. 'Well, one morning this man wakes up and sees he's been turned into a gigantic furry spider who....'

Charlie's story was cut short as Monster and Tate came into the room talking about their performance. Bare chested, shaggy damp hair curling around his shoulders, Monster moaned about the lousy sound system, the fact they had been paid a pittance and why they'd agreed to play at a dump like the Rat.

17

'We won't have to put up with it much longer,' Tate said, calmly. 'We'll get where we're going.'

'Yeah, take a chill pill, Mons,' Charlie said, trying to stuff peanuts in Monster's mouth.

Monster spat one out then brushed his chest. 'Fuck off delinquent!' he said. He pushed Charlie away and smiled at me. 'Sorry I had to leave you with that nutter. He behaves like a five year old!' He picked up the bottle of Jack and took a glug before passing it to me. 'We weren't provided with glasses in this dump but I've got everything we need at home, Melons.'

I waved the bottle away with a shake of my head, free hand holding down my hem. It was now or never to change my status from *Melons* to manager. 'Before you say anything else, I have a proposition.'

With a lazy smile on his face as if he was imagining the delights that lay in store, Monster rummaged through a bag under the table, pulled out a clean T-shirt, tugged it over his head, shook out his mane and winked. 'Sure you want to discuss your proposition in front of these two, Melons?'

I felt irked Monster's mind was still in shag land when I had deleted it from mine, and even more so, he was calling me Melons and encouraging Tate and Charlie to disrespect me. On the other hand, I brought it on myself by giving him my enticement treatment with all the trimmings. The only thing to do was stick to business until Monster's mind accepted our new relationship. 'My proposition concerns them as well,' I said, ignoring his reference to my boobs. His facial expression made clear he thought I was hinting at a gangbang and was in two minds whether he was for or against it. 'I meant in a business capacity.'

Confused, Monster sat down, opened a plastic bag, tipped out a little heap of coke on the table, flattened it with his cigarette box then used the edge of the box to cut it into lines.

'Somewhere between the back yard and here, you've lost me, Melons.' Tell us your proposition when you've had some of this.' He glanced at my hand, pressed against the table lid. 'Stop gripping that like you're afraid for your life.' He sniffed up two lines of coke then let Charlie, who was hanging over his shoulder, in on the act. Monster wiped his nose. 'I respect women. Relax.'

Tate, who studied me with mild curiosity, brought over the second chair. 'Here you go,' he smiled. Tate was the tallest of the three with bleach white cropped hair. He smelled of patchouli and gave the feeling he was a yoga teacher instead of bass guitarist. Even though he put the same effort into his performance and his T-shirt was soaked in sweat he looked cool and relaxed.

Gesturing to my hem as though Tate might guess the reason for my awkwardness, I smiled back. 'I'm fine thanks, Tate.'

Shoving Charlie away, Monster covered the last line of coke with his hand. 'If you want this you'd better get in fast.' In preference to saying I never touched it and ruining my chances of becoming manager to a heavy metal band, I said I didn't fancy any. 'That's a first.' Monster gave me a wink. 'Although something tells me you don't need any, Melons.'

My look of frustration prompted Tate to pass me a bottle of Perrier water. Charlie stared into space at something only he could see. Monster, hand propped up against his cheek, smiled at me with undisguised lust. I took a long sip of water. I knew from experience that when men had sex on the brain, they thought everything you said was a naughty innuendo. I had to delete from his mind that I was a girl called Melons with a penchant for gang bangs and make him take me seriously. 'I am aware that I may have given you the wrong impression earlier, Monster,' I said with authority. Monster looked around the room as though someone else was speaking through my mouth. 'And that seeing me in this mini, which was supposed to have matching leggings that laddered so I had to take off, that I am probably the last person you would imagine as your manager.' Monster screwed up his nose at Charlie who didn't see him since he was dabbing at coke powder remains on the table and licking them off his finger. Monster glanced at Tate and shook his head to let him know he had no idea what I was talking about. 'Yes, your *manager*,' I said to clarify matters. 'I have a deal you shouldn't refuse because it's a free three month trial offer - and I have the experience to get you signed to a major record label.'

Monster's expression changed from confused to gobsmacked. He took a swift glug of Jack. 'Manager? Fucking manager! Where did that come from?' Disgruntled he scratched between his legs. 'What do you mean you gave me the wrong impression? Two hours back you were coming onto me like a heat rash!'

Charlie puffed out his chubby cheeks. 'Let's listen.' He picked up his drumsticks and snapped at a bluebottle that seemed intent on landing on his T-shirt. 'A manager who's free and looks like Melons is a great deal.' The fly alighted on Monster's head. Sticks poised, Charlie snapped.

Monster grabbed the sticks. 'You're like a fucking hyperactive robot!' He threw them down on the table and shot Charlie a warning look. 'And what do we want with a manager who doesn't know the first thing about band management?'

Looking at me with his big round eyes, Charlie whispered in Monster's ear, 'Where are we going to find another manager. You chucked our last one out the window, remember?'

Even though it was a whisper, I heard because the four of us were so close. I knew the story. The newspapers said it was because their previous manager, Doc, slagged off Ian Gillan from Deep Purple and Monster lost his temper. I loved Deep Purple and Ian Gillan was number one on my 'must shag' list so I was on Monster's side.

Monster picked up the bottle of Jack and slammed it back down on the table. 'Doc was lucky it was only a ground floor window!' His eyes narrowed. 'Instead of overlooking that one minor mishap and protecting me, he told the newspapers I was a difficult, aggressive beast and when the press slammed us, said we were old news and my songs belonged in an incinerator!'

'Forget it Mons,' Tate tapped Monster's shoulder 'That was a year ago. We're starting over, remember?' Monster shook Tate's hand off and scowled in the mirror to relive his trauma.

Charlie, who'd taken off one of his shoes and sat picking at a brown and yellow striped sock that matched his T-shirt, sighed, flicked the hair out of his eyes and looked up sorrowfully at Monster. 'I'll never breathe Doc's name again. Sorry, Mons.'

'You deserve much better than Doc, and I am *that* person, Monster. Hear me out. Please?' Monster's response was to put his hands over his ears. 'My name is *Laura,*' I said it loudly to emphasize my name. 'I have a responsible position in a major travel company, know everything about PR, have great organization skills, am not afraid to knock on doors and more importantly see your potential, *really* get your music and my services including initial promo costs are free as stated.'

Monster's hands came off his ears. 'Hanging out with bikers doesn't make you an expert on anything. 'Who do you know in the music business?' he challenged. 'Who do you know?'

The only person I knew in the music business was a woman called Cassie who worked at WEA records. Randomly I got her a half price holiday deal for Tenerife and might be able to call in the favour by asking for advice. 'I can't believe you asked me that! Do you think I'd be standing here if I didn't know people?'

'Who?' Monster said. Until that moment I thought coke was supposed to make people more amenable. In Monster's case it was having the reverse effect. As I struggled to conjure up lies that couldn't be proved until further in the future, Tate jumped in to save me.

'Show a bit of respect Mons,' he said. 'You can see Laura's not comfortable because of the accident with her tights.'

'Thank you, Tate.' I looked back at Monster. 'Ask me a question related to music. Anything you can think of?'

Monster lit a cigarette and rested it on the edge of an overflowing ashtray of dog ends. He picked up a wet flannel and rubbed at his make up until the flannel turned murky brown. 'My only question is why you lead me up the garden path,' he sniffed.

Charlie, who was drumming a tune on the corner of the table, stopped and reached out to pick up two green balls. Monster slapped Charlie's hand off. 'Keep your thieving fingers to yourself! My therapist gave me those to roll in my hands to calm my nerves.'

Tate put the chair he offered me next to Monster and sat down. 'Ask Laura a question, Mons. Give her a chance to speak.'

Sighing heavily, Monster folded his arms. 'On the advice of my two fellow band members who think they know better than me, my question is how you'd go about getting us signed?'

I shook my hand because my fingers were numb and replaced it on the table. 'I have been employee of the year for three years and part of my job is to get travel agents excited by new destinations. I am the one who convinces them that wherever I suggest is the next major hot spot and...'

Monster waved me to a stop. 'That is all very fascinating and I don't doubt you get travel agents excited because I can see you have a lot going for you, but we are not a Benidorm holiday package. We're a fucking heavy metal band!'

Tate nodded at me as though urging me to ignore Monster and continue. I grabbed a denim shirt that hung on a hook beside me. 'Does whoever this belongs to, mind if I use it?'

Tate shrugged. 'Be my guest.'

Monster, sporting a bit of torn tissue that he'd slapped on an acne spot, watched me tie the shirt around my waist and knot the sleeves behind my back. 'What the fuck's the matter with you? This is the strangest meeting I've ever had.'

I gave my apron a contented pat. Finally able to protect myself against indecent exposure, I felt much more confident. 'Now I am one hundred percent ready to...'

'Cook a spaghetti Bolognese?' Monster pointed to the door. 'Since the proposition I was interested in no longer exists and I don't want to be managed by a travel rep - off you go Melons.'

Desperate not to be thrown out, I turned to my ally. 'Tate, ask me something related to music?'

Tate scratched his cropped hair. 'What could it be about?'

I zoomed in on his eyes and held steady. 'Music structure. Music origins. Popular musicians of the 50's and 60's. Which bands are signed to which record labels Who are considered the best guitarists?'

'Alright', Monster interrupted, 'Since you want to play games and my fellow band members aren't listening to a fucking word I say,' he shot Tate and Charlie a look which made clear he considered them traitors. 'What do you know about Hendrix?'

Stunned Monster asked such an easy question, I prepared to dazzle him with my knowledge. 'Apart from the fact he's your idol and arguably one of the world's best electric guitarists, Jimi Hendrix was born in Seattle on November 27th, 1942 and known as Buster growing up. His dad was drafted into the Second World War so he didn't meet him until he was 3. Jimi's first band was called The Casuals which was changed to King Casuals because...'

Monster turned his chair an inch to challenge me at closer quarters. 'For the title track on his album *Are you Experienced*, what was different about his playing?'

I shrugged to let him know anyone who appreciated Hendrix knew that. 'He recorded it backwards as well as forwards.'

Charlie, who sat at my feet, stopped fidgeting, sat up straight and lost his eyes in mine. 'She knows her stuff,' he said. 'Melons, I mean Laura, is a walking encyclopedia!'

'She just reads a lot of music mags,' Monster thumped Charlie on the head for paying me a compliment and turned his chair to face me. 'Alight, tell me why Jimi left the army?'

I flapped the question away. 'Next.'

Charlie put his hand up and waved excitedly. 'Why did Jimi leave the army? I wanna know that?'

'He was dismissed after he was caught masturbating in the platoon when he was supposed to be on detail,' Tate answered on my behalf.

Charlie's face took on an expression of shocked disbelief. 'Just for a wank? What a major injustice!'

'And it shows Laura's character that she didn't answer your stupid question Mons,' Tate said.

Monster spat out a mouthful of Jack. 'Fuck me! Now I'm the villain. I thought I was going to have a hot night playing naughty games and here I am on Twenty Questions!'

I decided the only way to get anywhere with Monster was to speak his language. 'Just so you know, I am as disappointed as you are that I missed out on what promised to be the best shag of my life because *you* are, I mean were, number three on my 'must shag' list. I however, unlike you, am willing to forsake the pleasure of the flesh for our mutual betterment and make sure you never play at dumps like the Rat again.' I flapped my apron at Monster's head. 'It took guts for me to come in here, feeling firstly like a slut and now looking like this, but when I heard you play tonight, I knew I was meant to be your manager and knew...'

Someone knocked on the door. 'We're closing up – need you out in fifteen minutes,' he shouted.

'What I propose,' I said, getting in what I wanted to say before my destiny moment was lost – 'is that we have a meeting tomorrow when I'll bring you a written plan of everything I intend to do over the next three months to get you signed.'

'Sounds a good plan,' Tate said, tipping Monster's stage make up into a bag. 'And you've got to give Laura ten out of ten for her honesty Mons. Anyone with her guts deserves a chance.' Monster flicked the hair out of his mouth and lit another cigarette.

Charlie jumped to his feet. 'Yeah, forget about the pleasures of the flesh where Laura is concerned, Mons.' Grinning, he poked Monster's arm. 'She hasn't blanked you out she just wants what's right for our betterment. And let's be honest, Mons, shags for you are two a penny.'

Monster gave me a filthy look and jotted down his address on a crumpled receipt. 'Don't know why I'm agreeing to something so stupid.'

'Time?' I said.

Monster scribbled it down, banged his pen against the table then looked up at me. The few seconds he said nothing felt like a minute. I held his gaze while his eyes probed mine, and prayed he wouldn't call off the meeting. 'It did take guts to deal with the shit I threw at you. I know I'm an awkward prat but since you want the chance,' he handed me the receipt. 'Let's give it a shot.'

# FOUR

Monster's flat was only ten minutes from mine in Queens Park. His place was over an antique shop in Ladbroke Grove. I found the number, rang the bell and waited to see his head come out of a third floor window.

'I'll send Tate down,' Monster said, waving a glass. It was still morning and he looked wasted. I just hoped I'd get enough sense out of him to have a professional meeting because I'd been up all night working on a schedule of what I thought a manager might do to get a band signed.

'Morning Laura,' Tate smiled, opening the door and pointing to the stairs. 'Just going next door to buy some juice. See you up there.'

When I walked into his front room, Monster sat stark naked on a red leather beanbag. His head was down in thought as he strummed on a guitar so I coughed to let him know I was there and glanced at the blonde sprawled out on a floor cushion. Her denim shorts were so tight, they cut right up the middle of her vagina. To avert my eyes, I glanced around the room. Apart from cushions in every size and shape that took up most of the floor, the only other items were an expensive looking music cabinet, an electric keyboard, three guitar cases propped up against the wall and a dining table strewn with music sheets.

'Hi,' the girl on cushion called out dreamily, high as a kite on something.

'Hi,' I said, looking over her head.

'When we gonna have our screw then?' Monster said, walking towards me bold as brass. His dick as I saw, wasn't the size he showed off on stage making it obvious he did have assistance in the underpants department. Monster caught me looking and misread my thoughts. 'We can have a threesome with Inge if you like?' he teased.

'I don't think Inge's up to it,' I said. 'What we can do is to talk about your career and how I intend to get you signed.'

Monster pursed his lips. 'I like girls who don't shock easily, shows strength of character - and I like your ponytail, your cowboy boots and that blue checked shirt you've got on.'

Relieved that Monster was having an amenable day, I smiled. 'Last night was a one-off situation as you'll find out, Monster.' I took a notepad out of my bag to prove I meant business. 'I saw Tate downstairs. Is Charlie coming?'

'He'll be here.' Monster pulled out a pair of boxer shorts from underneath a cushion, stepped into them and poured himself a Jack. 'What time is it?

'Noon,' I said.

Monster dragged his fingers through a mass of tangled curls. 'Who arranged a meeting for that fucking time on a Saturday?' he groaned.

'You did,' Tate said, coming back into the room. He handed me a glass of orange juice. 'Or would you prefer a cup of Earl Grey?'

'No, juice is fine.' I took a sip. 'Mmm, nice. Freshly squeezed?'

Tate nodded. 'Not all rockers are like Mons. I like to take care of my health.'

'Tate's a fucking vegetarian,' Monster said, lighting a spliff. 'Doesn't do drugs. Doesn't drink alcohol. Acts like a virgin. Right pain in the balls!' He had a toke and waved it at me.

'Too early,' I looked around the room. The first thing I needed to do was find a space for our meeting where I wouldn't be distracted by Inge. I pointed at the table. 'Mind if I clear that, Monster?'

'Yes, I do mind,' Monster said. 'You'll mess up my filing system and I won't be able to find anything.'

'Fair enough.' I shrugged. 'Then where do you suggest?'

'There's a table in the kitchen,' Tate said. 'Just need to clean things up a bit. And by the way, thanks for taking an interest in us Laura.'

'Oh, yeah that's *Laura,*' Monster said to Inge as if he just remembered my name. 'She's going to manage us. Did I mention it, babe?' Inge smiled, as vacant as a playing field with no-one on it.

Someone pressed the bell and kept pressing until Tate poked his head out of the window. 'Morning Charlie.' He threw down a bunch of keys and turned towards the kitchen at the end of the hall.

As soon as I saw the kitchen, I knew why Tate gave me a plastic glass for my juice. Every glass, cup, mug and plate Monster owned lay scattered around the room as though someone who despised cleaning up had a huge party but unable to face the disarray, took off into the night. Leaning at an angle on the side of the sink, a pile of plates with chunks of dried up meat and frizzled brown spaghetti tottered on the brink of crashing to the floor. Opened packets of corn flakes, cream crackers and tinned soups littered the sideboard. The table, used to dump coffee mugs, teacups and ashtrays didn't have space to fit a paperclip. I could envision Debs wearing a gas mask to hose down the walls with disinfectant. Assuming she wasn't stoned, because when I got home the night before, I found her propped up against our front door, one swamp boot on her head, the other in a geranium pot on the window sill.

'Sorry about this,' Tate said. 'Monster's been working on some new songs and when he gets carried away, he's oblivious to anything else'. Tate put up his hands as though he didn't know what else to say.

'We'll have the kitchen cleaned in no time,' I said to let him know I could take Monster in my stride, at the same time thinking how different he was to Monster.

Even the lazy way Tate stood spoke volumes about his patience. His skin, unlike Monster's was clear and glowing. His body was so lean it didn't have an ounce of spare fat. While Tate didn't have Monster's sex appeal, his deep brown eyes oozed kindness and his smile could melt a pyramid.

'Suppose we should get to work. Are there any bin bags?'

Tate rattled open a drawer and brought out a packet of bin bags together with a pair of plastic gloves. 'Thought these might come in useful to get that clogged up food off the plates since you're wearing nail polish and it might get chipped.'

'You obviously know a lot about women.' I laughed, wriggling my hands into the gloves.

Having dislodged a wooden spatula under the mountain of unwashed kitchen utensils, I scrubbed frizzled spaghetti off one of the plates, tipped it into the bin bag Tate held out, and got started on another plate. That one was three times worse because the remains of chicken wings had cemented themselves into the thick brown sauce. I scraped furiously at the plate with the tip of a carving knife. 'This plate must have been here for weeks!'

'Doc would never have dirtied his hands like you,' Tate said. 'But don't go thinking this is what we expect of you, Laura.'

'Tell me more about Doc?' I said, seizing the opportunity to learn more. 'What really went wrong?'

'Apart from the fact Doc couldn't deal with Monster's ups and downs, he mistook his insecurity for aggression. That stuff in the papers about Monster throwing Doc out of the window for insulting Gillan was untrue. The problem started when I realized Doc was syphoning money out of our bank account to feed his drug problem.'

Having finally given up their residency in cement valley, I tipped the chicken wings in the bin bag. 'Did they do drugs together?'

'Big time, sometimes they went on binges with some pretty heavy stuff,' Tate sighed. 'I told Monster to get rid of Doc because he was using him. Monster told me to mind my own business and you've seen how pigheaded he can be.'

'What proved the final straw?'

'Doc saw his days were numbered so kept blaming our lack of success on Monster's lousy song writing.'

I hurled dried up chunks of meat from the next two plates in the bin bag. 'What a damn nerve!'

'When Monster played Doc Everyone's a Mother Fucker, he tossed the tape in the bin.'

'*What?*'

'Yeah,' Tate sighed again. 'Doc said mainstream radio would never play it, that Monster had lost the plot and it was time for him to move on, so Monster said, "Let me help you" and pushed him out the window.'

Grabbing the frying pan, I clobbered a fly that buzzed around my nose and watched it drop to the floor. 'That's you put in your place!' I kicked its dead remains away with the tip of my cowboy boot and resumed washing up.

'Day one,' Tate smiled. 'Laura murders Doc. I assume that's who you had in mind when you knocked that fly senseless?'

'Doc was lucky Monster didn't chuck him out of a top floor window. Maybe *Everyone's* won't make it on mainstream radio but pirate stations will jump at it.'

'Love your faith,' Tate said. 'I think you'll handle Monster well.'

'Phwa,' I said. 'Monster will be a piece of cake compared to my boss.'

Tate chuckled. 'Hate to think what he's like then.' He nodded his head in the direction of the living room so I knew he was going to say something else about Monster. 'It's confidence Monster lacks. He often doesn't sleep for days, playing the same piece over and over because he never thinks anything is good enough. All those music sheets on the front room table are works in progress. Some have real commercial potential. You should get Monster to play them for you.'

'As soon as he trusts me I will.' I added another plate to the rinsed pile.

Tate started bringing dirty mugs and cups over from the table. 'What was Monster's mood like when you met him in the backyard of the Rat?'

'Hard to know,' I laughed. 'My friend Debs wouldn't stop bending his ear, but he seemed fearful and anxious.'

'That's how he is before most gigs. Sometimes his nerves get so bad he...'

Charlie bounced into the kitchen as though he had springs under his loafers. Shuffling his feet, he spun on the spot then tapped his fingers against the doorframe.

'Did you know that if you collected hydrogen in vast quantities and left it in a vacuum, it would eventually start thinking about itself?' He looked up in awe as though the universe was swirling through his head. 'Unbelievable. I wonder what it thinks about?' Coming back to earth, Charlie gave a gracious bow and nodded at the kettle. 'Any coffee on the go?' He watched Tate empty ashtrays then looked at me scrubbing the table. 'Perhaps not.'

Tate smiled. 'I'll put the kettle on.'

Charlie banged the door with his fist, his cheeks puffed out then hollowed as he flicked the gobstopper in his mouth from one place to the next. 'By the way, Monster won't be at our meeting.'

Afraid Monster had changed his mind about me managing Streetcrash, I scrubbed the table harder. 'Why?'

Charlie shrugged. 'Passed out, I'm afraid.'

31

Tate took the scrubbing brush out of my hand and pulled out a chair for me to sit down. 'Since he's already agreed, I suggest we carry on without him.'

# FIVE

'You're in a good mood, Babe.' Chris said, as we strolled out of the cinema.

I smiled into his eyes which were the same brown as his hair but held *tread softly* warning. I hadn't known him long enough to know how he'd react if I told him about my new career with Streetcrash. He didn't even know I'd gone to their gig at the Rat. Chris looked at me, waiting for an answer. 'I feel a promotion coming on,' I said, thinking it vague enough to mean anything.

Chris took my hand and squeezed it. 'Not many people on the streets tonight. They're probably all in bed with their arms around each other.'

I followed his eyes. Apart from a kebab shop, an all-night supermarket and a couple of bars everything was shut. 'Guess that's because it's nearly midnight.' I smiled at the traffic lights that stretched from Marble Arch far into the distance. Every one of them was green as if passing me a secret message. '*The road is clear. Run with the wind.*' My head was full of music. The lights swayed and winked.

'Don't do that,' Chris said. 'Not in public'

I looked down on my swishing hips. 'Why not?' I opened my arms and whirled around him.

Chris's creased brow softened. 'Wonder you can walk let alone dance, in heels as high as yours.'

'I run for the bus in these most mornings.' A slinky black satin jumpsuit in a boutique window caught my eye. My body gravitated towards it. 'I *love* that,' I said, imagining it swathed

33

around my curves as I walked a red carpet to pick up a music award. I saw flashlights going off as press clamoured for a few words from Monster. I could see screaming fans waving bits of paper to get autographs. I saw myself walking behind them, knowing that I was the brains behind their rise to fame. I saw my hair swept up in a French pleat as I slunk past my admirers in a waft of black satin.

Chris's nudge brought me out of my daydream. He pulled a face and pointed to the jumpsuit. 'There's hardly any material covering the front of that.' He kissed my cheek. 'Although I suppose it could be worn when you invite me over to dinner to meet Debs?'

I found it better to play along with men's deluded hopes than spoil the mood. 'As soon as she finishes painting the kitchen, you'll be the first guest.'

Chris took my hand and we started walking. 'What did you think of Blind Woman's Curse?' he said, referring to the Japanese sword fighting film we saw. 'The special effects when that woman's eye was gouged out and blood spurted out of her socket, looked authentic eh?'

'Too authentic!' I grimaced. 'But the actress who played that blind girl wanting revenge after her dad was snatched away, got to my heart.'

'Did it make you think of your Dad?' Chris said, hinting at what I told him so he wouldn't pester me to meet my parents. I told the lie so often, it rolled off my tongue like treacle. *"My mother's a nurse who went to India to aid dying children. My father died when I was three."* Making a sad face seemed appropriate so I answered with that.

I must have looked really sad since to cheer me up, Chris suggested we race to the car so he could see how fast I ran in stilettos. I liked my dates to be fun, so took off as fast as they would carry me. Chris overtook me in three strides, ran ahead and disappeared around a corner. I slowed down to listen to an

Arabic song that drifted out of a Lebanese restaurant. It was a woman singer and whatever she was singing, deserved a prize for erotic enticement. Exotic sounds hit my belly. My feet started to move. A man I guessed to be the owner, stood smoking a cigar on the pavement. There was no-one inside the restaurant so I guessed he was about to close.

'You like Arabic music?' His gold teeth glittered under the glow of the gaslight in the street.

'Don't know that I like all Arabic music but this song is so...' I was going to say sexy but changed my mind, 'Passionate.'

'Do you know what she is saying?'

'No idea.'

'She is saying ahlan ya habibi, enta hayat. This means hello my love, you are the love of my life.'

'Hmm,' I said, and imagined droves of men queueing outside the singer's door waiting to kiss the ruby in her belly button.

'You know how to belly dance?' He shimmied his shoulders, did something with his belly to make it wobble and raised his arms. 'Ahlan ya habibi, see? Easy. You try?'

'No time.' I pointed down the road.

'Bet you a bottle of raki on the house you can't do this?' Fingers forming intricate shapes above his head, he pumped his belly.

I couldn't care less about the raki but the *ya habibi* set me on fire. There was no-one in the street except a woman walking her dog and Chris was probably sitting in the car waiting. What difference would a minute make? 'Right. Bet on.' I swirled my hips in circles, wound my arms up and over my head and pumped my belly as he had done.

The Arab shimmied his shoulders and clapped. 'Ya habibi.'

Laughing, and about to say 'That's your lot,' someone poked me in the back. I turned to see Chris.

35

He was so furious his face looked like it would explode. 'So now you're an Arab's private dancer!'

'Come in,' the restaurant owner warmly welcomed us with an outstretched arm. 'Your girlfriend just won raki on the house.'

Chris machine gunned him with his eyes, grabbed my hand and yanked me away. He was a heavy weight boxer and gripped my fingers so brutally I thought they would snap. 'What kind of woman does what you just did?' he growled.

For all his play at being a man about town, Chris showed a narrow-minded thug side I didn't like. 'I wasn't planning it.' I ran alongside him because he marched at the speed of a marathon competitor.

Chris stopped walking, dug his hands in his pockets and glared at me. 'I think you're an attention seeker!'

'I might be an attention seeker but that's not why I danced. I was swept away by ya habibi.' I Irish jigged to make him laugh. 'Oh, be Jesus,' I said in an Irish accent. 'My feet are sweeping me away. Get me a pint of Guinness to make them stop.'

'*That,*' he pointed a stretched finger at my tapdancing feet. 'Is not the kind of woman I want to be seen with.'

'Fine.' I snapped. 'Maybe a miserable cow would suit you better!'

Chris sighed in recognition that he overacted since I'd done nothing wrong other than get caught up in the moment. He pushed the hair away from my face and cupped it with his hands. 'Sorry. Guess I don't know you well enough yet.'

I was furious but kept my mouth shut since for me a date that didn't end in a shag was a waste of time. Walking in silence, we turned the corner into the residential street where I suggested Chris parked his car. It was a quiet spot away from prying eyes.

'Are we OK now?' Chris said.

I looked at his taut, hard as marble chest, biceps and triceps that compensated for his rough edges and felt blood rush through my veins. 'One hundred percent.'

Chris unlocked the driver seat door. As soon as he did, I reached in, unlocked the handle on the back door and climbed in. 'What are you up to?' he said. 'Get back in the front so we can go to your place.'

'We can't go to my place. Debs is there with her fiancé.' That was another lie. I hadn't seen Debs all day because she had gone to see her grandmother at an old people's home in Barnet, her fiancé was working away in Cardiff and Debs was undoubtedly fast asleep.

'Then we'll go to my place,' Chris said, and watched me tug my hot pants down.

'Shagging in cars turns me on.' I opened my legs and stroked the pubic hair I trimmed at Chris's request, which seemed fair since he loaned me his equipment to satisfy my needs.

'Stop it. You'll make me go hard. Get in the front seat and behave.' Chris glanced about to see if anyone watched.

I undid the buttons on my green silk shirt and let it slide off my shoulders.

'Now I *am* getting hard. You look like one of those Botticelli women with no clothes on.'

I beckoned him with my middle finger. 'Come to buxom mama, she's got the hots for you.' I ran my tongue around my lips.

Chris unzipped his trousers. 'Alright, you can have a quickie, but having sex in a back seat isn't my best way of doing it, because I'm not exactly a small man am I?'

'No, you're not,' I patted the upholstery. 'Let buxom mama ride you like a wild horse.' Chris took his trousers off. I climbed on. Two minutes later, having satisfied ourselves, I pulled my hot pants on. 'Suppose we should get going. I've got a big day tomorrow.'

Chris looked stunned. 'Aren't you coming back to my place? I got a king size bed waiting for us.'

'I'll stay another night.' I pulled on my shirt, buttoned it, got out of the back and moved into the passenger seat.

As we took off down Edgeware Road, Chris went into silent mode. Since I wasn't the kind of woman who liked dates to end on a sour note in case I required their services again, I stroked his thigh. 'Penny for your thoughts?'

Chris nodded to himself, then me. 'I was just thinking. Twice we've had sex,' he said. 'The first time was in a hotel room when you couldn't wait to leave. The second was tonight in my car.' Clucking his tongue, Chris stared at the road ahead. 'Can I ask you a personal question?'.

From experience I knew the question, '*How many men have you slept with,*' and the route it would take. Me saying two to start, not being believed then working my way up to whatever number they felt comfortable with. Chris's grilling still went on after I admitted to fifteen lovers to shut him up. But would he? No. He tried to pin sixteen and seventeen on me. The number wasn't relevant. The point was he was turning two shags into a relationship. I was livid. 'How many times have you had steak and chips?'

'Dunno.' Chris shrugged. 'Once a week?'

'That's roughly the number.' I pointed to a lampshade with crystal dangly bits in a shop window. 'That would look perfect in my flat.' Chris breathed like a bull ready to plunder its hooves into concrete. He was a sulky shag but with two jobs on the go, I wouldn't have time to find a new one. 'Relax Chris, we'll be fine.'

Pulling up outside my flat, he reached out and stroked my hair, 'I can tell you're not the kind of girl who'd mess me around, but if I thought another man laid a finger on you,' Chris shook his head, 'I'd murder the pair of you, no remorse.'

I nodded, mind elsewhere as I thought about the paper work I needed to get through to pacify my tyrannous boss who called even on Sundays to pile more on my plate.

'See you soon,' I blew a kiss and jumped out of the car before Chris could pull me back in.

# SIX

Mr. Gibson rushed out of his office before I even had two feet in the door and loomed over me. 'Morning, Laura. Everything under control?'

'Everything under control,' I repeated, squeezing past.

Gibson looked at the clock on the wall and clicked his heels together. Something he did often. 'Hmm, five minutes past nine.' He said it with a smiley show of teeth but the accusation in his eyes read *'I've been in the office since 7am and expect you to show the same enthusiasm, you lazy cow'.*

'Take the three hundred seconds off the unpaid overtime you gave me to do yesterday, which happened to be another Sunday.' I returned the same fake smile wondering how many women murdered their bosses. If dreams counted, I'd tried countless times but somehow Mr. Gibson lived on. In my last dream, dressed as a Nazi, I ordered a firing squad to pump holes in him and watched him explode into particles until the only thing left was a dismembered cockroach's head that continued to bark out orders when the squad buried it under a mountain of hot coals.

Gibson sniffed, and impatiently tapped his excuse of a moustache that sat above his lip like a square of burned grass. I could feel his eyes boring into my back as I reached down to change my stilettos into platforms, which was one of Gibson's rules along with dresses must be knee length, red lipstick not allowed and dozens more. Gibson, who I suspected was a virgin, lived with his mother and was no narrowminded even jokes with the word bum caused the blotches on his cheeks to turn beetroot red. I knew the material of my dress was straining against my behind and making him squirm but it was up to him to turn his eyes away and not make me feel guilty for being generously built.

'Call Sissy into my office.' Gibson sounded flustered. 'I need her to run some errands.' I turned to see him pick up a phone that was ringing on my desk. 'Mr. Gibson here. Well of course Mr. Tyler, I most certainly will pass on your compliment to Laura.' Grimacing, Gibson looked at the clock again. 'She's *just* come into the office.' In my mind, my fist make contact with his thin pointed nose. ***BOOF.*** 'Laura is indeed an asset to our company,' Mr. Gibson chirped. 'I've already told her she's due for a pay rise.' I pursed my lips to show I doubted the truth of that promise since getting a penny out of his tight little fists was like trying to squeeze juice out of a prune. Gibson patted his toupee, which he plastered with Brylcreem to make it shine. 'Well, thank you again, Mr. Tyler.'

The second he put down the phone, I buzzed Sissy to come into my office and with Gibson hovering over my shoulder, took a file out of my bag. 'These are what I feel are our priorities for today.' I handed him the file. 'Would you like to check the order?' While Gibson combed through the list, ticking items off in a fluorescent marker pen that could have dazzled the blind, the phone rang again. It was Monster saying he had talked to Virgin Records and they wanted me to send them a demo tape. Instead of feeling thrilled that my new career was under way, I felt panic. 'In a meeting. Call you back.' I slammed the phone back on its stand.

Mr. Gibson carefully examined his manicured nails. 'Why did you say you were in a meeting?'

I lied to get into Gibsons Holidays with a CV that said I had five A levels and was an exemplary student even though I'd been expelled for bunking off school more than I attended class. The only reason I knew how to spell words such as *exemplary* was because I studied English at night college while waitressing for a year at fourteen. Naturally, I lied to the restaurant owner about my age and had lied ever since to survive my seven years with Gibson in Nazi prison. 'That was Bob from accounts,' I said, flippantly. 'I thought what we were doing was more important and didn't want to spoil your train of thought, Mr. Gibson.'

Gibson's chest puffed out. 'Quite right.' He handed me back the file. 'Carry on.' Patting his tweed jacket, he strode off swinging his arms as though he had a platoon of soldiers marching behind him.

'Oh Mr. Gibson,' I called out. I've told you twice that my fan's broken and the weather forecast says we're in for more hot spells.'

'I'll order a new one,' he said, straightening my stilettos as he passed so that they were in perfect alignment with the wall.

I watched Gibson sit down at his desk through the frosted glass window that separated our offices. There was no way I could leave my job until money started coming in from Streetcrash but how long would I be able to pull the wool over Gibson's eyes? I was having an anxious moment when Tod from press office walked in with a rose.

'Here you go sexy. A pink rose for my favourite girl.' Tod gave a low wolf whistle. 'Which happens to be a perfect match for that dynamite dress you're wearing. And *love* your hair. Very Sophia Loren.'

I smiled because Sophia Loren was the film star I had in mind that morning when styling it. 'Thanks Tod,' I looked up at all six foot five of him. 'I'll ask Sissy to bring something to put your rose in.'

Tod smoothed back his college boy haircut and gazed at me with innocent blue eyes. 'When are we going out on another date then?' As a clued-up historian who could quote the names of Henry V111's six wives, wax lyrically about the opium war between Britain and China in Victorian times and endless other stuff, I gave him ten out of ten. As regards women like me, he came last in class.

I checked Gibson wasn't peering through the frosted glass and strained my ears. He was talking to someone on the phone. 'For the second time, Tod, our date was a one off.'

'You were dynamite when you got up in that Mexican restaurant and started dancing with that waiter.' Tod patted his pristine V neck sweater. 'When you grabbed those maracas and starting playing them on your bum, the waiter nearly had a heart attack.' I could see the memory tickled him so smiled along. Tod took my hand and kissed it. 'I know a great Japanese restaurant where the chef cooks at your table and tosses knives in the air.'

I took my hand back and used it to shoo him towards the door. 'Apart from the fact Gibson would have a stroke if he thought two of his staff members were doing naughty things behind his back, you're eighteen and should be shagging girls your own age.'

Tod positioned himself in front of my hand. 'But that night we made love you were so into it.'

I laughed. 'I don't make love Tod, I shag.'

'See, girls my age don't talk like that and none of them make me feel as randy as you do.'

'Well you can think of me when you're having a wank. Now shove off. Mr. Gibson's being his usual pain in the neck.'

Tod dug his hands in his pockets, shook his head as if he couldn't figure me out and passed Sissy in the doorway as she rushed into my office. Sissy was wearing a polka dot bow on her head, a puffed polka dot skirt and looked like cartoon character Minnie Mouse.

'This is the letter you asked me to write regarding our Sierra Leone holiday promotion.' Sissy placed a piece of paper on my desk then handed me a mug. 'Here's your coffee – I'll go and see what Mr. Slave-driver wants- and I'll get something to put that in,' she said, spotting the rose.

Both my phones starting ringing. Picking them up I said. 'Gibsons Travel. How can I help you?' to one. Mr. Baldwin from Baldwin's travel agency asked me a question. 'Just need to answer another call Mr. Baldwin. I'll get back to you in a mo.' The person on the other phone was Pete from Virgin Records. I decided to give Mr. Baldwin priority so I could be more relaxed with Pete. 'Great to hear from you Pete, give me a mo, I'm on the other line.' Laying that phone on my desk I returned to Mr. Baldwin's call. 'That's right Mr. Baldwin. If you've got a group of thirty people who want to go to Majorca I can get you a 30% discount, on top of which I'll arrange free champagne for your guests and get the hotel to throw in free beach towels.'

Urgently waving a letter, Gibson strode into my office. Seeing the abandoned telephone, he picked it up. 'Mr. Gibson here,' he said.

Slamming the phone down on Mr. Baldwin after a galloped 'Call you back', I snatched the other from a bewildered Gibson, said 'Call you back, Pete' to Pete and slammed the phone down on him.

Gibson placed a hand on the small of back, creaked it upright and brought his eyes in line with mine. 'Which *Pete* might that have been?'

'Pete from the telephone company. My home phone isn't working. He's coming to fix it tomorrow before I come to work but can't confirm the time yet.'

'Hmph,' Gibson flapped a letter under my nose. 'I asked you to set up a meeting with the lawyers.'

'I wrote it in your diary last week. They're coming in at 3pm tomorrow.'

Gibson twisted his hands together then nodded at the telephone I'd said four words to Pete on. 'I accept the telephone company calling. However, I remind you that personal calls of any other nature are not allowed during office hours.' He strode away then turned, monocle pressed against one eye. 'Hmph. I smell something fishy.'

I smiled sweetly. 'Have no idea what you mean, Mr. Gibson.'

# SEVEN

Having never met Cassie from WEA Records, I had no idea what her personality was like or whether she would even agree to see me so felt a wave of relief when she said I could stop by her office that Monday night. I'd written pages of notes which I presented at my meeting with Tate and Charlie most of which were guesswork or lies. Guesses were as unpredictable as the weather but at least left space for hope. Regarding the 'lies' part I got carried away and pretended to know loads of big wigs in the industry that I'd only read about in magazines. I could see Tate didn't believe all I said because I caught him smiling to himself a couple of times. Charlie was so excited he leapt around the kitchen saying, 'Cor, Laura knows everything and everyone. She knows people we've never heard of and she had lunch with Ahmet Ertegun the other week.' Ahmet Ertegun was the founder of Atlantic Records. What I didn't know was that he'd been in Los Angeles for months and that another big wig I mentioned having chatted to over cocktails, died of a heart attack the year before. Cassie put me straight on both but I was *really* glad Monster passed out and wasn't at our meeting because he'd have seen through me within minutes.

While Cassie wrote her list of contacts, I took the opportunity to wander around the first floor hall of WEA Records. The exterior of the building was no different to Gibson Holidays. The interior was a vastly different world. At Gibson Holidays by 5.15 every day the place was as deserted as the Sahara Desert – apart from my boss who rattled around his office until all hours like a skeleton afraid to leave the cemetery. At WEA the buzz was electric. People dared to laugh, joke and pop into each other's offices without fear of being fired. I was so used to seeing Gibson's stern face and tight lips the contrast was a revelation.

My wondrousness made me think of a book I loved when I was little. The Lion the Witch and the Wardrobe. That book, together with music (which I listened to in my bedroom on a tinny, crackling radio I found on a dump and had to play quietly because music gave my mother migraines) helped me through my childhood. I used to imagine I was Lucy, the heroine in the book, and live out the adventures that awaited her in the magical world of Narnia. A world she entered by stepping through a door at the back of her wardrobe. Walking into WEA that night was like stepping through a door to find myself in a Narnia that wasn't a made-up world with imagined characters. This one was the home of famous flesh and blood singers and musicians I read about every week in the New Musical Express.

I made every footstep count as I trod the very same carpet Zeppelin, Yes, Velvet Underground, Crosby Stills and Nash and myriads of icons graced and imagined the feel of their footprints seeping into mine. Music blared out of every office all the way down the hall. Some of the songs I didn't know because they hadn't been released, but I hummed along to Ray Charles singing 'What'd I say' and Otis Redding singing 'On the dock of the Bay' as they competed to be heard among the rest. When Paranoid by Black Sabbath came on, my heart leapt out of my chest. Black Sabbath had risen from nowhere in a few short months and Streetcrash were in their league which meant once they were signed, we could be selling millions of records by the following year. Could it be that easy? I dared to believe it was and visualized myself dressed in Vivian Westwood, hair styled by Vidal Sassoon, lipstick by Chanel.

Most of the females I saw coming and going to grab a glass of juice, piece of fruit or a cup of tea from the bar where I stood sipping Earl Grey, wore jeans and trainers. A few wore embroidered Hungarian blouses, ankle length hippie skirts and Birkenstock leather sandals, but there was none of the glamour I expected to see in a building where you could bump into Mick Jagger – who was number two on my must shag list. I 'd taken a change of clothing into my office and was wearing navy blue crepe hot pants with matching fitted jacket, chisel toed orange sling backs and an orange silk scarf over my bouffant hairstyle. Compared to the other girls, I was too made up since the most they wore was a slick of mascara but I'd got so used to wearing false eyelashes my reflection had a fit when I left them off.

I was playing a guessing game with myself about where the Stones office might be and working out a list of questions to ask Mick, when a woman gave me a gentle poke in the back. 'Hey, pass me a banana, girl,' she drawled in an American accent. I snapped one off the bunch, happy to be of service to anyone who might prove useful in my new career and turned. It was ARETHA FRANKLIN!

Pointing at her, not a sound coming out of my mouth because I was in awe, I took in her flipped out hairdo and the halter neck dress I'd seen her wear on a TV talk show a few nights before and was instantly whooshed back to the yard where Debs and me danced to Respect. I must have swayed because Aretha said. 'The way you're waving that banana looks like you're warming it up for me or something?'

Embarrassed, I handed the banana to her in the regal manner she deserved. The letters '**R.E.S.P.E.C.T**' came out of my mouth.

'1967 that came out and still going strong,' Aretha hip bumped me. 'You sure got it all goin' on girl,' she said, admiring my outfit.

I couldn't believe it. *ARETHA* was admiring *ME* and my dress style. Glad my fashionista expressionism was appreciated in such exalted quarters, I gave her a feel of the fabric. 'Biba.'

'Beeeba?' Aretha gave the fabric a squeeze. 'Is that an English slang word for something?'

'It's the name of a shop in Kensington High Street,' I pointed vaguely to its vicinity as though she had radar eyes and could see through brick walls.

'Need to check it out while I'm in London,' she smiled.

My eyes were on her banana. She had just taken the last bite and was looking around for somewhere to throw the peel. Knowing Debs would pee her pants with excitement if I took it home for her to pickle and preserve, I said 'I'll take that,' and snatched it. Aretha didn't bat an eyelid which suggested banana thieves like me were an everyday part of life.

A woman poked her head around the door of Atlantic Records. She waved at Aretha to go in. 'Good talking to you.' Aretha gave me a mischievous smile. 'If you want a couple of tickets to my show at Hammersmith, tell her they're on me.'

*What! Half an hour at WEA and I'd scored Aretha's banana peel and tickets to her show.* I nodded at Aretha's behind like a twat until the door closed behind it, then protecting my prize, went back into Cassie's office. 'Have you got a paper bag I can put this in?'

Laughing, Cassie, who was a freckle faced blonde with a gentle nature, opened a drawer and gave me an envelope. 'Who did that belong to?'

'Aretha Franklin,' I breathed, trying to remember every syllable that passed between us.

'You remind me of me when I started working for the Squeaks. You'll soon get over it, Cassie said, patting the chair next to hers for me to sit down. 'By the way, thanks again for getting me that 50% discount to Tenerife. My boyfriend and I had a great time.' She stroked my arm as her way of saying thanks then ran her finger down the names on her list. I pinched myself to erase Aretha from my mind so I could concentrate. 'Apart from Derek at Warners here, try Vince at EMI, Jamil at Break Neck and Robert at Scorch – Scorch have their offices next door - all four could be interested in a band like Streetcrash since they have bands in a similar vein. Send them tapes, biogs and photos but push for a meeting.' She ran her finger down another list. 'Send everything to all these people as well but know that the majority don't listen to stuff they're sent because they receive hundreds of demo tapes every week. Try to get as many as you can to come to a gig, front VIP seats with the names on of those who say yes, free drinks and fancy vol au vents etc. because freebies help, and make sure it's a venue they can easily get to.' It was suddenly sounding like there wouldn't just be a lot of work but managing Streetcrash would take a massive chunk out of my meagre savings. I had a moment of panic wondering what I'd got myself into. Cassie handed me a membership card for the Speakeasy club. 'It's got my name on but they don't know me because I've only been twice. The action doesn't start until after midnight but it's worth showing your face. Talk to agents, managers, roadies, session musicians, journalists, producers, A&R people and glean information.' Still trying to take it all in I fanned my face. 'It won't be a stroll through the park but...'she tapped my hand. 'Stop shaking, you'll be fine.'

I placed the Speakeasy membership card, the list of contacts and Aretha's banana safely in my bag, overwhelmed by the mammoth journey ahead. Then I remembered the demo tape I put in the post to Virgin Records. Convinced Pete would snap Streetcrash up having listened to it and that I'd be able to skip the majority of Cassie's suggestions, I cast her my most confident smile. 'I'll let you know soon as I get them signed.'

# EIGHT

The following six weeks felt like I'd been slapped by a tornado, both mentally and physically. I ran myself ragged trying to get record labels interested in signing Streetcrash but it was definitely not the piece of cake I imagined. I sent demo tapes to everyone on Cassie's list, which resulted in six paltry meetings. Four wanted to sign Streetcrash without paying an advance and one even dared to suggest I paid them money to help with recording fees! Only Jamil from Break Neck gave me a spark of hope but he had an iffy partner so I wasn't holding my breath.

Going to the Speakeasy proved another sorry saga – apart from the fact I got Ginger Baker from Cream to write his autograph on a paper napkin, (which Debs framed). The manager of the Speakeasy wouldn't hear of Streetcrash playing there again because they'd caused so much damage the first time with Charlie letting off fire distinguishers and covering everyone in foam and Monster bopping one of his VIP guests on the nose. In desperation, I gave out my newly printed business card left, right and centre to anyone I came across but apart from a few calls from sleazy men who wanted dates, my Narnia adventure verged on a tragic comedy.

During that time Monster crashed into a lamp-post and dented the fender on his van so was in a stinking mood for days. That was partly because of the accident but mainly because he lost a bag of coke somewhere. He insulted me on a regular basis driving home that someone who hung out with bikers wasn't an expert on anything and that Tate and Charlie should have listened to his advice. There were times I wanted to chuck Monster out of a window and wash my hands of him. If Tate hadn't been there to calm me, I might have done so. Working round the clock proved exhausting. There were mornings I couldn't drag myself out of bed so was ten minutes late for work on two occasions which didn't sit well with my boss. When he sent me to Sierra Leone, he made sure I worked like a Trojan as punishment. I missed Aretha's Franklyn's show because I was abroad and had a black eye thanks to Chris, which meant taking a day off work. I told Gibson I'd fallen off my bicycle. 'Funny that in all the years you've worked for me this is the first time I've heard of a bicycle,' he spat down the phone. I told him I bought a second hand one to help me lose weight but knew he didn't believe a word and dreaded the Nazi inquisition that awaited when I returned to work.

Quite a list of calamities and to make things worse, that morning Robert Bauman from Scorch Records asked me to go and see him and Streetcrash had a gig at the Trade Club in Camden Town two nights later. My black eye couldn't have come at a worse time. I felt gutted, depressed and ugly.

When Debs got home from work, she served me a plate of pasta she named 'spaghetti bolaneska' which had so much garlic I couldn't stop burping. Her latest fad was to use tons of it on everything she cooked. I watched her clear the plates from the coffee table then give it a squirt of wood polish. 'We've got lemon curd pie for afters,' she said. 'It's another new recipe I made up. Thought I'd make it for Dave when he comes back from Cardiff.'

'I'm sure Dave will love it.' Trying to stretch my jaw, I looked down at the pyjamas I'd been in all day and felt sorry for myself.

Stepping over to our 'new' record cabinet in a floaty boho dress I bought her in Portobello Market, she fondly fingered it.

'And what about the great swap I did for this while you in Sierra Leone?' The record cabinet was as scratched as if an army of cats had been at it with their claws and was a stupid swap for a set of six aluminum saucepans. I didn't have the strength to open my mouth so said nothing.

Debs handed me the piece of raw stewing steak that I put on a napkin while I ate. 'Put this back on your eye.' Tutting, she peered at it. 'That Chris should be in jail for doing this to you. Men can't go around punching women in the face. Dave says you should tell the police.' Debs grabbed my legs and made me lie straight out on the couch, then plumped up a cushion and pushed my head against it. 'Explain to me exactly what happened last night because so far nothing you said makes sense.' She sat down on the carpet and crossed her legs. 'Start from the beginning.'

I squinted at her through my available eye. 'I don't know what happened except that when Chris slapped me, I saw the faces of all the rotten sods who slapped my Mum so I slapped him back – not for her because she got what she deserved but because of the nasty, vicious look in his eyes. When Chris punched me in chest, all the pent up fury I felt came back again so I spat in his face. Then he punched me in the eye,' I gave Debs a weak smile in an attempt to make less of my ordeal.

Debs arms flopped in dismay. 'There's something seriously wrong with you, Laura! Anyone normal would have walked away –who else but you would pick a fight with a heavy weight boxer?' She gave me her hand on hip fretful mother look. 'How many Bacardi's had you had?'

'Two, but it wasn't the drink. It didn't matter what I said, he kept getting more aggressive, poking me, calling me a prostitute and worse - and all because I said he was too possessive and I didn't want to see him anymore.'

Debs spied a tiddly piece of spaghetti on the carpet, gathered it in a napkin and rubbed at a non- existent stain with her thumb. 'I know what happened. You let the cat out of the bag and he guessed you shagged someone in Sierra Leone?'

'I didn't shag anyone in Sierra Leone, Debs.'

'Oh *really!*' Debs crossed her arms. 'You couldn't last a week without a willie fix.'

'Well I didn't have a willie fix alright! Mr. Gibson sent three of our top UK travel agents with me and they took up every spare minute.' I took the piece of steak off my eye, sat up and faced Debs. 'Anyway, I've decided to give up sex for three months because my priority is getting Streetcrash signed.'

Huffing, Debs leapt to her feet. 'Three *whole* months! I'd like to see that!' Glowering, she pointed at my black eye. 'If Streetcrash are so important to you, you wouldn't have got yourself beaten up by a thug the day before your meeting with Scorch Records! What do you think Mr. Bonniman or whatever his name is will think when he sees that orange atrocity?'

'How could I have known Mr. Bauman would choose today to call?' I felt as upset as Debs because my jaw ached from the punch, my eye throbbed, the fingers of my right hand were numb and I could barely twist my neck. 'I'll wear sun glasses.'

Debs glanced at the rain slashing against the window pane. 'Then let's hope the weather changes or you'll have to wear an eye patch!' She took off for the kitchen mumbling under her breath while I settled back to listen to Crosby, Stills and Nash singing Woodstock on the record player. They were singing the lines *'We are stardust, we are golden. We are caught in the devil's bargain and we've got to get ourselves back to the garden'*. I knew I was caught in the devil's bargain, otherwise I wouldn't lead men on and use them to satisfy my needs. How I got back to the garden was my dilemma but not one I could think about with so many issues to deal with, especially how I was going to face the press at the Trade Club. I could see the headline 'Streetcrash takes on Mafia manager in last bid for recognision'.

Debs put a plate down in front of me and pushed a spoon into my hand. 'Lemon curd pie. Tell me what you think and let's forget everything we talked about. Listening to you has given me stomach cramps.'

I sat up and ate a spoonful under Deb's watchful eyes as she waited for the verdict. 'I think Mrs. Beeton might have put a bit more sugar in this,' I said, wincing at the sharpness of the lemony taste.

'It's because my mind's on you!' Debs shouted. 'If you carry on like this, you'll end up with broken legs, your jaw hanging off your face and no teeth. You have got to pull yourself together and....' Debs picked up the phone because it was ringing. 'Hello Monster,' she said curtly. 'Yes, Laura's here. I'll pass her over.' Debs reeled out the telephone wire, gave me the phone and stomped back into the kitchen while I sat with my ear to the ear piece unable to get a word in as Monster rattled on without stopping for breath.

'Stop worrying, Monster,' I said. 'I've already sorted out everything for the Trade Club gig,' The knot in my stomach tightened knowing the VIP row was still half empty. 'Yes, I've arranged for the press to be there. Yes, there's interest from a couple of record labels – Oh, and I've got a meeting with Scorch tomorrow,' I threw in casually. 'Yes, with Robert Bauman. He called this morning.' I listened to Monster's do and don'ts agreeing with what he said until he ran out of suggestions then remembered my black eye. 'By the way, just so you know I fell off my bicycle.'

Not really listening, Monster said, 'You should be more careful,' and moved onto a story about the night Streetcrash played at the Marquis Club and Keith Richards from the Stones got up and played with them on stage. That was Monster all over. Some days I barely got two words out of him and others I was his confidante, agony aunt and best friend. That phone call fell into the latter category. I could feel something building under the surface but whether he took another minute or hour to spit it out was anyone's guess. I waited patiently for a gap to reply.

'Yes,' I said when part one of his story was over. 'If we get Scorch, you will be able to go next door to the Stones office at WEA and ask Keith how he's doing.' Debs plonked a cup of tea in my hands. I nodded my thanks and took a sip adding a burning tongue to my injuries due to the fact it was scalding hot. 'Yeah, The Stones were clever moving to France to avoid paying tax in the UK.' Debs started vacuuming the carpet. I waved at her to stop because I couldn't hear myself. 'Anything else on your mind, Monster?'

'I'm working on a new single. I'll play it for you next week.' Monster said. The line went quiet. I heard him take a few long sniffs. 'The song's about how that fucking Capricorn bitch, Inge, screwed me over.' Monster disappeared off the line again. I could hear the clink of glass and sound of pouring so guessed he was fixing himself a Jack. 'I'd have done anything for her,' he said, picking up where he left off. 'And what does she do? Not only fucks two guys behind my back but has the fucking nerve to tell me I lack intellect!'

I called Debs over and mouthed that her prophesy had come true. 'Told him,' she whispered, chuffed she had been right about Capricorns.

'What d'you think of that then?' Monster screamed down the phone.

Having got lost under the rubble of misery that possessed me that day, I hadn't registered the importance of getting a meeting with Scorch. The record label we most wanted to sign us. I thought of making more of it to calm Monster down, and was on the verge of saying something when he screamed '*What d'you think of that then?*' again.

'If Inge was the inspiration for your song, can't be all bad,' I said calmly. 'Keep thinking how close you are to success and…'

'Fuck success, I don't give a shit,' Monster slammed down the phone.

My face must have changed colour because Debs raced off and brought me back a glass of water. 'I think you should lie down.' She eased the phone from my fingers. 'What did Monster say?'

Lost for words, I waved Debs away, put the piece of steak back on my eye and lay flat out on the couch to bask in more misery. I was a band manager with a black eye on the verge of being sacked from my day job, my three month trial period was nearing its end and Monster was so unpredictable he could cancel the Trade Club gig. Worse than that was listening to Monster come unhinged over Inge. I thought he was a rocker who shagged for pleasure but I'd seen another side and what scared me witless was his slide back to depression and drug binges.

# NINE

I shook out my dripping umbrella and dropped it in the stand as I passed through the front door into the grandeur of a mosaic tiled hall. It was obvious the building that housed Scorch Records had once been an apartment block inhabited by posh people. As I wandered towards the bronze gated lift that cranked its way to the ground floor, I imagined ladies in satin bustle dresses and wide brimmed hats coming to take tea in dainty cups with their lady friends. I wore a wide brimmed hat with oversized sunglasses to disguise my black eye. My outfit was a black Mary Quant tent dress with big white pockets on the front and black Cuban heeled shoes that had squares of white leather clipped to the front. They cost thirty three guineas in the sales at Harvey Nichols but due to the sudden downpour, squelched with water. The hem of my dress was also soaked – the price of not wearing a raincoat - but could I have known the sky would open with such violence when the weather forecast predicted sunny spells?

Whilst waiting for the lift to descend, I took off my shoes. The dye had come off and my toes were black. Having wiped the inside of my shoes with tissues, I squeezed my feet back into them and since the lift decided to go up a floor instead of coming down, took out my compact mirror and used the time to tuck wet, frizzing strands of hair back under my hat. With a heavy clank, the lift arrived at the ground floor, the door slowly opened and a colonel style gentleman with a bristly moustache got out as I passed him to go in. 'Good weather for ducks,' he beamed, taking in my soggy appearance. I could see that rain

58

drenched or not he was impressed by my stylishness since he went on to comment on my hat saying how refreshing it was to see a woman who wasn't afraid to stand out and asked if I worked for Models International who apparently had an office on the fifth floor. His compliments brought back my confidence. I tried out a smile I intended to use on Mr. Bauman to convince him Streetcrash were the next big thing. 'Actually,' the colonel wagged a finger. 'You could be an actress – didn't I see you on that BBC period drama last week?'

'I manage a heavy metal band called Streetcrash.' How I loved saying those words even if it was to a stranger who didn't have a clue who they were. I waltzed past him into the lift. 'They are going to be *huge,*' I said proudly as the lift door rattled shut.

It seemed to take forever to reach the fourth floor. When I got out, I glanced down the hall debating whether to turn left or right and saw identical twins come out of one of the doors. From their punky strawberry pink hair and red jeans, I knew they were singers so headed in their direction. On passing one said. 'Two months he messed us about before saying no!'

'He's a prat,' said the other. 'I told you that the first time we met him.'

I smiled at Mr. Bauman being called a prat. Having Gibson as a boss made me an expert prat handler and I knew how to handle them. The only reason I'd broken out of prison fifteen minutes early was because Gibson thought I was going to a meeting to clinch a deal with an airline who would sell us half price tickets if we used them exclusively for six months. I'd already clinched it but if the only way to get what I wanted was to lie, I was also an expert on that, and would lie through my teeth until fortune smiled.

Having shaken out the drips from the hem of my dress, I took a deep breath and pressed the buzzer for Scorch Records. A girl in a blue tailored suit and crisp white shirt opened it.

'You must be Laura.' She smiled and waved me in. 'Take a seat in the waiting area.' She pointed to a kitchenette. 'Or you can make coffee if you like?'

I made coffee, took the mug with me into the waiting area and surveyed the layout to get my bearings. Behind a closed door with *Rehearsal Studio* written on it, I could hear a Ginnie Linnie track playing that I didn't know. Ginnie Linnie were one of Robert's bands. They had just entered the charts at No28 with their new single but from what I heard, were losing fans.

Shortly afterwards Max Oliver, the lead guitarist of Ginnie Linnie, came out of the rehearsal studio followed by Mr. Bauman. Max's fingers were sunk into the pockets of his jeans as he stared down at the parquet floor. He looked more miserable than a condemned convict on his way to the gas chamber.

Mr. Bauman unclenched his jaw. 'Pull yourself together, Max. 'I'm just pointing out that you need to come up with better material for your next album. From what I've heard today when your single peaks and dies, you've got nothing to follow it with. I sunk a lot of money into Ginnie. I was expecting more that's all.'

Max ambled by me into the kitchenette, swinging his ponytail and heavily sighing as he poured a mug of coffee then went back to the rehearsal room. Mr. Bauman disappeared into another room further down the hall. The minutes ticked by. Having witnessed the strawberry haired twins' fate and seen Max's abject misery, something told me I should arrange another meeting for when Mr. Bauman was feeling better disposed, but what if he was always like that and the next meeting took weeks to come around? To get me through my trial period, I sold every piece of jewellery I owned and had nothing else to sell.

His secretary appeared like a leaf on the breeze cutting through the icy atmosphere that clung to my wet dress. 'Mr.

Bauman's ready to see you now'. She took me on one side. 'He's in a rotten mood,' she whispered. 'Just agree with whatever he says or you won't last long in the lion's den.' She opened the door for me to go in. 'Good luck,' she mouthed.

I walked in head held high to mask my anxiousness but Mr. Bauman was oblivious to my presence. His head was down at his huge oblong glass topped desk as he scribbled something on a notepad. Passing the mahogany conference table with its twelve high backed dining chairs I continued walking towards a semi-circular maroon velvet sofa, which again could easily sit twelve people. Since I hadn't been told where to sit, I chose the middle and waited, crossing and uncrossing my legs as I listened to the faint rattle of traffic going up and down New Oxford Street outside the glass paneled wall.

'I'm sorry to have brought you in today but I've decided against Streetcrash.' Mr. Bauman said without bothering to look up.

Straightening my back, I placed both hands over my crossed knee. 'Well, since I'm here,' I used my most businesslike voice, 'I'd appreciate hearing the reason why you've changed your mind?'

'I don't have to have a reason,' Mr. Bauman looked up briefly. His pen dropped on the glass and rolled towards me. Instinctively I picked it up and placed it in the box where he kept a supply of silver, gold pens and letter openers which I assumed were gifts because who needed seven of everything? Mr. Bauman selected another pen and continued writing.

'I know the tape I sent you was rough but to call this meeting you must have listened to it and thought Streetcrash had potential?' I leaned forwards to force him to look at me.

'I've got enough headaches,' he said, continuing to ignore me. 'Streetcrash will only add to them!'

*How did I react to that?* 'I have no idea what you mean about Streetcrash adding to your headaches because I can assure you Mr. Bauman that they are one of the easiest bands in the music business to work with.'

'Monster and Charlie are erratic hooligans. On their last tour they smashed up a hotel room.' He waved his pen at the door. 'I've wasted enough money this year.'

The prat still didn't look up. If I had to be carried bodily from his office, I would go pleading my case until such time. 'Charlie and Monster might be a bit erratic but I can think of a lot worse. Look at the number of hotel rooms the Stones or the Who trashed and the number of times they were slammed by the pressed. That didn't stop them becoming icons.'

Mr. Bauman finally looked up. 'The Who and the Stones are superstars. Streetcrash are an unknown band,' he sniffed.

'Exactly, but I bet Dick Rowe from Decca is still kicking himself for turning the Beatles down. He said *guitar bands were on their way out* and look where the Beatles are today?' Since I was on a roll, I thought I might as well keep going. 'In addition, Monster is one of the best songwriters in the UK and has enough material to write as many albums as you want because his talent never dries up.' I added the last bit because of what I heard him say to Max.

'I've said all I have to say,' Mr. Bauman said.

He had a way of looking at me without seeing me so I stood up, arms placed by my sides, and gave him my deal clincher smile. 'I'm aware how many people must have sat on that sofa,' I pointed to where I sat, 'trying to convince you they've found the next big band but Streetcrash are one of the hottest heavy metal bands around and they are going to be huge.'

My deal clincher smile made him scowl. 'And what makes *you* an authority on that?'

'I know their songs and I know what kids of today want. Streetcrash just keep getting better and I believe one hundred percent that with the right guidance they could be up there with Zeppelin, which is where you come in.' I dug a tape I'd brought along out of my handbag. 'Here are two new songs Monster wrote in the past month. Truth Kills could be a No1 hit.'

'I've already told you I'm not...'

'Why not listen to Truth Kills then give me your opinion.' I pushed the tape under his hand.

Mr. Bauman flipped the tape over then pointed to the door. 'Why don't you give in gracefully and leave?'

'Because I've got the guts to fight for what I believe in,' I said, thumping his table for effect. Mr. Bauman looked at his watch as if saying my time was up. *Sod what his secretary said about agreeing. I was going to stand up to him the way I should have stood up to Gibson.* 'Are all men in the music business as rude as you are?' I think I probably glared but he wouldn't have seen that through my sunglasses. 'I have come here to tell you about a band who could be selling you millions of records by this time next year and *you*,' I shook my index finger at him, '*You* are missing out on one of the greatest opportunities of your career and will prove to be another Dick Rowe.' Mr. Bauman looked ready to leap out of his chair and toss me out of the window. His hand reached for the buzzer on his desk.

Unable to stop myself, I covered his hand with mine. 'I'm asking you with all the respect I can to give Streetcrash a chance. Listen to the new demo tape. Come and see them live tomorrow night at the Trade Club, and if you're still not...'

'Could you please take your hand off mine?' His steely grey eyes glittered with fury. 'Your behavior is outrageous.'

I could see that my tactics rubbed him up the wrong way so took my hand back. It was sink or swim time. If I sank to the bottom at least I'd know I had done everything humanly possible to win him over and could leave feeling proud that I left no stone unturned. But what could I offer? What could I say to twist his arm? He called me outrageous. The idea that popped into my head had a capitol O. 'How would you and your girlfriend or wife like to go on an exotic holiday?' I made a grand gesture with my hand, and knocked his pencil box flying. For a moment I stood there as if pens weren't rolling off my shoes but since I couldn't leave it like that, asked Mr. Baumann to excuse me for a second. Falling to my knees, I crawled about the floor catching rolling pencils and pens. Who knew pens moved at the speed of light? Some travelled so far afield I scrabbled about underneath the conference table capturing them under my dress and pinned them down so I could pick them up. I knew Mr. Bauman was witnessing a woman in a big floppy hat and giant sunglasses leaping about like a puppy catching sticks for its master. Cheeks burning with embarrassment, I stood in my most lady like manner, collected the rest by kicking them in a pile then bent over to pick them up and deposited them in his pencil box. I straightened my sunglasses, tucked my hair back under my hat and gave it an adjustment so it wasn't hanging over one ear. 'Sorry about that.'

Mr. Bauman's stony eyed glare softened. His arm twitched. A faint smile appeared on his upper lip. He burst out laughing. 'Hahaha. So now you're selling exotic holidays!' He looked me up and down with a mixture of disbelief and amusement. 'You're like no-one I've ever come across - and where might you send me and my wife?'

He sounded like he was teasing but I couldn't take the chance. 'Djerba or perhaps Sierra Leone?

Mr. Baumann rocked slowly back and forth on his plush swivel chair. 'I've got no idea how you managed it but you made me laugh for the first time in days.' He tapped his cheeks with long, tapered fingers then turned to study me as though I was a curious species that had yet to be named. 'Do you always go around trying to blackmail people?'

Opting for a cheeky reply to show I wasn't perturbed at being called a blackmailer, I gave a casual shrug. 'It seemed a better idea than offering you a pen since you've got a plentiful supply of those.'

Mr. Bauman's forehead creased as he suppressed a smile. 'Well you're not doing Streetcrash any favours.' He pointed to my eyes. 'And do you always wear sunglasses when it's pouring with rain?'

'Slight accident with my bike. I slid into a ditch and came face to face with a tree trunk.'

Mr. Bauman absently nodded then stared into space and drummed his fingers on the desk. His face was turned sideways so I didn't have to worry about his steely eyes penetrating my sunglasses. He had a nose that might have looked too pointed on someone else. It suited him. His trimmed beard gave him a look of elegance. The faint stripes on his crisp cotton shirt were the same grey as his eyes. He wasn't good looking, but for a man I guessed to be in his thirties, he had an appeal that had something to do with his concentration and suggested a man of mysterious depths. Mr. Bauman's tongue flicked snakelike around his lips. He rested his hand against his elbow and stared at the demo tape on his desk. In the random way the mind goes off, I wondered whether he preferred Italian or French food, then if he wore pyjamas or went to bed naked. The silence was so quiet, I could hear the beat of my heart. To help time pass until Mr. Bauman said something, I recited a passage from The Lion the Witch and the Wardrobe. *Call out the werewolves and the spirits of the trees who are on our side. Call out the Ghouls, the Boggles the Ogres and Minataurs. Call the Cruels, Hags and Spectres and the people of the Toadstools. We will fight.*

I had just mouthed, 'We will fight,' when Mr. Bauman came out of his trance.

'Let me listen to the tape,' he said. 'It's rare for someone to stand up to me the way you did.'

I was so surprised I think I said 'Errr?' before I changed my grin to something less readable. 'Assuming you like it, would you consider coming to hear them live on Saturday night at the Trade Club?'

'That's unlikely.' He picked up the demo tape with Truth Kills and gave it a rattle. 'But I'll give this a listen.'

Deciding there was nothing more to be done and reminding myself that I had scored a goal if not the game, I held out my hand for a shake. 'Then I look forward to hearing your opinion about Truth kills.'

Robert didn't take my hand. 'If you don't hear from me in a week, take it I'm not interested and won't be in the future.'

# TEN

The Trade Club dressing room was a big step up from the Rat being three times its size, had proper make up lights around the mirror and came supplied with coffee making facilities, a plate of sandwiches, savoury snacks and soft drinks. My sleek tonged hair gave the illusion of a serene mermaid and while nothing could erase my huge boobs or tribal woman's bum, the high-necked jumpsuit with wide legs didn't emphasize my assets and Monster's acne-erase makeup stick ensured the bruises under my eye couldn't be seen from stage when I introduced Streetcrash.

On the outside I looked calm and collected. Anxiety caused me to devour three sandwiches that I practically swallowed whole due to the fact my mouth felt like singed hay and I couldn't chew, and also because eating fast stopped the guilt associated with supposedly being on a diet. I was saved from mindlessly grabbing a piece of quiche by the manager who poked his head round the door to ask me to check the catering arrangements and to let me know the girl who was handling the press list wanted a few words. That proved a major learning curve since I knew diddle about press lists or arranging gigs for five hundred people. Having successfully bluffed my way through, I went back into the dressing room to see Monster practically sobbing in the mirror.

'Fuck! The way I've made my eyes up makes me look like Alice Cooper!' Monster groaned and slammed down the shadow pot he used to create a smoky effect. 'Look, I've got the shakes.' Monster held out his hand to prove it. 'Where's my coke, I need a line,' he screwed his eyes up at Tate who chatted to Charlie in the corner. 'Tell me where you've hidden it?'

'We agreed,' Tate said calmly.

'I need it for my nerves. What if I forget the words and fuck up one of the songs?

'You never forget the words,' Tate said. He picked up a copy of Melody Maker and scanned the pages.

Sweat seeping through his T shirt, Monster sniffed under his armpits. 'I smell like shit!' Groaning he pressed his fingers against his stomach. 'I've got stomach cramps, Laura.'

Monster took a slug of Jack then pointed to his face and sighed miserably. 'What am I going to do about Alice?'

'Start your make up over?' I squirted make up remover on a tissue. 'I'll do it.'

'You'd better not mess it up!' Monster waved his hand for me to get started, then swung around on his chair to glare firstly at Tate who was engrossed in an article he was reading then at Charlie whose fingers were going ten to the dozen tying elastic bands in a chain. 'How come you two are so fucking calm?' he said.

Grinning, Charlie cast the elastic bands to one side and threw a banana at him. 'You forgot to stuff these down your trousers, Mons.'

Monster caught it, stood up, unzipped his leather trousers and lodged the banana in his underpants. 'I need a clean T shirt. Where's my bag?' Monster knew where it was because he tipped everything out of it three times searching for his coke. Taking off his soaked T shirt he used it to wipe his armpits, pulled a fresh one out of the bag and sat down again.

'Close your eyes so I can rub your old makeup off,' I said, trying not to let Monster's agitation get to me because I felt sick wondering if the VIP front row would be empty.

Monster closed his eyes. I used one of Charlie's elastic bands to tie his hair back from his face and wiped off his old makeup. 'Tate's a prat, Laura,' he said. 'Don't know who he thinks he is confiscating my coke!'

'Laura's done a lot of work trying to get us signed,' Tate said. 'I don't want anything to spoil our chances.' As usual Tate was so calm, he gave the impression he could detonate a bomb without a change of voice tone. 'Not only that, more often than not coke turns you into a dickhead and I don't want you insulting the press if we're lucky enough to get any interviews.'

For a few moments Monster was quiet as I massaged his neck but I could sense his mind ticking away under the surface. His eyes shot open. 'See what Tate thinks of me, Laura?' Monster scratched an acne spot on his cheek then waved me back to work. 'By the way, I am grateful for everything you're doing.' He grinned. 'Shame our relationship is strictly business though 'cos I'd still love to give you a good seeing to.' I knew Monster so well by then his remark went over my head.

'Cut it out Mons,' Charlie stood up, pushed in front of me and pelted Monster's head with popcorn. 'Show our manager a bit of respect.'

'I was fucking joking!' Monster picked bits of popcorn out of his hair and hurled them back at Charlie who jumped in the air shouting 'Goal' each time he caught one. 'You're the reason I can't relax,' Monster huffed and tilted his face so I could apply pan stick to his throat. Trying not to laugh at Charlie who made rude faces at Monster's skull, I smudged eye shadow in his sockets then drew a black line over his eyelids and softened it with my fingertip. 'Did any of the record labels call to confirm or cancel?' Monster asked, opening one eye.

'No-one. I guess they decide at the last minute – but I saw Jamil from Break Neck at the bar,' I said, to cheer him up.

'I'm so nervous,' Monster blew out a stream of breath. 'My balls are knocking against each other.' When I glanced up at the clock, my fingers shook. We only had another ten minutes before Streetcrash were due on and I should have been doing something useful like buttering up Jamil instead of administering to Monster who couldn't stop fidgeting, wouldn't keep his eyes shut and farted due to the fact he scoffed three bags of cheese and onion crisps. I told Monster everyone got nervous but there were techniques people used to lessen their anxiety. 'Like what?' Monster said. He opened his eyes to stare up at me and caused his still wet black eyeliner to mess up the eye shadow I applied. I wanted to scream '*keep your bloody eyes shut before I turn you into Alice again,*' but calmed myself. 'I know a great technique but you have to keep your eyes closed and take deep breaths.'

'I'm too hyper to breathe,' Monster said, eyes trained on mine like beanstalks.

I glanced at the clock. Nine minutes left. 'Alright, let's begin by repeating a few quotes. You know, things people say to give themselves courage?'

'Like, what?'

'Like...' I sped up my voice to gain time. 'There are no great people in the world just ordinary people with the courage to rise to great challenges.'

'That's no use because we don't know *how* they rose to their great challenges.' Monster sat up and had a glug of Jack. 'Give me something more visual to work with.'

'Alright.' I relieved Monster of the bottle of Jack and pulled his head back by tugging his ponytail. 'Close your eyes, keep them shut, and tell me which book characters you liked as a boy.'

Monster closed his eyes. I dabbed off the four wavy lines of black eyeliner that had worked themselves into his eyebrows and started over. 'How do you expect me to remember that?' he snapped. 'Who did you like?'

'Lucy from *The Lion the Witch and the Wardrobe*,' I said.

'*Velveteen Rabbit*, 'Tate chipped in.

'*King Kong*,' Charlie shouted.

'Who was *Lucy*? - and fuck *Velveteen Rabbit*. No wonder you're such a fairy, Tate!' Still with his eyes closed, Monster threw a bit of popcorn he found on his lap in the direction of Charlie. 'And the only thing King Kong could do was grunt!'

My hand jogged as a spurt of nervous laughter rose to my throat. My knees buckled under the weight of nerves as valuable seconds slipped away. 'So, who did you like best, Monster?' I prompted.

'Tarzan,' Monster said. 'Yeah, he was my favourite.'

Despite my agitation, I softened. I kissed his head. 'Why?'

'Because,' Monster used his arms to express himself, 'he could swing across the jungle on a rope.'

'So, imagine the stage is a jungle. You are Tarzan and...

Charlie made **HU HU** sounds and beat his chest.

'Charlie go and play with King Kong somewhere else,' Monster said. 'Yeah, I'm Tarzan. What am I doing?'

I tapped his lips shut so I could apply brown lipstick. 'You're looking out over the jungle and in the distance, you see a golden guitar. You know that when you play this guitar the world will fall at your feet under its spell. Can you see the guitar, Monster?'

'Yeah. I can see it. It's perched on a rock behind a water fall.' Monster mumbled. 'But where am I standing looking over the jungle?'

'You've climbed to the top of the tallest tree. It's so tall it touches the sky. Were you frightened climbing to the top of the tallest tree?'

'Course not,' Monster said, 'I'm swinging from the top branch.'

'Can you see a rope dangling down?'

'Erm, yes. Now I'm holding it in my hands.'

'See yourself flying through the air.'

The movement behind Monster's closed eyelids told me he was imagining it. 'I am flying through the air.'

Tate covered his face with his hands, trying to laugh quietly so he didn't disturb Monster's concentration. I wanted to laugh through sheer nerves because there were five minutes left until I introduced them.

'And King Kong's lumbering towards your golden guitar because he wants it,' Charlie said, making gorilla faces no-one but I could see as he beat his chest to the cry of HU.

'Well King Kong's not fucking getting it,' Monster said. 'I knocked him out with my feet when I swooped down.'

'Grab the guitar,' I urged. 'Can you see it, Monster?'

I could tell by Monster's twitching fingers that he was excited. 'Yeah, the sun's shining on the gold.'

'Have you got it?' Is it in your hands?' I sped my voice up for the climax.

'Yeah, fuck!' Monster's fingers strummed as he played his imaginary guitar. 'I'm playing notes I've never heard. I'm even better than Hendrix on Watchtower.'

I ignored Charlie, who stood next to me mimicking a mad scientist playing guitar 'See how amazing you are?' I said. 'Stop worrying.' I tapped him on the shoulder. 'Open your eyes and tell me what you think.'

Monster opened them and inspected his make-up. 'Not bad. Just smudge a bit of something more under my lower eyelids?' When I finished he preened like a peacock. 'Your ugly mug could do with Laura's help.' He turned to look at Tate who playfully punched Monster's arm.

'I can live with my ugly mug.' Tate glanced at the clock. 'Nearly time to go on. Let's show whoever came to hear us, why we're worth signing.'

'We are worth signing,' Monster rummaged through the bag at his feet, pulled out a black cotton scarf and tied it around his forehead. 'I'm going to wear this like a bandana to remember I'm Tarzan.'

'If Jesus had been a highwayman who wore makeup that's probably what he'd have looked like,' Charlie thrust his pretend sword at Monster before turning it on himself. 'Jesus don't kill me. Jesus have mercy on…'

'Can't you ever be fucking serious?' Monster said. He snatched Charlie's pretend sword and snapped it in two. 'What do you think?' he glanced at Tate who gave him a nod of approval. 'You?' he said to me. The bandana suited the sultry eye look I gave him and I had to agree with the highwayman part of what Charlie said. With the bandana pressed to the sides of Monster's head, his shaggy hair sleeked into a mass of tumbling waves that made his mouth look cherubic and framed his perfectly angled face in a way that could bring out a cavalier, devil or saint depending on the song he sang. 'We should make bandanas your trademark.'

Fluffing out his hair, Monster pouted in the mirror. ''Yeah, I look alright! We'll have a party at my place after the gig to celebrate eh, Laura?' Monster called as I rushed out of the door with twenty seconds to make it to stage.

# ELEVEN

Spotlights dazzling my eyes, I shielded them with my hand and smiled into the blurry crowd to see a roomful of full chairs from the second row back. My heart beat faster than an overwound clock. People were still pouring in and having to stand inside the entrance door because the bar was packed to heaving.

Debs chatted to a girl with huge sparkly glasses. Jamil sat in his VIP seat in the front row and further along was another man from a record label but he already said he wouldn't give Streetcrash an advance so his only purpose was filling one of the seats. Next to him was a record producer, an agent, a top journalist from NME magazine, a couple of session musicians and some random people I met at the Speakeasy, but it wasn't the turn out I imagined unless there were latecomers. On the off chance, I reserved a chair for Scorch records but that was empty.

I let my hand drop, counted to three and started talking. 'I'm pleased to see so many Streetcrash fans here tonight. How are you all feeling?' The audience whistled and banged their wine and beer glasses on tables. Flashlights went off as members of the press took photographs. 'Since you didn't come here to listen to me, let me hear you give Streetcrash a warm welcome.' The audience whooped and chanted *Streetcrash*, waiting for them to appear on stage. I watched Robert Bauman push his way through the crowd and my stomach did a somersault. He must have listened to Truth Kills and seen its potential, otherwise why had he come?

Charlie bounced on stage and ran around the drums. Monster and Tate picked up their guitars to the sound of deafening applause.

'Enjoy the show,' I said, making sure I caught Mr. Bauman's eyes before I left stage.

Streetcrash were at their best and it wasn't long before the audience were singing the choruses and stamping their feet with such electrically charged energy, the walls and floor vibrated with sound. I stood peering out from behind the curtain as Monster strutted, did mid-air splits and slid across stage on his knees, making his guitar moan, groan and zing to the ceiling and back. Tate's right leg was anchored to the ground while his left knee twisted, jerked and shook and his foot twizzled or thudded the floor, his forehead creased in furrows as he dragged howling notes out of his guitar. Charlie was on top form. His face contorted into weird shapes then broke into grins as he hit the drums, as though even he didn't know where the sticks would land. He twirled his sticks in the air, caught them then pounded on the cymbals as he laughed at Monster.

Monster picked up a pair of panties a girl threw, sniffed them as if he appreciated where they'd been, tucked them in his belt, winked and started to play again. Screaming 'MONSTER, I LOVE YOU,' the panty thrower went into a swoon. Her girlfriend slapped her face to bring her around. Two burly security guards forced people back as they tried to climb on stage. The photographers were having a field day. Jamil was so into Streetcrash, his eyes never left them. Mr. Bauman's face was a blank canvas and he left immediately after the last song. When Jamil stood up and pushed his way towards the exit, my heart sank wondering what I was going to say to Monster.

# TWELVE

'Don't be upset we got no response tonight. It'll happen soon 'cos you're a grafter,' Monster said, as we climbed the stairs to his flat. I sniffed. I was a grafter with practically nothing in the bank due to some sneaky sod in the VIP row who bought ten bottles of champagne. I was livid for not setting a one drink per person limit, felt gutted not one record company showed interest and felt furious I had to be at a party when I wanted to go home and rip the stuffing out of my pillow.

Monster's arm was around a tall, skinny blonde on the stair above me so couldn't see my miserable face. His pre gig nerves forgotten, Monster looked down at me and smiled. 'I can feel your mood from here. Chill. It's party time.' He hugged the blonde who was a replica of Inge, other than his current one had had straggly bleached hair. 'You didn't mind me bringing the girls eh?' Monster asked. The blonde brazened me out daring me not to like her. All I could think about was that when I first met Monster, even though it wasn't intentional, I looked like her. A half-dressed slut. I must have looked at her micro mini skirt in a derogatory manner because when I glanced up, her eyes were fierce. Giving her my Audrey Hepburn smile, to transfer the meaning of class, I made a meal of smoothing down the legs of my satin jump suit. The blonde raised her eyebrows which didn't appear to have seen a pair of tweezers in their life. She was like an ugly sister who wanted to banish me to a life of sweeping chimneys.

'The more the merrier,' I shrugged.

The blonde kept her hand glued to his behind until we reached his front door. Lapping it up, Monster looked over the banister and glanced down at Charlie. Charlie was on the second landing and regaled two brunettes with a comedy scene from a Tony Hancock TV show. It was the one where Hancock went to a blood donor's centre to give blood for the first time. 'What do you mean, you want a pint of blood? That's nearly an armful. I'm not walking round with an empty arm.' It was funny but not as hilarious as the brunettes made out. One, legs crossed, jiggled on the spot ready to pee herself. The other flapped a wrist and screeched with such laughter, a neighbor came out to see what was going on. 'Come on Charlie, let's get the party started.' Monster shouted. Charlie gave Monster a thumbs up and carried on regaling. I looked at Debs who stood on the first landing chatting with Monster's second blonde. She was also tall and skinny but whereas the first had long hair, that one had an urchin haircut with kiss curls lacquered to her cheeks.

Monster inserted the key in his front door, rattled his missing bag of coke which Tate attached to his key chain and sighed. 'Now I come to think of it, Tate was right to confiscate it. 'Don't know how he puts up with me half the time.'

Charlie pelted up the stairs and came level with Monster. 'Have you got any Presley, the girls want to rock 'n roll?'

Monster winked. 'The girls will be rocking all night. I think we can keep them happy, Presley or not.'

Monster's blonde stayed wrapped around him like cling film as he fished bottles of pills and a bag of weed out of a drawer and arranged them on top of the music cabinet. 'Where d'ya keep the glasses, Monster?' Her hand reached around and fondled his private parts.

'In the kitchen,' Monster pointed without turning. 'And while you're in there, fill a bucket with ice would you, Sophie?'

The blonde giggled but the expression in her eyes was hostile. 'My name's Lulu,' she said.

Monster shrugged. 'Not much difference.'

Giving me a filthy look as if I was responsible for Monster's name mistake, she jogged me as she passed and left a trail of cologne that smelled like cat's pee mixed with dead geraniums. I felt like having a few words to bring home the meaning of respect but doubted she could even spell the word so bit my tongue. As I waved the cat stink away, Debs came into the room, deep in conversation with the second blonde.

'So fuschia leather shorts are the *'in thing'* then are they?' Debs asked, as excited as if she had discovered a new recipe for master chefs.

That blonde ran her fingernails over her shorts. 'Nah, not only fuschia. Any colour's in. Yella. Green.'

Debs patted the leather. 'Where did you get them?'

That blonde blew a kiss at Monster who blew one back then carried on cutting lines of coke. 'Got 'em down Chapel Street market,' she said. 'From one of the stalls at the end, next to the man who sells pet food.' She wiped Debs hand off her shorts. 'Anyway, it's been nice talking, love.' She sauntered towards Monster, exaggerated her steps to make her bum wobble and smacked his bum as though he was a naughty child. Monster lapped it up.

'I love her hair and shorts but Monster *can't* fancy her,' Debs said, 'she's so obvious.'

'Monster gets his kicks from the obvious,' I said.

Charlie waved his brunettes into the room. Giggling they took off for the bathroom. 'What do you want doing with the music sheets on the table?' Charlie asked as he buzzed around moving cushions to the back of the room and formed them into a mattress.

'I'll take care of that,' Monster said. He slapped the blonde's lips off his neck. 'Anything else but no love bites!' He passed her a spliff then waved his hand along the selection of available drugs. 'And whatever else you fancy, be my guest, Lulu.'

'My friend's Lulu.' She drew furiously on the spliff. 'I'm Samantha. The one you said turned you on the most!'

'So you do Samantha,' Monster said. 'And I can't wait to lick your furry cupcake.'

'Oh, Monster,' Samantha gushed like Popeye's Olive. 'You can have as much furry cupcake as you want.'

I couldn't believe I was listening to such pathetic sex talk so busied myself stacking music sheets under the table as Monster shouted. 'Alphabetical order, facing East and cover them with a dust sheet.'

Debs kneeled down beside me. She labeled three pieces of paper with the names LAURA, DEBS, TATE and pinned them to cushions she took to the kitchen to scrub to be sure we didn't come in contact with dried up spunk stains. 'What they're doing to him in public is disgusting!' She rested the cushions against the wall under the window.

I glanced over to see what Debs meant. Lulu and Samantha took it in turns to rub their body against Monster's crotch. Eyes shut, he writhed in delight. 'It's called a rock n' roll lifestyle,' I said. Debs gave the table a squirt of polish, rubbed away with her duster, picked up a bottle of Jack from the carpet and plonked it on the table. 'Stop cleaning everything.' I said. 'This is supposed to be a party.' Debs looked back to see what Samantha and Lulu were up to. They were helping themselves to lines of coke, their voices getting more irritating with every sentence.

'Excuse me Monster,' Debs walked towards him waving her duster, and for some reason dusted the girls. 'I am sorry to interrupt your rock n' roll lifestyle but I noticed the only food you had in the fridge was a bit of dried up salami so I was thinking maybe you, Tate and Charlie might like to come over tomorrow for Sunday dinner?'

'Yeah. Right on,' Monster said, as he sorted through LPs in his music cabinet. Charlie emerged from a tangle of body parts to inform us it was his twenty second birthday and his parents had arranged a family knees up at the... We didn't hear the rest because the octopuses sucked him back into the fray. Tate, who'd come back from the all night supermarket and sipped a bottle of raspberry juice, said he was spending the day with Lotte. Debs said to bring her as well.

Monster opened the top of his record player and eased a record in. 'I want everyone on the dance floor. Here's Blue Suede Shoes by Presley.'

Tate strolled over. 'Because Monster gets his kicks from booze and drugs, he assumes I've got one foot in the grave.' He held out his hand. 'Don't suppose you jitterbug?'

I covered Monster's music sheets with the dustsheet. It was time to end my pity party and join the fun. 'Honey,' I said in an American accent. 'I am the *queen* of jitterbug.'

Tate took hold of my hand. Within seconds we tuned into each other's rhythm. Seeing that, he grabbed both hands. 'I'll slide you through my legs then we'll jitterbug.' When I came up, Tate let go of my hands. We twisted our feet, added razzle-dazzle hands, twisted to the floor and came back up.

'Fuck me, elephants do fly,' Monster said, watching Tate twirl me. 'You never told me you could dance?' Tate winked at me then slid me through his legs again. Beside us, Monster's blondes took to the floor to compete in a lewd version of the mashed potato. 'That's right. Give 'em a good shake, girls,' Monster clapped them on. Tate nodded. I knew it meant, *ready to stop*?' Nodding, I pulled my hair back, tied it in a knot, kicked off my green high heels and threw myself down on my cushion next to Tate. As I watched Lulu and Samantha caress their boobs while Monster encouraged them to take off their tops, my mind drifted back to the night in the Rat. It felt like another lifetime. I hid my growing lack of confidence as well as I could but facts were facts. I couldn't afford one more expense and time was running out. 'Look at those two show offs.' Debs bent down to give me a Bacardi and coke. 'And here's a plate of cream crackers and cheese for you, Tate.' She flopped down on her cushion and ripped the blondes to shreds with her eyes.

The neighbor above banged on the floor with something that sounded like a brick. Monster came to the window, stepped between me and Tate, opened it and called up 'If it gets too noisy Mr. Krakowski, come down and join the party.' Mr. Krakowski kept knocking. Monster's answer was to turn the music up. He strolled over with a spliff. 'Want some of this?' Monster gave it a general wave. I shook my head. 'How come you're not dancing?' he said to Debs. 'You gave the impression you were a right raver.'

Debs blew her fringe out of her eyes then tossed her bobbed haircut at him. 'I'm warming up.' She grabbed the spliff and puffed until it was half the size but I wasn't in the mood to play mother so let her get on with it. I expected that any minute she'd get going with one of her random topics. Instead, her expressions played roles of actors sharing their thoughts on pollution or something to do with dirt. She drew heavily on the spliff, huffed at Lulu and Samantha and puffed until it was down to a dog end. Tate and me watched as Debs settled into an imaginary conversation with someone. The disgust on her face turned to defiance. She jumped to her feet. 'I can do what they're doing.'

Another side effect when Debs got stoned was that people who disgusted her became bosom buddies, and that's what happened. Lulu and Samantha were competing to see whose moves were sexiest. Having become one of them, Debs

81

waggled her bum shouting. 'Sexy' – which was the last thing she looked in her swamp boots and baggy camouflage trousers.

Tate settled back to watch Debs antics and smiled. 'She's so different when she's had a smoke.'

'You have no idea what I have to put up with,' I laughed.

Tate ran a hand through his bleached cropped hair. 'Like?'

My mind rolled through half a dozen stoned incidents. 'Like the time her brother Pete spiked her tea with something. Whatever it was made Debs thirsty so she went around the corner to buy a bottle of lemonade from the off license. When she came out, she bumped into Mrs. McClory – one of our neighbours – who according to Debs had a blue vibrating face and frog's eyes the size of saucers.' Enjoying the sound of Tate's laughter, I carried on. 'She took Mrs. McClory to one side and asked if she'd been abducted by aliens.' Tate laughed harder. I waited until he stopped. 'It took Debs weeks to believe Pete spiked her tea. In the meantime, every time she saw Mrs. McClory, she grilled her to find out what the aliens had done to her. Mrs. McClory still crosses the road when she sees her.'

Monster danced around Lulu, Samantha and Debs clapping his hands. Debs pushed in front of Lulu to shake her boobs at him. It was unlike Debs but I couldn't help smiling at how funny she looked and how happy Monster seemed.

'I often wish I had your patience with Monster,' I said to Tate.

Tate smiled fondly at him. 'We met at primary school when we were nine so we've known each other eighteen years. His real name is Montague but any kids who called him that got bopped. Mons became Monster and it stuck. We formed our first band when we were eleven. He'd just got his first electric guitar. His gran said as soon as he saved fifty pounds she'd put the rest towards it and buy it on the quiet, so for two years he washed cars and did a paper round.'

'On the quiet?'

'Monster's dad was a sergeant in the army. He wanted Mons to have a military career so refused to buy him one.'

'He sounds a bit like Hendrix's dad?'

Tate nodded. 'Monster hasn't got one good word to say about his dad but he'd walk over burning coals for his gran – and grandad come to that. They still go out once a week for pie 'n mash and he slips them a bit of extra money whenever he's got some to spare. Talking of which,' Tate looked into my eyes. 'Unless you've got rich parents, I'm guessing you might be strapped for cash with everything you've done for us so if you need a loan I...'

As much as I felt close to Tate, there was no way I'd tell him I was close to bankruptcy. 'Loan?' I brushed the idea away as though it was ridiculous.

Our chat was interrupted by the sound of someone furiously banging on the door. Monster went to open it. An exhausted looking man of about eighty with hair sprouting out of his ears and more waving like grass stalks on top of his head, stood there in crumpled pyjamas. He shook his head in misery. 'Hello Mr. Krakowski,' Monster slapped him fondly on the shoulder. 'Come on in and I'll fix you up with a nice girl to put a bit of fire back in your pecker.'

'My pecker hasn't pecked since my wife died ten years ago,' Mr. Krakowski snapped. 'And I'd appreciate it if you turned the music down so I can get some sleep.'

'Just for you Mr. Krakowski.' Monster said, 'Because you remind me of my grandad, I *will* turn the music down.'

Mr. Krakowski peered through the door to see Lulu take off her top. She jiggled her boobs at Debs chanting 'Sexy.'

'Never once in my life did I see nipples as big as hers.' Sighing, Mr. Krakowski patted Monster's chest. 'Use your pecker on my behalf Monster.'

'Night, Mr. Kraw,' Monster said, closing the door. He winked at me and Tate. 'Think I just made his night.'

Tate stood up. 'Think it's time for me to go.'

'Me as well,' I said. Tate held out his hand and helped me up.

'We're already three party goers short since Charlie vanished with his brunettes in the bedroom and I can't see him emerging anytime soon,' Monster said. 'You can't leave now. Things are just warming up.'

I glanced at Debs. She was doing some sort of African tribal dance and had the bottle of Jack rammed between her legs. 'Sexy,' she chanted, pretending to shag herself with bottle. Lulu had her hands around Debs waist and gyrated her hips as if she was shagging Debs from behind. Not only was Lulu a groupie, but from the way her hand stroked Debs thigh, she showed lesbian tendencies. Debs wouldn't know what hit her if that hand found its way around to the front.

Monster followed my eyes. 'If Debs wants to stay, she's welcome'. he said innocently. I imagined Debs shame if I told her she allowed herself to be touched up by a woman. It would be enough to make her rush out and buy a yashmak to hide her face.

'Debs,' I called out. 'Time to go.' Debs carried on shagging the bottle. I marched over and grabbed it from between her legs. 'Unless you fancy getting involved in a gang-bang of a particularly suspicious nature.' I slapped Lulu's hand off Debs inner thigh. 'It's time to go home.'

Debs snatched the bottle back, unscrewed the top and had a slug. 'I was just starting to enjoy myself,' she moaned.

# THIRTEEN

'Mmmm, that beef smells yummy,' Charlotte said, rubbing her tummy. 'But don't forget I don't want any of that cabbage you put in a pan Laura because the only green thing I eat is peas.'

I covered the joint of roast beef I'd taken out of the oven with a tea towel and left it to rest while the roast potatoes crisped up. 'About another twenty minutes and we can have our dinner,' I smiled. I'd perched Charlotte on the sideboard in the kitchen because she wanted to watch me cook but it was more than that. From the minute Tate brought her into the flat she hardly left my side. Charlotte gently banged her shoes against the kitchen cabinet door.

'You look pretty in your pink gingham bell bottoms, Laura. And we've got the same hair,' she announced. Charlotte had a mass of long golden ringlets whereas mine was black and wavy. The only thing our hair had in common was that it around the same length.

'And you look very pretty in your dungarees,' I said. My hair, which I'd left down, kept getting in my mouth. I picked out a hair from the carrots I was chopping. 'Reach down and get me a chopstick out of that open drawer would you Charlotte?'

'There are tons of chopsticks in the drawer Laura. You can have,' – she counted the number out loud. 'Ten if you want.'

'One's all I need.'

Charlotte held one up. I took it from her, twisted my hair into a bun at the nape of my neck and stuck the chopstick through the middle to hold my hair in place.

'You look like a Chinese girl now,' Charlotte said. 'Can I have a chopstick in my hair?' She eagerly held up another one.

'Course you can,' I laughed, gathering her hair at the back to give her the same hairstyle as mine.

'Now we look like twins,' Charlotte held her arms out. 'Can you put me down please, I want to go and show Daddy and Monster.' As I lifted her into my arms, Debs hobbled into the kitchen.

'I should be doing that,' she pointed at my half-chopped carrots.

'Go back in the front room and rest your foot,' I said, putting Charlotte down on the floor.

'I can't relax,' Debs said. She lifted her foot to take the weight off her sprained ankle. 'I can't believe I slipped off the side of the bath. This is *so* painful.'

'You shouldn't have climbed on to wipe a speck of dust off the light bulb! We didn't invite the Queen for Sunday dinner.'

'It's the first time Monster and Tate have been to our flat. I wanted it to be nice.'

'It is nice. And cleaner than most hospitals. Now buzz off and leave me in peace.' Debs hesitated. 'I'll call you if I need you,' I said to pacify her.

With a defeated grunt, Debs hobbled back down the hall. 'Don't forget to take any lumps out of the gravy,' she called out 'Oh and by the way, Chris called again. I said you were abroad as asked.'

I returned to chopping carrots. 'Need any help?' Tate asked, coming into the kitchen.

'No. I'm enjoying cooking Sunday dinner. Normally the kitchen is off limits since Debs wants to do everything.'

Tate ran the tap, poured a glass of water and leaned against the sideboard. 'So, what do you think of my Lotte?'

'She's really cute.' I chopped the last carrot. 'When you said Lotte last night, I thought you were talking about your girlfriend. Or are you married to Charlotte's mum?'

'Not married. Lotte's mum was 19 when she got pregnant. We'd only been going out six months. Getting hitched wasn't on the agenda then but we decided to keep Lotte. Lotte calls herself *our happy accident*.' Tate smiled.

'You said '*then*,' does that mean you're thinking of tying the knot?'

'I'd be up for it but Kate, Lotte's mum, never brings it up so I'm letting it ride until money starts coming in from Streetcrash.' Tate took a sip of water. 'Monster doesn't get it but Kate's the only woman I've been to bed with. I'd feel like I was betraying her if I slept around, although we still, you know, get together,' he said, to indicate their relationship was more than platonic.

Charlotte ran back into the kitchen and tugged at Tate's jeans. 'Daddy, can you put me back where I was sitting before?' Tate scooped Charlotte into his arms and sat her on the sideboard. Charlotte squished his cheeks with her fingers and kissed his forehead. 'You smell like orange marmalade daddy.' Bringing her attention back to me, she watched as I tipped cut carrots into a pan of water. 'You can put some of those on my plate Laura. I like orange vegetables – ooh and I like lots and lots and lots of gravy.' I turned to smile at her. Charlotte looked back at Tate. 'And from today I'm going to very careful when I ride my bicycle daddy, because I don't want to get a black eye like Laura.'

Tate gave Charlotte a hug. 'Your bicycle is a three-wheeler, but it's good to be careful eh?'

Monster came into the kitchen. 'Think we need more red wine,' he uncorked the third bottle of four he brought with him. 'Come with me for a minute, Tate,' he said. 'I wanted to ask you something.'

Tate followed on behind him. I was busy piling Yorkshire puddings on a platter when Charlotte said 'What's this? It looks like a big fat worm.'

I turned to see what she meant. Charlotte was carefully holding the jar with Aretha's banana peel. 'That's Aretha Franklyn's banana peel. She's a famous singer but I don't suppose you know who she is?'

'No, I don't, but why did you put her banana peel in here?'

'To pickle and preserve so that even when she dies, we'll be able to say, Aretha lives on in that banana.'

'Oh,' Charlotte said as Tate came back into the kitchen. 'That's a clever idea. When my grandad dies, I'm going to pickle his false teeth.'

'What are you going to do with grandad's teeth?' Tate said.

Charlotte pointed at the contents in the jar. 'Pickle them like Aretha Bumpkin's banana.'

'Haaaaaaaaaaaahaha.' One of the Yorkshire puddings, flipped off my spoon and landed on the floor. 'Haaaahaha,' I held the sideboard and crossed my legs as a bit of pee trickled out. 'She means Aretha Franklyn.' Tate started to laugh although he didn't know what he was laughing about. 'Haahaha, I'll explain another time.'

'Look forward to hearing the story,' Tate chuckled. He nodded at the joint of beef. 'While you're finishing up, I'll carve that for you if you like?' I waved at him to get on with it because I was still laughing.

'Do you like my dad's music Laura? Charlotte asked. I picked up the Yorkshire pudding, threw it in the bin, wiped the tears from my eyes and told her I loved it. 'Hmm, and me,' she said. 'I specially like their song called Everyone's a – I can't say the rest because there's a swear word.' Tate and I shared a smile because she sounded so serious.

'And Uncle Monster knows we don't swear in real life eh, Lotte?' Tate winked at me.

'He does forget sometimes,' Charlotte sighed. 'But I make him say fudge when he forgets.'

Another giggle escaped my lips. I coughed over it pretending I had pepper up my nose. 'Think we're about ready Tate. If you want to get plates out of that cupboard,' I nodded to which one, 'we can plate up.'

Grabbing a carton of orange juice, I went in the front room and set five tight places around the coffee table. Monster rubbed Debs sprained ankle. They were having a conversation about Monster's acne.

'I know the *best* cure ever to get rid of spots,' Debs said.

Monster ran a hand over his pockmarked cheeks and scratched at a blistering scab. He had his hair in a ponytail so every pimple stood out. Even his neck was covered in them. 'I've been trying to get rid of these monstrosities for years!' he said.

Charlotte ran back in at that point, headed straight for Monster and sat on his lap. 'Are you talking about your pimples uncle Monster?'

'Yeah,' Monster said, stroking Charlotte's head. 'Debs is going to tell me about a cure.'

'I want to know as well – in case I get spots when I grow up,' Charlotte looked expectantly at Debs, while I doled out paper napkins for each place setting.

'Go on, what's your cure?' Monster asked Debs.

'Urine.'

Charlotte let the word settle in her mind. 'What does urine mean, uncle Monster?'

'Pee pee.'

'Pee pee like wee wee?'

'Yeah, pee pee like wee wee,' Monster said. 'Now let's hear Debs tell us about the cure.'

'It's called urine therapy,' Debs said, having a glug of wine. 'I read about it in a natural health medicine book. You catch the middle flow when you're having a pee in a plastic cup and dab it on your spots. I tried it once when I came out in a rash and it was gone in five days.'

'Yuk that's disgusting,' Charlotte piped up, watching Tate bring in the first two plates. 'Daddy, uncle Monster is going to put urine on his face when he goes home.'

'Nothing surprises me about uncle Monster.' Tate laughed, and laid the plates on the coffee table. 'Here you go Lotte, carrots but no cabbage.'

'Very good daddy,' Charlotte said, scrambling off Monster's lap. She sat on the floor, crossed her legs, picked up her knife and fork and tucked in. 'Mmmmm, this is yummy,' she said. 'Hurry up and bring the other plates daddy.' Tate kissed the top of her head. 'Yes madam,' he said.

Lunch went down well with not one complaint from Debs although that was probably because of the amount of wine she drank.

'That was fu....fudging amazing and I'm fudging stuffed,' Monster said. He undid the top button on his jeans because he'd polished off Charlotte's left overs when she gave up half way through, as well as everyone else's scraps.

Charlotte looked at me and tutted. 'Uncle Monster nearly forgot didn't he Laura?'

'He did,' I laughed. 'Now, who'd like strawberry ice cream?'

Charlotte's hand shot up. 'Me, me, me.'

Monster settled back on the sofa and raised his hand. 'Me as well. I'd forgotten what it was like for someone to take care of me. That f—fudging Inge, couldn't toast a bit of bread.'

'Come over again tomorrow night Monster,' Debs slurred. 'My foot should be alright by then. I'll make a pie with the leftovers.'

'I might,' Monster said. 'Cos I'm working on that song I was telling you about Laura. I can play it and see what you think?'

Tate wiped strawberry ice cream off Charlotte's mouth. 'Can I come and have dinner with Laura again, daddy?' she pleaded.

'Course you can,' I answered for Tate. Charlotte shook her hair. 'Can we be Chinese girls again?'

'Yeah, and I'll teach you my Chinese dance,' I flapped my arms like chicken wings and flicked my feet out. 'Ying tong, ying tong.'

'Hihihi.' Charlotta ran around her dad, flapping her arms. 'Ying tong, ying tong.'

'You'd make a great mum,' Tate laughed. 'You're a natural.'

Debs who was propped against Monster's shoulder, burped. 'I keep telling her she should find a...' Her head dropped forwards. She snorted then nodded off.

'Too much plonk by the looks of it,' Monster said, shifting over on the couch.

'Uncle Monster, can I sit on your lap again?'

'Yep, my lap's all yours.' He patted it.

Charlotte jumped on, threw her arms around his neck and looked up in adoration. 'I love you more than all the sand on all the beaches in the whole world.'

'And I love you more than double pepperoni pizza,' Monster smiled.

'Hihi. You're silly.' Charlotte clasped her hands together. 'Can you play your monika Uncle Monster?

Monster shifted her over to one knee and tugged out a harmonica from a pocket in his jeans. 'What do you want to hear, princess?

'Lay lady lay.'

'And who sings that?' Monster asked.

'Bob Dylan,' Charlotte said proudly.

'OK then, just for you, here's Lay Lady Lay.'

It was such a melancholy version it brought a lump to my throat as I watched Tate gaze at his daughter with fatherly love. Charlotte sang the lines *'Why wait any longer for the world to begin, when you can have your cake and eat it too'.* I started to feel sad wondering how different I would have been if I had a dad to guide me in life, or even knew his name. When Monster finished playing, Charlotte tugged at his T shirt. 'Play it again. Play it again Uncle Monster.'

'Next time,' Monster said. He looked at me 'You OK Laura? You've got a bit white.'

I shrugged. 'Just – feelings.'

Tate looked at his watch. 'We had a long night last night Monster and I'm sure Laura could do with a bit of quiet time. What do you say we get going?' He called Charlotte over. 'Come on Lotte, go and get your cardi from the bedroom.' Charlotte ran off to get it.

Monster stood up and squeezed my shoulders. 'I don't want you worrying about Break Neck, Scorch or any other record label, Laura,' he said, thinking that was what upset me.

# FOUR

There was me in my flared cotton sailor trousers, matching top with anchor motif and blue headband looking as if I'd come off the set of a sports commercial and hanging out of a red lit first floor window was a girl in a negligee touting for clients. Wondering if I made a mistake and scribbled the address down incorrectly, I glanced at the panel of buzzers that listed the occupants of the Soho building. *Suzy. Oriental Massage. Crabtree Surveyors. Kamasutra Yoga. Lolita. Flip Records.* I figured if Crabtree Surveyors had an office there, Flip Records was on the level and I was simply being oversensitive because I couldn't recall meeting Roger, the record company boss - one of dozens I randomly gave my business card to in the Speakeasy.

With ten minutes to kill before my appointment at 6pm, I wandered into the sex-toy shop next door. I'd seen tame versions before but 'Anything You Can Think of For Pleasure' seemed more about sadistic torture than erotic titillation. I couldn't see the pleasure anyone got from a game called Electric Roulette which had a banner on the box that said 'How close would you venture to death to experience the ultimate orgasm?' Equally off-putting was the man with the stern look of a judge who sucked with rapturous delight on an adult size dummy. He couldn't see me spying on him through my sunglasses. I made it look as though I was engrossed in a spiked ball on a chain and thrust it at an imaginary Chris. A furtive weasly man with sunglasses bigger than mine, made his way towards me from the Dominatrix department. From behind his back, he produced a leather corset, pressed it against his chest and wiggled his tongue at me. Since there was no point hitting him with my weapon in case it gave him a hard on, which he wasn't getting on my account, I slid through an arched door to the Emporium of Clitoral Stimulators and Dildos.

The item that caught my attention was a lifelike dildo, curved at the top like a penis with hard, plump testicles. At first I just browsed. No intention of buying, but my feet kept taking me back. I had another two months and seven days of sex abstinence to make it to my three month goal. A dildo wasn't the same as the real thing but might do the trick. My dilemma was whether it would tempt me back to dick and the devil's garden. Then I thought of Eve. Perhaps if she'd been given a dildo instead of an apple, things would have turned out differently for mankind? I picked it up and ran my finger down its length. It was heavy, solid and felt like real skin. I pressed a button. It performed a series of thrust variations to equal any stud. The dildo, a deluxe model, was expensive at twenty pounds but seemed a better option than ending up on a psychiatrist's couch. I handed my credit card to the man at the till before I dithered. The box the dildo came in was the size of a small shoebox. I didn't want to walk around with that and certainly didn't want to go to Flip Records with a purple bag that had 'Anything You Can Think of For Pleasure' emblazoned across its front, so I tossed box and plastic bag in the bin, threw the dildo in my hand bag, went next door and pressed Roger's bell.

'Come up to the first floor,' Roger said in a jolly, happy-clappy voice.

The inside of the building was better than expected. It had a theatrical feel with tied back Bordeaux velvet curtains on both sides of the hall and black carpet on the stairs. On the way up, I felt an excitement close to delirium that my ship might have

94

come in and determined to behave like a professional, come rain, shine or pencil box incidents.

The door to Flip Records was open. The smell coming out was of strong French cigarettes and reminded me of an underground Paris jazz club. I poked my head around the door.

Roger waved. 'Come in, come in.'

His office was a converted studio flat with kitchenette, filing cabinet, his desk and chair and a velvet sofa I assumed turned into a bed. There was so much smoke it made me cough. 'Is there any chance you could open a window, Roger?'

'Ah yes, soon fix that, I forget that not everyone likes the smell of these wretched things.' Roger held up a packet of Gauloise cigarettes. 'Since we'll be working together, I'm going to do what I've been meaning to do for months.' With a flick of his chubby wrist, he tossed the cigarette box in the bin, grabbed a magazine from the top of his desk and waddled to the window in his shiny striped trousers and glary orange shirt. Having prised the window open, he fanned the air with his magazine. 'There's some air spray in my drawer, give the room a squirt would you, my lovely?' Underneath a roll of toilet paper, hand wipes and a bar of soap, I found the can and squirted. 'Ah much better, yes much better.' Roger glanced at the open drawer as he sat down, causing the chair to creak with his girth. 'Shared toilet down the hall,' he said to explain the items I saw. He rattled the drawer shut. 'Let's get down to business.' Roger retrieved his pack of cigarettes from the bin, lit one, crumpled the pack and threw it away again. 'This will definitely be my last.' He took a long drag, tilted his neck upwards and blew smoke at the ceiling. 'You know who I used to be don't you?' He chuckled and nodded at a gold disc on the wall. 'Sold over a million records for Frilly Vanilla - you must know them?' They sounded like one of the cheesy boy bands Debs watched on Top of the Pops. I shrugged my shoulders. 'It was four years ago,' he said. 'They didn't make it in the UK but were *huge* in Australia.' Roger drew the shape of Australia with his thumb.

I scratched my thigh wanting to warm to him since he seemed normal enough despite his obnoxious taste in clothes. 'What kind of band were they? I mean do you have anything I can listen to?'

'I have plenty you can listen to but the question you should be asking is…' Roger's eyes twitched. 'Am I the right man to make *you* and Streetcrash a lot of money and the answer to that is…' He thumped the desk with his pudgy fist. 'Yes!' I walked over to take a closer look at the gold disc. Frilly Vanilla had indeed sold a million records. As I turned, I caught him looking at my bum in a way that creeped me out. 'I hope you're not doubting my words?' Roger said.

I sat down on the sofa. 'I don't doubt your words, Roger, I'm just the kind of woman who likes to dot her i's.'

'Then ask away and we'll fill in the dots.' He rested his jowly cheeks that folded into three chins on his knuckle. His lips twitched involuntarily. There was something about Roger that reminded me of one of mum's loser boyfriends who tried to grope me behind her back.

'Are you a one-man band or do you have a partner?' For some obscure reason I felt like a detective on the trail of a criminal.

'Partner? Not anymore. Filthy swine screwed me over big time.' Roger scratched his hairy chest. I could see it was hairy because his shirt strained so tightly around his middle, two of the buttons no longer met the button holes. 'Anyway, let's not talk about the past.'

I asked Roger what he liked about Streetcrash. He assured me it was their raw, earthy sound and rattled on how about how he knew everyone in the music business to ensure Streetcrash's success. What bothered me was the way he kept emphasizing '*you*' as if he was hinting at how much I would gain from the deal. 'I have other record companies who've shown interest in Streetcrash,' I said. 'What are you offering as an advance?' When Roger said thirty thousand pounds I nearly fainted. I had been led to believe around fifteen thousand was the going rate.

'Don't worry your pretty head about money', Roger said. I've got a villa in the South of France complete with butlers and an Olympic size swimming pool.' He wagged a confident finger. 'You'll be able to wallow in it all when we become business associates.'

I asked which Streetcrash songs Roger liked best to which he glibly answered the ones I mentioned in the Speakeasy. I studied his pointed crocodile shoes. What was it about Roger that make me think of a mafia boss? *Was the money laundered? Had he killed his partner to get it*? I kept my gaze on his shifty eyes and brushed an imaginary crumb off my trousers wishing Mr. Bauman was there to see my calm collectiveness. 'Did you sign any other bands after Frilly Vanilla and how have you been occupying yourself since because four years is a long gap?'

'I don't need to occupy myself.' Roger struck himself across the chest. 'I'm a rich man. When we become partners, it will be first class all the way.'

Had fate given me a blackmailer to pay me back for bribing Mr. Bauman? 'Can I ask a question, Roger? Cards on the table?'

Roger pretended to lay out a deck of cards. 'Cards on the table – Honest Joe that's me.'

'Then *Honest* Joe. Short and sweet. Are you interested in Streetcrash? If not, I am a very busy woman.'

'As Honest Joe, I am interested in Streetcrash. Very much so but the reason behind it is that *you* are their manager.' Roger's smile stretched across his cheeks like a happy frog. 'I believe in you. You're a tough, gritty tour de force who I have no doubt will stop at nothing until you see their names in lights.'

All of those things about me were true but if Roger thought I would jeopardise Streetcrash's career by handing them over to a deluded basket case who bribed me with butlers, he was wrong. 'It's been a pleasure meeting you,' I said in my most ladylike manner, 'However, I've decided to decline your offer.' I stood up.

'No, no please sit down. Let Honest Joe finish what he has to say.' Since I was still in professional mode and it seemed a reasonable request, I sat down to hear him out.

'From the minute I set eyes on your flowing hair, pouty mouth and curvaceous plumpness, you knocked me for six. Cards on the table.' He pointed at me, then him. 'How would you feel about us getting together in a more personal sense?' I guffawed at his gall to voice the words, and wanted to punch Gibson for making me slam the phone down on Roger in the middle of questioning, thus landing me in seedy Soho with a wheezing lothario.

I stood up and walked towards the door. 'I wouldn't be seen dead with a man with sweaty armpits. Look at our clothes? Do we look like a match?'

'Don't get upset my lovely.' Roger cranked himself out of his chair. 'I went about things all wrong due to the delirious passion you make me feel but I still want to help. Please? I know how tough it must be for a woman like you to have to go without luxuries.'

For someone who waddled he was the fastest duck on the pond. He stood in front of me blocking the door, his arms stretched out as if they were nailed to a cross. 'Perhaps you'd like to be a partner in my other business next door? Sex toys make a *lot* more money than selling records.'

My mouth dropped open in shock. Of all the people in the world I bought one of *Roger's* dildos. 'I have no interest whatsoever in sex toys or the needy people who use them.' I tossed my head for effect. 'On that note, I shall take my leave.' I hit him across the chest with my handbag. 'Move away.'

'What kind of man would I be if I let you get away so easily, you feisty prickly porcupine?' His fat fingers strayed to one of my boobs as his fat hand patted my arm.

'I said, move away from the door.'

Somehow, my display of anger turned Roger on. His hand left the cross to slap my bum then resumed its position on the doorframe. I could feel myself sliding out of control. 'I gave you the benefit of doubt when your fingers interfered with my boob but that slap wasn't accidental.'

Roger thought it was a game and slapped my other bum cheek, that time adding a pinch.

My head filled with swear words I never said out loud. With mum's groper boyfriend I was too small to defend myself which was why I resorted to leaving a skate on the stairs to break his leg. Maybe heavy weight boxers like Chris were out of my league but I'd wrestled many a pig like Roger since my youth.

'Touch me again and...' The slimy bugger pinched my nipple. He still thought I was playing hard to get. The lady in me took off with the fairies as my rage reached boiling point.

'I've seen your version of foreplay. Would you like to see mine?'

Roger laughed with glee. Laughing back theatrically to put him off the scent, I threw my sunglasses in the bag, whipped out the dildo and licked it like a lollipop.

Roger panted.

'Would you like to see what else I do with this?'

A trickle of spit dribbled out of his mouth. Before he could react, I kneed Roger in the groin and hammered his head with the dildo.

'Little less force prickly porcupine,' Roger shrieked as he tried to snatch the dildo from my fingers.

I karate chopped his neck, wrestled him to the floor, sat on his chest and forced the testicles down his throat.

Roger's arms flailed by his sides as he spluttered, 'Stopppppp. I'm sorrrrrrry.'

His repentance meant nothing. I'd been taken over by a killer bent on taking revenge on scumbags. Whipping Roger's face with the dildo, I heard someone scream and looked up to see the girl in the frilly negligee. I have no idea what she said because it was in Russian.

I extracted the dildo from Roger's mouth, gave him a final kick and slapped it in her hand. 'Thrill yourself with this,' I said, preparing to scream my head off the second my feet hit the pavement.

# FIFTEEN

When I got back home, Debs and Monster were lying on the floor staring at the ceiling. They were playing a Ravi Shankar album and it was like being in an opium den except the smell was ylang ylang, which burned in pots all around the room. I bent over to look into their eyes. Both were wasted. I went into the kitchen to make a cup of tea wanting to hit Monster over the head for encouraging Laura to take drugs when he knew she was easily led.

Debs left me a portion of left over beef and vegetable pie on a plate that she covered with a tea towel. The pinned note said. '*Laura's xxx*' I wasn't in the mood to eat. Apart from seeing the state Debs and Monster were in, on the way home I'd picked up a copy of the Guardian newspaper. Their Streetcrash review had the headline: *Heavy metal? Listening to them play sounded like scrap metal falling from the sky.* Seriously doubting my ability as a manager. especially after my encounter with Roger, I went back in the front room and sat gloomily on the sofa.

'What are you seeing now Monster?' Debs said. 'I'm seeing twirling purple umbrellas, women in kimonos and golden maggots falling out of pineapples.'

'I'm seeing Inge's luscious lips everywhere.'

'What else?' Debs said

'Inge's bum.' Monster said.

'Think about something else,' Debs said. She was wearing yellow leather shorts and a skimpy tight top which wasn't like her. I needed to have a word because I had the feeling she was infatuated with Monster.

Noticing I was there, Monster turned and looked at me out of one eye. 'Hello Laura, fancy some psychedelic mushrooms? Debs seems to be enjoying them.'

'Now I'm seeing blue elephants wearing Christmas hats,' Debs said. 'Hahaha, they're dancing with aliens. One of them looks like our neighbor Mrs. McClory.'

'Monster, I said. 'Are you too out of it or can we talk?' Monster patted the carpet. 'Come and talk here. Come on, don't be shy.'

*If you can't beat them, join them* I thought, laying down beside him as I thought about what to say. There was no way I'd tell him about Flip Records because he'd think I was useless and there was no way I was mentioning the Guardian review in case he freaked out. 'Jamil from Breakneck called earlier today. He said he would have signed you but his partner didn't agree because of budget cuts.'

'Fuck Breakneck,' Monster said. 'Talk to me about the last man you screwed?''

'Why would I want to remember that!' I snapped.

'You're in a bad mood.' Monster nudged me. 'Have a cup of tea. We left you some in the pot.'

'I don't do mushrooms. Drink it yourself and I hope it makes you sick.'

'Lighten up. Take some deep breaths,' Monster gave me a lopsided smile. 'Think about your favourite character from a book, and if you can't do that stop talking because you're spoiling my trip.'

I stared at the ceiling listening to Debs who had taken off with pixies and was collecting odd socks to make them winter coats. 'Hahaha, the rabbit from Alice in Wonderland has lost his pocket watch. What are you seeing now, Monster?'

'Inge and me are flying in a space machine. Whoa! The colours flashing past are so bright, they're filling our heads with rainbows.'

'How long will it take before those mushrooms wear off?' I sighed.

'In Debs case it could be all night because she drank three cups before I could stop her. In my case about half an hour. Can't you go and do something until then because you keep bringing me back and I was enjoying being in that spaceship.' Monster tutted. 'Now you've made me lose Inge.'

'I saw your guitar when I came in,' I said determined to ruin his trip so he'd think twice before using my flat as a drug den again. 'Did you bring it to play me your new song?'

'I will play it for you in a while.' He poked Debs. 'What you seeing now?' Debs started crying. 'My granny.'

'What's she doing?' Monster asked.

'She's pulling the stone off my grandad's grave and spitting on it,' Debs said.

Monster rolled over and hugged her. Debs clung to him. 'Come on little Sis, blank it out. Change the picture in your head. Go back to your herd of blue elephants.'

'I can't,' Debs said.

'Why not?' Monster asked.

'Gran's gobbling Grandad's arm.'

'I knew this would bloody well happen!' I jumped up, ran into the kitchen, wet a kitchen towel with water, ran back and put it on Deb's forehead. 'It's OK Debs, you're tripping. Right now your gran and grandad are holding hands and running over daisy fields together in heaven. Can you see how happy they are? Hahaha,' I pretended I could see everything they were doing. 'Oh look, your gran and grandad have just gone in the Cambridge Arms to have a pint. Remember how your grandad loved to get up stage and sing your gran that Sinatra song?'

'No, no,' Debs quivered and squeezed her eyes shut. 'Gran's feeding Grandad to a tarantula.' She started screaming. 'Tarantulas are coming up from under our floorboards. Help! Get them off me!'

'Fuck, her trip's gone sour,' Monster said, sitting up.

'I'll mop her face,' I said. 'You go and put some strong coffee on – No, bring a mug of salty water. Let her drink that and vomit it up then we'll let her sleep it off.'

# SIXTEEN

'I've never seen so much sick,' Monster said after I put Debs to bed. 'She must have brought up all the food she's eaten in the last month – and what the fuck was all that red stuff?'

'All the wine you plied her with yesterday,' I said. 'Look Monster, I need to ask a favour. Debs doesn't know a lot about life or men. She's a virgin who's been with Dave since she left school and your rock 'n roll lifestyle is going to her head.'

Monster reached over to the coffee table, picked up his third bottle of Pepsi and downed half of it in a couple of gulps. 'Yeah? So, what you saying?' He wiped his face with Deb's wet towel because the psychedelic mushrooms had the effect of making him burn up as well as wanting to drink me out of house and home.

'Weed's OK, but don't give her any other drugs, Monster.'

'What, are you her mother? Let her enjoy herself.'

'Would you call what we just saw *enjoying* herself?' I glared at him until the message sank in.

'OK, fair enough. Spliffs and nothing else - and come to think of it, I might hold back with my weed because she's a greedy cow when she gets started.' He wiped his neck and forehead with the towel. 'There's nothing worse than having to come back from a trip before it's worn off.'

*Serves you bloody well right*, I thought. 'Let's just hope it wears off Debs by morning.' I said, listening to her scream at something with fifty nine legs.

'Do you want me to get your guitar so you can play me your new song?'

'Yeah, that might be a good idea. It'll take my mind off being so hot.'

I picked up the guitar case he propped against the record cabinet and gave it to him. Monster took his guitar out. 'I'm taking it this is the song Inge inspired?' I said.

Monster's face dropped. He shook his head. 'I don't get it. I can screw any girl I want and my mind's still on that cow day and night.'

From what I'd seen the *cow* was nothing to write home about but I stopped myself from being one. 'What was it about Inge you liked so much?'

'Have you ever met a man you couldn't stop thinking about but couldn't put your finger on why?'

'No,' I said, since I couldn't recall one who stuck in my mind.

'Well Inge – who by the way wasn't always out of it like the time you saw her – made me feel like I wanted her to be part of everything. Even walking down the road, I wanted to hold her hand. She made me laugh. She made me feel the kind of special I wanted to feel. Yeah, we had mind blowing sex but that wasn't it with Inge - and we all know she was a lazy bitch when it came to housework. It was Inge who got me into Chinese food, took me to art exhibitions and taught me about Dali and Ernst. You probably never noticed that big painting in my bedroom…no well you wouldn't have noticed because you never came in my bedroom – Inge painted that'. Monster idly strummed chords on his guitar.

'So you admired her talent, is that it?'

'I admired her talent but I've got mixed feelings about that painting, although as Inge said, I lack intellect so what do I know.'

'What's intellect?' I shrugged. 'We either like something or we don't.'

'Yeah suppose so – so we're back to whatever it is you can't put your finger on. But whatever it was, Inge was right for me. She was just right for me.'

'Play me the song?' I said gently.

'Alright, but remember it's not finished. This is still an idea in my head. I'll run through the instrumental part, then second time round I'll sing some of the words.' Monster started to play. The tune reminded me of Zeppelin's Stairway to Heaven which had just been released. It had a faster rhythm than Stairway and the chords were deeper but it had the same hypnotic feel that lifted you one stair at a time. The way he plucked at the strings sounded like three electric pianos playing as one, then he did something with his guitar that turned it into a weeping violin. 'What I'm thinking,' Monster said, 'is to overlay the sound to make it sound like an orchestra with cellos.' As Monster played, his long blonde shaggy hair fell over his face and the light from the lampshade shone down on his head making him look like a fallen angel. Tapping his foot, Monster picked up the beat. 'This is where I want Tate to come in strong so his base notes bounce off my high notes. Charlie will be drumming double time and I'm thinking of getting a session musician to play rhythm guitar for some other bits I've got in my head.' Monster stopped playing. 'What d'ya think?

'It's great. I can already hear where you're going,' I felt so excited I almost forgot the psychedelic mushroom episode.

'Alright,' Monster placed his fingers back on the strings. 'Here are the words for the chorus of Heart Trapped in a Jar – which is what I'm calling this song.' Monster started strumming again, looked into my eyes and sang. *When all you're left with are lies, who to trust or believe in. What heart can you give when it's trapped in a jar? Bleeding. Bleeding. Bleeding.* Monster stopped singing and put his guitar back in its case. 'That's the gist.'

107

'Monster, that song's going to be amazing. You've already got your third single.'

'Dunno, if it's that good.'

'Monster, you've got more talent than you realise.' I hugged him because I felt so emotional. 'I'm the luckiest manager in the world.'

Monster pushed me away. 'Get off me before you make me go soppy.' His eyes clouded over. I knew he was thinking about Inge. 'Fucking psychedelic mushrooms,' he said, wiping away a tear.

# SEVENTEEN

'GHWAAAPH.' The living dead, meaning Debs, threw up in the chamber pot I'd put on the floor beside her and returned to the land of the dead on the couch. She'd kept me up most of the night and when I woke up in the morning, I slept through my alarm call. That meant I would have been late for work again but looking at the state of Debs, couldn't have gone in anyway.

Pacing up and down the front room, I thought about what to say to Mr. Gibson. I couldn't say I was ill on top of my bicycle fall for which I'd already taken a day off, and I couldn't say I had to go to a funeral because he would have expected notification. I needed to invent a relative who had a spectacular accident. Placing the back of my hand against my forehead as you saw actresses do in silent black and white films when something terrible had befallen them, I imagined what might have happened to my invented relative and practiced my speech in the mirror before calling. 'Mr. Gibson,' I wailed down the 'phone. 'The most terrible thing has happened to my aunt Priscilla.'

'What Aunt Priscilla?' he snapped.

'My only living relative on my mother's side. Boohooo.' I thought my crying style sounded real and carried on. 'I'm in the hospital now.'

'What hospital?'

'A hospital in Kent where she lives and had her terrible accident.'

'Her accident?'

'She was flattened by a tractor. They've just amputated one of her legs.' I pretended to sniff into a hankie.

'One of her legs did you say?'

'Yes, one of her legs,' I wailed.

'You must look on the bright side. It could have been two.' I stuck my tongue out at him down the phone. Only someone like Mr. Gibson could say something like that.

'And since she was flattened, what about her arms?'

'She lost the thumb on one of her hands.'

'At least she's still got fingers,' Mr. Gibson said.

The living dead threw up in the chamber pot again. GWWAAAAAA.'

'What was that noise?' Mr. Gibson asked.

'My Aunt Priscilla threw up again. It's the shock. She's just soaked her hospital bed sheet in vomit. I need to get back to her Mr. Gibson, she's calling me with her one good arm.'

'Yes, you must before the poor woman chokes.'

'MONSTER, MONSTER, I love you,' Debs shrieked. *As I thought, Debs was infatuated with him.*

'Now Aunt Priscilla thinks she's seeing monsters.' I sighed, to signify how wretched I felt about my aunt's rapid demise.

'She said she loved a Monster,' Gibson said, correcting me.

'That's how bad she is.'

Tugging the telephone wire with me, I clapped my free hand over Deb's mouth, before she gave the game away. 'I will be at work early tomorrow morning because I know Gibsons Holiday needs me.'

'You're right Gibson Holidays does need you – and appreciates you,' Mr. Gibson was talking to me in a soothing voice which happened about once a year. 'I was thinking I may have been a bit hard on you lately and I'm going to give you a pay rise starting the end of this month.'

I held the ear piece away from my ear. *Wonders would never cease.* I looked up at the ceiling. *Bless you whoever you are Aunt Priscilla.* Debs blubbered something under my hand. It sounded like she was drowning in a sea of bubbles.

'Quick, go. Your Aunt Priscilla needs you,' Mr. Gibson said, putting down the phone.

I wrung out the ice-cold flannel sitting in a bowl on the coffee table and put it over Debs eyes. She was sweating not only due to the after effects of three cups of psychedelic mushroom tea but because the promised hot spell had arrived with a vengeance. I went around opening all the windows in our flat then opened the cupboard in the hall. As I thought, our dedicated homemaker Debs had everything in there I needed to sand down and repaint the record cabinet she swapped for a set of saucepans. Tying my hair in a knot to keep my hair off my face, I gathered the tin of undercoat, a tin of Wedgewood blue paint, a plane to sand down the wood, a couple of different sized paintbrushes and some plastic clothes bags from the cleaners.

In the front room, I took the records out of the cabinet, covered them with a dustsheet and lay plastic bags on the carpet ready to get started. 'Laura,' Debs called out weakly. 'Can you switch the electric blanket off, it's burning my bones.'

'You're not laying on an electric blanket Debs, it's the heat from the weather.' I looked down at her chamber pot. A fly was licking her vomit. I picked up the chamber pot, emptied it down the toilet, gave the pot a swill and took it back in.

'Water, water,' Debs croaked. I poured her a glass of water from the jug on the coffee table, helped her to sit up and held it to her mouth.

'Laura, Laura?' Someone called from outside our basement window. The voice sounded like Charlie's. I turned my head. Charlie nervously looked in. 'Monster told me you called him this morning to tell him off again about letting Debs overindulge so I knew you'd be here.' He scratched like a monkey.

'Water, water,' Debs groaned. I let her sip some from the glass.

In one leap, Charlie scrambled through the window and was at my side. 'Something bad happened to me,' he said scratching his penis, then his bum, then his head. 'I've got crabs.' Charlie rubbed his legs together and scratched his arms. 'Can crabs travel up your body?' I shrugged because in despite of the number of men I shagged I'd managed to avoid them. 'It must have been one of those two brunettes,' Charlie said. 'I came because Monster told me Debs gave him a cure for acne so I wondered if she could give me one for crabs?'

Debs threw up in the chamber pot then flopped back down on the coach. Fortunately, her vomit had dwindled to a runny dribble so she was in recovery mode. 'You might have to wait a bit,' I said.

Scratching and nodding, Charlie picked up a paintbrush, pulled his jeans out at the back and stuffed the paintbrush down to have a scratch.

'Did you shave the hairs off your willie?' Debs mumbled.

'Yes, but I couldn't get to the hairs underneath and around my bum and I think the crabs may have made nests there,' Charlie shouted to make sure Debs heard.

'Shave the rest of your hairs off,' Debs said faintly.

Charlie gave me an appealing look because he couldn't do it himself. I nodded my OK and he knelt down in front of her. 'Then what?'

'Clove of garlic in... half a pot... of yoghurt...' Debs' voice trailed off, she burped and returned to the land of the dead. I assumed she meant I needed to mix garlic with yoghurt and spread it over Charlie's private parts.

Charlie stood, scratched his dick then jumped around, arms going up and down by his sides. 'I'll keep active while you make the cure.'

In the kitchen, I concocted his mix in a plastic dish, took a wooden spatula out of the drawer to apply it then went in the bathroom, grabbed a towel, a razor and made a bowl of soapy water. *Hmm, Debs hadn't said anything about what to do after Charlie was covered in yoghurt?* I took a sanitary towel out of the bathroom cupboard, added it to my doctor's kit went into my bedroom and lay the towel down on my bed. 'Ready, Charlie,' I called out.

Charlie bounced in pulling off his jeans and underpants and threw himself down on the towel. His sore, limp dick was very sorry looking and the area around it post box red where he'd scratched himself raw. Having wet his private parts with soapy water, I held up his dick and shaved underneath. It felt a bit like what you saw mothers of baby boys do when they held up the baby's willy to sprinkle it with talcum powder. 'Turn over and I'll do around your bum.' I shaved away the hairs, smothered him in the yoghurt mix then slapped a sanitary towel on him. *Oh, the duties of a manager* I thought. 'Your underpants will hold this in place but I think it's best to leave your jeans off a while.'

Charlie stood and pulled on his underpants. 'I look like an overgrown baby wearing a nappy.' I bit my tongue so I didn't laugh because I'd never seen anything as funny as a twenty two year old baby with purple hair streaks, patting his nappy bulge. 'I saw you were about to paint the record cabinet in the front room.' Charlie said. 'I'll do that, it'll keep me busy.' He hopscotched across the bedroom. 'I'm still as itchy as scratching powder. How long will this cure take?

'Dunno,' I wiped my hands on my shorts before going into the kitchen to make a jug of icy lemonade.

113

When I went back in, Charlie was sanding down the cabinet as if he was on speed. *Sand, sand, sand. Scratch, scratch, scratch. Sand, sand, sand.* With the sanitary towel bulging out of his underpants he looked like a giant baby who pooped himself. While I was silently laughing myself silly about that, Charlie announced he'd been laughing himself silly thinking about the three of us. 'You with your black eye, me with crabs and vomit girl over there. If we were a band, we could call ourselves Black Crabs and Vomit.

On the word *vomit*, Debs got up, stumbled to the bathroom like a sleepwalker, stumbled back like a sleepwalker and crashed out again. Having a scratch, Charlie turned to look at me, tongue rolling about his cheeks as though it was chasing a fly. 'In her sleep she kept mumbling Monster and telling him about wedding dresses.'

'She's got weddings on the brain,' I said, as Debs sat up looking startled.

'Where am I?' Trying to focus, Debs pointed at Charlie. 'Charlie?' She squinted her eyes at the record cabinet. 'That wasn't blue yesterday.'

She went to lay down again so I propped her up and held her steady. 'Charlie painted it after I gave him your cure.'

'Yeah, I owe you,' Charlie said making a face as though he was sucking sherbet through a straw. 'What am I supposed to do with my nappy 'cos I've got to go and see Mons and if he sees me like this, he'll have a right laugh.'

'Stuff a wodge of toilet roll in your underpants.' Debs stood up then sat on her heels on a plastic bag. 'What time is it? Am I late for work?' Returning to the land of the living she stared at the newly painted cabinet in awe. 'If you need any more cures Charlie, just ask because I know loads about natural remedies, don't I Laura?'

'You're an ever spurting fountain of knowledge,' I laughed, glad to see her coming back to normal.

114

I watched her mind tick over. She looked at me in defiance. 'I'm going to college next year to get a diploma in natural medicine. You found a new profession so why can't I change?'

Charlie stretched his neck, touched his toes and stood up again. 'Where d'you work now?'

'Near here, for two dinosaur accountants who talk nothing but numbers and make me nod off when they dictate letters because it takes them five minutes to get further than 'dear sir.' Debs sighed as if the end of the world had come. 'It's *so* boring. My whole life's boring!'

Charlie painted a picture in the air with his hands. 'You could call yourself Witch Doctor Debs, healer extraordinaire. Cures you with urine, garlic and rat's tails.'

'I don't know a cure with rat's tails but I read bull's semen is great for men with thinning hair,' Debs said.

Lips curling downwards, Charlie gave his glossy, thick hair a ruffle. 'Even if went bald, I'd never rub bull's spunk in my hair. Men who do that must be bonkers!' He looked at the clock on the wall. 'Anyway, better go. Mons will be waiting. If you're not doing anything later Laura, come over. We'll talk music and stuff.'

'Yeah might,' I said following Charlie to the window where he jumped out the same way he jumped in. I turned to see Debs folding the plastic covers on the carpet. She was in deep thought. I had the feeling I knew what she was thinking so asked if there was anything she wanted to talk about. When she shook her head, I told her Monster apologised for giving her the magic mushrooms. She wanted to know if he said anything else. 'That he loves you like a sister and doesn't want you to get hurt.'

Debs threw herself down on the carpet and buried her face on her arms. 'Why is this happening to me? I thought Dave was my one and only but I can't get Monster off my mind,' she whimpered.

'It's called infatuation Debs – how long has it been since you've seen Dave?'

'I don't want to marry Dave anymore,' Debs said, shaking her head at the carpet. 'If Monster got to know me better, why couldn't he fall in love with me?'

'Because...' How did I say Debs wasn't Monster's type? 'Because he's a lunatic and a drug addict with no sense of what being faithful means. Once he's over Inge, he'll be shagging someone new every night. Monster would break your heart Debs. Is that what you want?'

Debs sat up straight. 'I feel like my heart's trapped in a jar bleeding – like the words of the song Monster played you last night.'

'You heard that?'

Debs nodded. 'It was the last thing I heard before a giant buzzard flew me off to the land of dustbins.'

'Come here,' I said. 'You need is a cuddle.' Debs threw herself in my arms and I stroked her hair. 'What a mess we are. Monster's heart is trapped in a jar, yours is and so is mine.'

'But you don't love anyone,' Debs mumbled into my tank top.

'You're both suffering because you think you're in love. I'm suffering because all I've felt is emptiness,' I said.

# EIGHTEEN

On the way to Monster's flat, I picked up copies of Music Secret and the Daily Echo. Music Secret tipped Streetcrash as the band most likely to rise to fame in 1971 saying they were 'scalded by the electricity in both the playing and the songs.' The Daily Echo said 'Top marks Streetcrash. Another Zeppelin in the making.'

Since we finally had something to celebrate, I picked up a couple of pizzas for us to share. When I walked into Monster's front room, he chatted to Mr. Krakowski who sat none too comfortably in the red leather beanbag.

'Yes, a randy sod like you shouldn't have to live out the rest of your days without a woman to give you a good seeing to,' Monster said in all seriousness as he lounged next to Mr. Krakowski on a cushion. Monster's acne had started to disappear. He wore a baggy green shirt tucked into his jeans and looked like a matador. I imagined him in a shirt like that with a green bandana for a photo shoot I had in mind to accompany a Truth Kills round of demos I intended to send out since Robert was the only person who heard it, and I was more convinced than ever it was chart material. 'I think a Lonely Hearts ad is definitely something you should do, Mr. Krakowski,' Monster said. 'And Laura's going to tell you what she thinks of my wording when she's made herself comfy.' He smiled up at me. 'Thanks for bringing those. Is one of them a double pepperoni by any chance?'

'Yeah, I remembered from last Sunday, I handed the pizza boxes to Tate. 'There's a plain cheese one too.' Tate's hair was newly bleached and silvery white, he was wearing brown jeans and a brown silky T-shirt and seemed more handsome each time I saw him although I knew it was partly to do with the kindness that shone through his eyes. He winked then headed for the kitchen.

Charlie used the edge of Monster's table as a drum to keep his fingers occupied. 'Nearly got it under control.' His cheeks puffed out as he grinned at me.

'Give me a mo.' Monster patted Mr. Krakowski's knee and swiveled his head around. 'What have you nearly got under control, Charlie? Ever since you came here you've been running about like a headless chicken!

I sat on a cushion opposite Monster and he passed me a piece of paper which I read out loud: 'Not bad looking randy old sod, who enjoys the cinema, theatre and days out at the weekend, would like a feisty woman to cuddle on cold nights.' Charlie chuckled his head off. 'Mr. Krakowski can't write that in his ad,' I said. 'Imagine the kind of women who'll reply?'

'Mr. Krakowski's interest is getting some fire put back in his pecker. He's got to aim at the right audience,' Monster reached up and squeezed Mr. Krakowski's thigh in a male-bonding gesture. Mr. Krakowski coughed in embarrassment.

Mr. Krakowski was freshly shaved and smelled of Old Spice. He was dressed in neatly pressed trousers, a patterned silk waistcoat and his shoes although old were highly polished. I thought about what to say to attract the right type of woman and rewrote the ad. *Nice looking, elderly gentleman with cultural interests, takes good care of himself and has lots to offer, seeks warm, attractive lady companion to share interests and cuddles on cold nights.* 'How does that sound, Mr. Krakowski?'

'Much better.' Mr. Krakowski nodded in delight.

'Ads should be specific,' Monster insisted. 'Krakowski will only get replies from old dodderers.'

118

'I just want a companion,' Mr. Krakowski said, sounding flustered. 'I see enough going on in your life Monster to remind me of the old days. Not that mine were a patch on yours. We were lucky if we got a kiss goodnight back then.'

Tate came back in with the pizzas on two plates, some napkins, a bottle of wine and glasses. He put them on the carpet, sat down next to me and kissed my cheek.

'Want to stay and have a slice?' Monster asked Mr. Krakowski.

'No, no. I'll leave you young 'uns to get on with it.' Mr. Krakowski heaved himself out of the beanbag and Monster walked him to the door.

'Off you go, you randy old sod,' Monster said. 'Let me know how you get on with the ad. I'll help you interview the ladies if you like?'

After Monster closed the door he sat down again and helped himself to a slice of pepperoni. Charlie plonked himself down on a cushion next to Monster then put another one on top of his lap. 'Ooh look, Charlie's gone all posh. He has to have a table to eat on now.'

Charlie blew a raspberry and nabbed a piece of pepperoni while I extracted the newspapers from my bag and lay them down in front of Monster. I pointed to the reviews I'd circled in red and watched their delighted expressions as they consumed the words. Squashed into Monster's side, Charlie read them out.

'Great result,' Monster said to Tate. 'I think we're on our way up.' Monster smiled at me. 'And well done to you.'

Tate hugged me. 'From the minute you walked in our dressing room at the Rat, I knew you were a winner, Laura.' I wanted to feel like a winner but my meeting with Roger played heavily on my mind and I couldn't erase the memory.

Charlie, still with the second cushion on his lap, grabbed another piece of pepperoni and greedily gobbled. 'You've already have two slices. Have some of the cheese one.' Monster said. He smiled at me. 'Have a slice before Charlie scoffs the lot.'

I took a piece and bit into it like a hungry bricklayer. It was the first thing I'd eaten all day. By rights I should have been as thin as a stick considering the effort I put into losing weight but my beach ball bum refused to deflate and my breasts were still 38EE which caused low life's like Roger to assume I was an easy target to be swayed by butlers and Olympic size swimming pools.

Charlie's top cushion had gone. He scratched himself over his jeans. 'OK,' Monster said. 'What the fuck's going on?'

Charlie's mouth screwed into a knot then he grinned. 'One of the brunettes gave me crabs.' He enlisted the help of a plastic fork to scratch between his legs.

Monster spat out a mouthful of pizza. 'Hwaaaaaahaaha, that's rich. So that's what you were doing at Laura's. Getting a cure from Debs.' In the middle of his next spurt of laughter, Monster's face turned serious. 'Since it's honesty time, I'm going to share my latest embarrassment.' He looked at Tate who smiled as he contently nibbled on pizza. 'No. This embarrassment is nothing to smile about, Tate, it was *the* most embarrassing thing in my life. In fact, no, fuck it, I'm keeping it to myself.'

'You can't keep us suspended, Mons,' Charlie said. 'You had a laugh at my crabs.'

Monster shook out his tousled mane, wiped a pizza crumb off his shirt and cleared his throat. 'I couldn't get it up with those blondes on Saturday night.'

'HAWHAWHAW,' Charlie slapped his thighs. 'You said you were taking them in the bathroom because you fancied seeing yourself doing it in the mirror?' HAWHAHA. 'What did you tell 'em?

'That I burned my dick on a sunbed and would get back to them when it healed.' Monster squirmed, uncomfortable with the memory of being unable to perform. 'It's all that fucking Inge's fault.' Tate tapped Monster's arm to show his understanding. Monster thumped Charlie on the head. 'Stop laughing. It's not funny.'

Fiddling with my blouse, I thought about all I had endured those past days due to Roger and Deb's heart-break. My intestines were in knots. Perhaps sharing my anxiety would stop my need to pee at 3am, 4am and 5am? 'Since we're being honest, I'm going to get my embarrassment off my chest.'

'Yeah, you've got enough weight on your chest without adding extra,' Monster pretended to hold out two melons to represent the size of my boobs. Seeing I was not amused, he wiped the smile off his face. 'No, go on – what's your embarrassment?'

When I told him it had to do with a meeting I had with Roger at Flip Records, he nearly had a heart attack and wanted to know how I ended up going to see the wanker before I told him the story. Apparently, Roger spent three years in jail for embezzling his partner out of a fortune and nobody in the music business would touch him with a barge pole. I waited for one of them to tell me how stupid I was but apart from Tate who patted my knee and said I couldn't be expected to know everything, Charlie and Monster stayed quiet. When I got to the part where Roger suggested that I got involved with his sex toy business and mentioned the nipple pinch incident that slipped through my tongue before I realized what I said, Monster nearly choked on his pepperoni.

'That's ripe!' He shook his head as though it was the most outrageous thing he'd heard. 'I hope you told the psycho to fuck off?' Monster gave me his glass of Jack and jumped to his feet. 'I'm going around there to give that perv a piece of my mind. Where's his office?' He patted his jean pockets. 'Where are my van keys?

I tugged at his jeans. 'We can't afford bad press, Monster.'

'Bad press or not, I'll have his fucking guts for garters.' Tugging harder, I told Monster I got my revenge.

Charlie yanked at Monster's foot. 'Sit down. Laura got her revenge.' He turned his eyes on me. 'What d'ya do? Stab him with a letter opener, set fire to his office?'

It was only then I realized I had to tell them how I came to be in the possession of a dildo. I took a slug of Monster's Jack. 'A friend of mine's boyfriend has been away for months working so I bought her a dildo from Roger's sex toy shop so she could…'

'Hwaaaahaaaha, a dildo? You can't fool us,' Monster said. 'Now we know what you do when you disappear to the toilet for half an hour. I'm going to call you Dildo Laura from now on.'

Charlie rolled in a ball laughing. Tate bit his tongue, trying to contain himself. 'OK, so it was for me,' I said. 'I felt sex starved! Satisfied?'

'HAAHAAHAA. I told you no other band had a manager like Laura.' Charlie threw his legs in the air and shook his feet, tears of laughter running down his cheeks. 'HOHOHAHAHA.'

I glared at Monster. 'Did I laugh at your sunbed story?' I grabbed Charlie's foot. 'Did I laugh when you had a sanitary towel stuffed in your underpants?' Tate patted my knee and told me to save the story for another time.

Monster stuffed a napkin in his mouth until he stopped laughing. 'You can't leave us on this cliffhanger! How did a dildo come into the story?'

Charlie rolled to his knees and put his hand over his mouth so he could laugh behind that. 'She twisted Roger's arm off until he gave her another six dildos so she had a different one

122

for every night of the week.' Monster tucked his head into his neck, shoulders shaking with mirth.

Tate sighed at Charlie and Monster. 'You know what those two are like. Keep your story.' Monster clapped his hand over Charlie's mouth and assured me that from then on, they wouldn't crack a smile.

From the minute I gave them the vision of Roger nailed to the door, their eyes bunched up, their cheeks puffed out but not much as a snigger left their lips. I closed my eyes. If I couldn't see their expressions, I could exorcise myself more thoroughly. 'Anyway, I gave Roger the benefit of the doubt when his fingers caressed my boob, but after the second slap on the bum, followed by the nipple pinch, I lost it. Next thing I was kneeing him, hammering his head with the dildo and forcing the testicles....'My head filled with the sound of hysterical laughter. I opened my eyes to see Monster, Charlie and Tate flat out on the carpet. Shoulders touching, tears of laughter rolled down their cheeks. Even Tate had succumbed.

'This is so funny,' Monster held his dick so he didn't pee himself. 'They should make a film of it.' Monster laughed even harder. 'They could call it The Dildo Diaries.'

They tumbled around the floor like five year old kids. I grabbed my bag. 'It's the last time I'm sharing anything with you three!' Tate tried to say they weren't laughing at me but never got past three words because he laughed as much as the others. They were still hysterical when I slammed the door shut.

# NINETEEN

The journey on the No.6 bus from Queens Park to Piccadilly the following morning was stifling. The weather forecast said it would be the hottest day for thirty years and it could be felt at 8.30 a.m. I sat on the front seat of the top deck, reading the headline of a newspaper I picked up off the floor. 'BEATLES OFFICIAL BREAKUP' It was like reading the Pope got a divorce from the Vatican. To digest the shock, I fanned my face with the paper and watched a group of Hare Krishna's dance down Oxford Street in orange robes. How they couldn't feel the heat was beyond me.

'It'll be hot enough to fry eggs on the pavement soon, eh duckie?' the woman sitting next to me said.

'And bacon,' I opened my legs and discreetly fanned my private parts which felt sticky as a current bun.

'At least you've got something cool on,' she said. I wore a short sleeved cotton tank top that showed my midriff and a matching mid-calf floral sarong, tied in a knot at the back. The woman next to me looked ready to faint so I fanned her to cool her off.

'Very kind, duckie,' she said.' See you like to take care of yourself? Matching green headband. Matching high heels. Going somewhere special?'

'Just work,' I said, wishing I could spend the day in a tub of ice.

As I thought, when I got to work, Gibson hadn't bothered to get me a new fan so my office felt hotter than a boiler room on a cargo ship. Changing as usual from stiletto's into platforms, I thought about what to say to give Mr. Gibson a piece of my mind. Two things stopped me. I was supposed to be grieving for Aunt Priscilla and needed the job until money came in from Streetcrash, because financially my situation was dire.

'My dear girl,' Mr. Gibson said, as he marched into my office from his. 'How's your Aunt Priscilla?'

There was no point forcing fake tears into my eyes because I wore sunglasses, so I sighed, raised my hands to the sky and said 'It's in God's hands now, Mr. Gibson. We have a lot of work to do so I am casting her fate from my mind.' I sat down at my desk looking glum. 'By the way, did you order my fan because I might pass out in my weak emotional state?'

'I'll order one now,' Mr. Gibson said as the phone rang on my desk. I'll take this call to give you a chance to adjust. 'Hello,' he said in his usual nauseating manner. 'Who? What's your name? Did you say Monster?' Mr. Gibson covered the mouth piece with his hand. 'Yesterday we had your aunt Priscilla calling out Monster's name. Now we have one on the phone.'

'Oh, he's calling about a survey I've been doing.' I said it with such sincerity I nearly fooled myself. 'Let me take the call. Gibson's business must carry on.' Mr. Gibson handed me the phone. 'Thanks for calling back Monster. So, what I would like to know is whether you and your wife enjoyed your holiday in our Sierra Leone hotel and whether you have any suggestions to improve our service?'

Monster understood straight away and laughed. 'Me and my wife fucked day and night and enjoyed every minute of our holiday.'

'We're very glad to hear that, I will make a note for the survey,' I said, putting down the phone.

'What an excellent idea.' Gibson tapped his piddly patch of moustache with glee. 'Have the survey finished and on my desk by tomorrow morning. I could learn a lot from that.'

So much for his sympathetic phase I thought, thinking about all the holidaymakers I needed to call to give him the survey by the next day. 'I will do my best,' I feigned delicacy to hint I might be slower than usual due to stress.

'You will rise above this like the star employee you are.' He said, and strode off like a sergeant major.

The phone rang again for the twentieth time. I had so many calls to make and so much work to catch up on I thought of taking one of the two phones off the hook but with Gibson back to his usual selfish self and bothering me every few minutes, thought better of it. 'Oh hello Mrs. Levin – yes I can certainly get your ladies golf group a weekend in Portugal. I have the perfect hotel in mind. Let me get back to you.' I put that phone down. The other one rang as Mr. Gibson marched towards me again. 'Gibsons Holidays,' I answered.

'Can you talk?' Debs whispered. 'It's urgent.'

'Thank you for taking the time to talk to me about your holiday Mr. Hitchcock. Knowing our customers are happy with our service means a lot.'

'Stop wasting time on that survey,' Mr. Gibson screamed. 'Where's the in-house travel magazine you were supposed to be putting together?' It should be at the printers by now.'

'I will show you the layout and everything else I've done so far, Mr. Gibson,' I pulled out a file from a drawer in my desk. 'The only reason I'm behind is because circumstances forced me to take two days off work.'

'I'm aware of that.' Glancing at my face, Gibson walked around in a circle, hands held behind his back. He stopped to smooth his hair and clicked his heels together. That meant it was Nazi inquisition time. 'You took two days off?

'Two days, yes.'

'On one of those days you fell off your bicycle?' He brought his eyes level with mine.

'Yes.'

Mr. Gibson squashed his monacle to his eye and peered closer. It was then I remembered I took off my sunglasses to read the small print on a contract and forgot to put them back on. He examined my eye in microscopic detail. 'I will not be lied to!'

'You are right, Mr. Gibson. I was protecting the innocent.'

Gibson made the figure eight with his lips. 'Now an innocent has entered the story?'

'I am the innocent, Mr. Gibson. I was attacked by a man with a vicious temper but couldn't bring myself to talk about it.'

'And that is the truth?'

'One hundred percent.'

'Now let's discuss your second day off. The way you were laughing with Sissy earlier, makes me think Aunt Priscilla wasn't flattened by a tractor and that somewhere in the story *Monster* plays a part.'

I made my face look like a wronged prisoner. If he wanted to play at war, this was one I would win. 'You are a very suspicious and unfeeling human being, Mr. Gibson! Perhaps you'd like me to bring you Aunt Priscilla's amputated leg and thumb?' I jabbed myself in the chest. 'And I can't be held responsible for all the Monsters roaming the world.'

'HMPH.' Stony faced, he flipped through the pages and let the subject drop.

I pointed to where hotel pics would go. 'I've chosen three pictures for each hotel and location and...' I turned to the last page. 'I thought we could include a competition to make sure travel agents read the blurb.'

'Hmm.' Mr. Gibson patted his jacket with the fondness you might pat a dog. That was a good sign. It meant even if he didn't believe my lies, he was calming down. 'Quite good.' He nodded his head. 'What are we offering the winner of this competition?'

I pointed to the paragraph at the bottom of the page. 'A weekend for two at their favourite hotel from those listed in our in brochure.'

Gibson picked up the Kit Kat Tod left on my desk earlier that morning. 'Mind if I...?' Snapping it in half he slapped a stick of gooey chocolate in my palm. 'Take this as a peace offering.' Giving me a *carry on with your work* flick of his wrist, he marched back to his cool, airy office where his industrial fan blew full blast.

I threw the Kit Kat in the bin, wiped the chocolate off my hands, took an elastic band out of a box on my desk and pulled my hair back in a ponytail. With one hand I wrote a list of people to call and ask whether they loved or hated their holiday and the other one to fan my face with a travel brochure.

'Phew. It must be a hundred degrees in here,' Sissy said, leaving a file on my desk and going back out.

Debs called again as Mr. Gibson appeared from nowhere like the invisible man and breathed down my neck. 'Yes, Mrs. Morris,' I said. 'We've just put the price down on that holiday package so it's an excellent deal. Yes, fine. Call me back.' I replaced the receiver and looked up at Gibson feeling agitated. 'Can I help you with something Mr. Gibson?'

'I was looking for my black marker pen,' he said.

'Haven't seen it,' I shrugged. Mr. Gibson looked up at the wall clock. It was 1pm. 'At 2pm precisely I'd like Sissy to bring me in an egg mayonnaise sandwich and some fruit. A bunch of green grapes instead of my usual orange for a change. I shall now, as usual, take my power nap.'

'Yes, Mr. Gibson.' I watched him go back into his office and close the door then buzzed Sissy. 'When you get a minute, Mr. Gibson wants an egg mayonnaise sandwich and a bunch of green grapes.'

Having made a few more calls, I tiptoed to Mr. Gibson's office and listened. He was snoring. Hip Hip Hooray. The best time of the day had arrived when I didn't have to see him for a whole hour. Back at my desk I opened my legs and fanned myself with my skirt.

'You should learn to pick up the phone!' Chris said, storming into my office. 'Five times I've called Debs and not once have you called back!'

I looked up in shock, realising what Debs had been trying to warn me about, quickly shut my legs and made myself look decent. 'I had nothing to say,' I said in a low voice. 'And how dare you come in my office. My boss is in there. Wasn't giving me a black eye enough or are you trying to get me sacked as well?'

Chris got down on his knees. 'I'm here to ask for forgiveness. The way I behaved wasn't what a babe like you deserves. Give me another chance? Let me make it up to you?'

'I told you it was over,' I hissed. 'Sling your hook!'

'I said I was sorry.'

'Since you don't understand English let me tell you in Italian. We are FINITO!'

'I don't know what came over me,' he pleaded with his hands. 'I've never hit a woman before you. I haven't slept a wink since I did it,' he looked guiltily at my eye. Since Mr. Gibson had seen it, I hadn't bothered to put my sunglasses back on.

'I had to take a day off work to recover from your handiwork! Get this through your head. I *never* want to see you again.'

Chris's face changed. He growled like a starved lion. 'You *are* going to forgive me and we *are* getting back together.'

Sissy stood in the doorway of my office with Mr. Gibson's lunch in her hands. She rested two paper bags on top of a filing cabinet. 'Ooh, just remembered something. Back in a flash.'

I sneered at Chris. 'You don't scare me.' In the background, Mr. Gibson's fan whirred and clunked as he snored. 'Get out before I call the police.'

'Don't threaten me with the cops,' Chris snarled.

Sissy edged Tod in through my office door. 'Everything alright in here?' He looked confused.

'I was just telling Chris that *friends* of ours are not permitted to walk in off the streets and bother us during office hours. He seems to be having trouble understanding.'

Putting on a swagger, Tod approached Chris and placed a hand on his shoulder. 'Listen mate, let's…'

Chris shrugged Tod's hand off. 'Take your hand off my silk shirt.'

Tod sneered. 'Expensive clothes don't mean you've got taste and the lady asked you to leave.'

'Oh, the *lady*, and what business is it of yours what I do with her?'

Chris and Tod moved around each other like cats ready to strike. Tod so tall and skinny it looked as if he'd been squeezed through a tube of tooth paste to reach his 6' 5" height and Chris so squat, round and solid he looked as if his body was made of Michelin truck tyres. Chris was considerably shorter so had to look a long way up to glare into Tod's eyes. I positioned myself between them. 'Leave Chris. Let's not have any trouble.'

'I'm getting the feeling that you two,' Chris poked Tod in the stomach then pointed his finger at me. 'Might know each other outside office hours.'

Tod retaliated by poking Chris on the shoulder. 'Don't poke me, mate.'

Turning to one side, I put a hand on their chests to push them apart. 'STOP IT Tod, go back to your office.'

'Mr. Gibson will give Laura the sack if you don't go away.' Sissy timidly shook a rolled up umbrella at Chris.

'Laura doesn't need a job. I've got *more* than enough money.' Chris looked at Tod as if he was a lowly worm. 'Where d'you get your trousers from *mate*? Was it C&A or British Home Stores?'

'You're asking for it,' Tod said, swelling his chest. 'This is no longer between you and Laura, it's between me and you. If you want to make a fight of it, let's take it outside.'

'You screwed her, didn't you?' Chris's mouth twitched.

'None of your business,' Tod said.

'You effing well did screw her.' Chris turned and grabbed me by my ponytail. 'Is that tall, skinny runt, with his college boy haircut the reason you went off me?'

'I hope I am. You're not worthy to lick her shoes,' Tod looked at my black eye, his face darkening. 'Did you do that?' he hissed at Chris.

'None of your business,' Chris said. He tugged at my hair until the elastic band plinked off. Sissy hit him over the head with the umbrella. He pushed her off to ruffle my hair in my face. 'Now you look like the prostitute I know!' Boiling with fury, I spat in his face. 'You little bitch,' he hissed.

Tod's hand shot out from nowhere to punch Chris around the ear.' Pick a fight with someone your own size.'

'GRAAAAAAAAAH,' Chris's face turned blue. He jumped up and punched Tod in the eye. BOOF.'

Reeling back, Tod picked up my broken fan. 'You'll get this over your head if you don't back off, mate.'

Chris punched Todd in the gut, grabbed the fan and smashed it on the floor. 'Now what you gonna do, *mate*?

'Stop. Go test your testosterone somewhere else,' I screamed.

Squaring up to Chris, blood dripping off his chin, Tod rolled his fists, reached over me and bopped Chris in the eye. BOOF. Chris hit back aiming at Tod's stomach. BOOF, BOOF, WHACK. Squealing like a petrified mouse, Sissy thrashed

131

Chris on the back, while I lashed out hitting whoever was closest to make them stop. Stumbling to his feet, Tod flew at Chris's legs. 'Now you're really gonna get it, mate!'

Chris fell backwards into my desk where it scraped its way towards the window sending up a gust of papers and scattering a box of paper clips on the floor as my swivel chair spun off into a corner of the room. Armed with my metal waste bin, I went at Chris from behind and whacked him on the skull. 'CLONK, CLONKKKK. Chris wrestled the bin out of my hands and threw it. Sissy chased and caught it while I crouched down and sank my teeth into Chris's shin.

'Last round,' Chris said to Tod, shaking me off. RATATATAT. His fists came at Tod's gut like spitfires. BOOF, BOOF, BOOOOOF. Tod's feet left the floor, his body flew backwards through the air and he crashed to the floor like a sack of stones.

Running to him, I bent over and slapped his face to bring him round. 'Tod, Tod.'

In one stride, Chris was behind me tugging at the knot on the back of my skirt to pull me off. 'You did screw him, you slut.' In the background Sissy screamed.

In all the commotion and hoo ha, no-one heard Mr. Gibson's door open. All we heard was: 'WHAT ON EARTH IS GOING ON?' The three of us reeled round to see Gibson standing there, his mouth hanging open in horror.

'Here's another reason to sack Laura.' Chris punched Mr. Gibson squarely between the eyes.

*D-O-I-N-N-NG.* Gibson's eye balls swam around like marbles. He held the filing cabinet to steady himself. From my crouched position I started to rise, knowing my hair looked as wild and woolly as a cavewoman, but not knowing my tank top no longer covered one boob and that Gibson was getting an eyeful of nipple. Pulling my tank top down in haste I straightened my shoulders and stood to face the music when

*Floop*, my sarong wrap around skirt dropped to the ground. Gasping in shock, Mr. Gibson was presented with a bird's eye view of my vagina but couldn't tear his eyes away. Sissy, grabbed the bunch of grapes and held them in front of me trying to cover what she could but with Tod lying spark out on the floor and me looking like Eve in the garden of condemnation, there wasn't much I could do to redeem myself.

Mr. Gibson stumbled to my desk arms held out to steer himself because he'd been rendered half blind from Chris's punch. Searching the floor until his hand felt a telephone, he picked it up and asked to be connected to the police, at least that's what I understood from reading his lips since the shock had rendered him speechless. Chris stuck two fingers up and stormed out of my office.

I tied my skirt then picked up my handbag and sunglasses. 'I imagine Mr. Gibson that this is goodbye?'

Sissy cried and tried to tell Gibson it wasn't my fault. Gibson silenced her with a Nazi swoosh of his hand before pointing me to the EXIT sign.

'Actually Mr. Gibson, I am happy to be leaving. Would you like to see my vagina again as a keepsake before I go?' Even though I couldn't hear him, it was obvious by the shape of his mouth that he was screaming *OUT.*

# TWENTY

With no job and nowhere to go, I ended up at a pub in Great Portland Street to drown my sorrows. My mistake was getting involved with a hen party and accepting every Bacardi and coke that came my way. When the hen party left, I hailed a taxi and told the driver to take me somewhere classy where I could continue getting sloshed.

The receptionist at Morton's in Mayfair, didn't take too well to me turning up with no shoes. I handed them to her explaining through a slur that my heel broke off in a pavement grid and she could throw them away. She looked down her nose, probably because I burped in her face, put my shoes in a plastic bag and handed it to me. 'This is a private members club. Do you have a membership or do you know someone here who can sign you in as their guest?'

My arm slipped off the reception desk. 'I know everybody, the whole world are my friends.' I chose a stranger who was standing inside the club at the bar,' That's my friend David.' I gave him a wave and winked at him to come over. He was about 55 with puffed out mongoose cheeks but I knew my men well enough to know his type, and out he came. I threw my arms around his neck. 'David, thanks for inviting me. It's so luzely to see you again. Tell her my name's Laura and how we've known each other for *years.'*

'Do you know her John?' the reception asked frostily.

John threw his arm around my shoulder. 'She always calls me David because I remind her of David Niven.' I focused on his features. If he looked like Niven I was a monkey's aunt.

'Exactly,' I slurred, aiming the plastic bag with my shoes at the bin behind the reception desk. 'Bullseye.'

'Well I hope your friend Laura isn't going to cause trouble,' the receptionist said, allowing John to sign me in a guest. He ushered me into the bar and patted the stool next to his.

'This must be my lucky night,' John rubbed his hands together with glee. Hiccuping, I told him it had been one of the worst days of my life so that should even things out a bit. 'Let me order a bottle of champagne.' John rubbed my thigh. 'The night is young and I can tell that you and I are going to have lots of fun together.'

I gestured him to come closer with my index finger. John put his ear to my mouth. 'You John, look to be a very sexy man, but I don't have a vagina under this skirt and unless you're partial to a nice long dick, you might not want to waste your money.'

John jumped off his stool as if he'd stung by a wasp. 'I've just seen a business colleague at the other end of the bar.'

I went to take my sunglasses off, then remembering my black eye, left them on, propped my head on my elbow and flicked a peanut across the bar. 'One coke for a beautiful lady with a lot on her mind from what I am seeing,' the barman said.

'You wouldn't want to know,' I sighed.

'A word of advice,' the barman said in a low voice. 'Go and sit in one of the booths. I'll bring your coke over – and a coffee on the house. From his accent I guessed he was probably Italian and was exactly the kind of man I'd have chatted up, if I'd been sober enough to string two words together. I started sliding sideways off the stool. The barman caught my arm. 'Go, before they throw you out.'

'You deserve a medal,' I slurred. 'You get my vote for barman of the year.' I stood up and carefully putting one foot in front of the other, zigzagged my way to the closest booth and sat down. I glugged down the coke and coffee when they came then picked up the salt shaker, tipped salt out on the table and made patterns of smiley faces until there was a row of them from one end to the other.

A man appeared and put his finger on one. 'That one looks like me? Mind if I join you?'

'Join me at your peril,' I said glumly. 'Or perhaps you'd like to see my vagina? Everyone else has today.'

The man guffawed and sat down opposite me across the table. 'Interesting day you've had. Can I buy you a drink?'

'Yeah, why not. Bacardi and coke with lots of ice'.

The man ordered drinks from a passing waitress. 'Want to tell me your fanny story,' he said. 'I'm stuck in a studio most days with people who think they're better at my job than I am. And I had a distressing experience recently. You're like a breath of fresh air in my morbidly, dingy, dark world'.

I exhaled over him. 'Bet my breath stinks.'

He sat back. 'Let me order you something to eat to settle your stomach?'

'It's not food I need. I need to change my whole, entire, screwed up life.'

'What's with the sunglasses?' he said. I lifted them to show him my black eye. 'I'm assuming you didn't get that walking into a door?'

'No. I got this for being a slapper.' The man laughed over my words as the waitress put our drinks down on the table.

'A slapper?' He kept his voice down. 'Are you a - woman of the night?'

'Oh no. I wouldn't take money for having sex.'

'Uhaha, Is the fanny incident related to you being a slapper?' He asked, trying to piece together my nonsensical sentences.

'No. I'm taking a break from shagging.' I hiccupped. 'I'm a recovering sex addict.'

'Wawawa,' the man guffawed. 'How long has it been since you last had sex?'

I took a slug of Bacardi. 'Phew! More than three weeks.'

'Wawaa, I think I should hire you to make me laugh.'

'Well, I'm available,' I hiccupped again. 'I got the sack today.'

'HAHA. Get it off your chest. Tell uncle Bob. I prefer men,' he whispered. I looked at his pink jacket and purple flamingo shirt imagining him to be popular on the gay scene. His lips had bunched into a knot. 'Or I did before my so-called lover took off with a prancing, tutu wearing, ballet dancer!'

'Would you like to tell me your story, Uncle Bob?' My elbow slid off the table.

'Maybe another time when I don't feel so distressed. Tell me yours?'

I folded my arms and rested my chin against them so I could stare at the table while I opened my heart. 'Well uncle Bob, this particular part of the story about my miserable life, started seven weeks ago when I was dating this heavy weight boxer, before which I shagged Tod from press office. During that time there was also an incident with a sicko I ended up whacking with a dildo.'

'WAHAHA, stop darling. Let me get my breath back.' Uncle Bob wiped his eyes with a napkin.

'In the same time period I got involved in a new business which was affecting my day job due to the number of personal calls I got. My boss was on the warpath.' I went through the story, recalling the torturous things I suffered until my skirt flooped off. 'And that's how I ended up in the garden of condemnation – Tod now with a black eye like mine I suspect, and my boss possibly lying in a funeral parlour!'

Bob flapped his arms, and giggled his head off. 'I'm sorry. I'm not laughing at you. I'm laughing at the story.' He passed me a bowl of crisps. 'How are you feeling darling?'

'Much better Uncle Bob.'

'I shall take that story with me to the grave,' Bob said. He tapped my arm. 'Sit up. Look at me. I don't even know your name?'

I pushed myself off my elbows, sat up and offered him my hand to shake. 'I'm Laura the loser.'

'You're not a loser. You're one of the funniest, most honest women I've met – and I've got many stories to rival yours. You'll find your way,' he nodded at my handbag which lay open on the table. 'Here, give me that?'

He had such a lovely smile it seemed a shame he was gay. 'Why, do you want it to take me on a date?'

'You are a breath of sunshine.' Bob popped a business card in my bag and closed it. 'I haven't got the vaguest idea what you do and I've got to go to France for a couple of weeks, but any time after that give me a call. I'll help in any way I can.'

'That's very kind of you.' I folded my arms, turned my head to one side and let it flop against them. 'Goodnight Uncle Bob'.

He gently shook me. 'Let me call you a cab.'

# TWENTY-ONE

The next few days I was tense and anxious, half expecting someone to turn up with a writ summoning me to court for exposing myself in public, damaging office property and causing Mr. Gibson's death. I couldn't bring myself to tell Debs what happened, and in her fragile state, she wouldn't have heard. She cried at the drop of a hat, had the face of a tragedy queen and took to cleaning with the ferocity of a ferret.

I busied myself stuffing envelopes with Truth Kills tapes and the new Streetcrash photo from the photoshoot. The photo showed Monster wearing a green satin shirt and bandana. Tate and Charlie stood back to back on either side wearing green T-shirts.

Debs pinned one of the photos above her bed and had candles going day and night on our bedroom windowsill. She bought a book of witch's spells and chanted incantations as she cleaned spotless cupboards, wiped down scrupulously scrubbed shelves, mopped floors and vacuumed carpets until they gleamed. Debs had gone to live in the land of heartbreak. I let her get on with it to digest the horrors that had befallen me.

Debs concocted a potion in a copper pot on the coffee table. She was mumbling something like Mitar Kumbala under her breath. I rolled a joint and blew smoke in her face trying to tempt her. Stop that,' Debs said. She waved the smoke away. 'You're spoiling my incantation.'

I looked at the clock on the wall. I told Monster to call and ask Debs for advice about his love problem then say something disgusting to end her infatuation. Thus far he hadn't called.

'Maybe it would help your incantation if you weren't so stressed?'

'Shh, I'm concentrating.' Debs mumbled another part of her incantation. She wore a robe with half-moons and a pointed witch's hat so she felt authentic. I wore a pirate eye patch and red spotted scarf to show her how silly she looked. She was too far gone to notice.

'Mmm, this Acapulco Gold your brother Pete brought over is really mellow,' I said. 'Sure you don't want some?'

'No. Shh.' Debs closed her eyes to chant more rubbish.

'Witchcraft isn't going to make Monster love you,' I said, hardly knowing the Debs who had emerged those past weeks. 'One day you'll look back on this and we'll laugh our heads off like we do with Mrs. McClory.'

'Monster's not in love with Inge,' Debs said, ignoring my words. 'What we have could last forever.'

Just then the phone rang. 'Oh, hello Monster.' Debs ears pricked up. 'What's up?' I said innocently. 'Oh, you don't want to talk to me, you want to talk to Debs. Yeah, she's here, I'll pass you over.'

Debs took off her hat and grabbed the joint. 'Told you it would work,' she said, taking a puff. 'Yesss Monster?' She purred as though her prince had ridden up on his stallion to ask her hand in marriage. 'What did you want to ask me?' I watched Debs face drop a fraction. 'Oh, about Inge. Yes, go on, I'm listening.' Debs kept puffing on the joint. Her eyes filled with tears as her chin dropped through the floor. 'No, I don't have any cures to make someone love you. You should forget Inge and find....'Debs stopped talking as Monster took over. 'Inge liked WHAT? That's disgusting Monster. Dogs weren't born to do that! And no, I wouldn't consider letting your neighbour's pug do that to me! Anyway, sorry. Haven't got time for more advice. I'm busy making homemade apple pie with custard.' Debs threw the phone on the receiver, gave me the joint, grabbed the copper pot and marched off. I listened as she ripped Monster's photo off the wall then marched back in. 'I'll never be able to look at a pug again without thinking about what Monster makes them do!' She flopped down beside me on the couch.

'Disgusting,' I said.

Debs grabbed the joint back and puffed away. 'This Moroccan is mellow – and it's made me see the light. To think I was going to throw my lovely, faithful Dave away for a monster like Monster. I can't believe I thought I was in love with him!' Debs peered at me. 'Why are you dressed like a pirate and why aren't you at work?'

'I gave my notice in,' I said, rather than telling her I got the sack and get a scolding.

The phone rang again.

'If it's Monster, tell him I'm busy.' Debs said.

Nodding, I answered it. 'Hello.'

'Laura?'

'Yes.'

'It's Robert Bauman from Scorch Records. I've decided to sign Streetcrash. Can you come and see me tomorrow before I leave for L.A.?'

# TWENTY-TWO

'Bye, Audrey Hepburn.' The taxi driver tipped his cap as I got out of his cab. 'Enjoy your premiere,' he joked. Jim and I had become best mates during the taxi ride from my flat to Holland Park. It turned out that he not only knew who Streetcrash were but was at their gig at the Trade Club and asked for my autograph so he could boast to his friends.

'Bye. Jim.' I raised my hand to my mouth and blew him a flirty kiss that was more Marilyn Monroe than Hepburn because I couldn't imagine someone as skinny as Hepburn doing it with the same panache. I wore a fifties style dress from a shop called Rock-a-Billie off Portobello Road. It was pink, V necked with pearl buttons, had a wide belt and flounced skirt. I patted my hair which was styled into a French pleat. 'Look out for me at the Music Awards next year.'

Jim winked. 'Get me and my wife an invite.'

Clickety-clacking up the front steps of Robert's house in my pink high heels, I felt like a celebrity on a red carpet. He didn't have a bell to press so I knocked on the huge brass lion head knocker half expecting to be received by a butler in tails because the houses in his street were so posh. Excited, I smoothed down my dress. To be invited to his house had to mean something positive since he was seeing me between international flights.

When Robert opened the door, I was struck by his elegantly cut blue trousers and blue shirt with faint white stripes. Maybe it was the sandy coloured hair and his trimmed stubbly beard, but he reminded me of a Scottish highlander who would have been equally suited to wearing a kilt. 'Come in Laura,' he smiled and ushered me into his front room. 'Make yourself comfortable.'

'Thanks,' I mumbled, aware the butterflies in my stomach had solidified my tongue. I chose the singular green leather armchair and sat down. Cool air was being piped through ventilators on the walls and wafted the scent of pinecones although I couldn't see pinecones anywhere.

'If you're wondering where the smell's coming from, I had a special unit fitted.' He pointed to a tiny round grid on the ceiling.

'It's amazing,' I said, the smell of pine bringing me round. 'The weather's still so warm, we could be in the tropics.'

'Somewhere like Sierra Leone perhaps?' Smiling to himself, Robert sat down on the green leather sofa opposite. 'Still haven't stopped laughing about that day. I'm assuming your day job has something to do with travel?'

Keeping my back straight, I crossed my legs Audrey Hepburn style wondering if I would ever live that cringey embarrassment down. 'It did. I handed my notice in to concentrate on Streetcrash.'

'Sensible because you'll be rushed off your feet from now on.' He picked up a brown envelope from his coffee table that was so shiny I could see my reflection in it. 'The offer I'm prepared to make is twenty thousand pounds. I'm not known to be a penny pincher when I believe in a band and having considered it, I believe Streetcrash *do* have something unique – and you were right about Truth Kills.'

I opened my mouth to speak. The excitement froze my tongue. I coughed into my nails to gain composure. 'Twenty thousand is more than generous. I won't disappoint you, Mr. Bauman.'

'I'm thinking Streetcrash should go on tour,' Robert announced. 'The whole of the UK and Scotland.' I coughed out

143

loud in shock. We hadn't yet signed the contract and I was a tour manager! 'I want to bring Truth Kills out before Christmas – With Everyone's on the B side.' Robert said. 'I'll give you a budget, won't be much for a first tour but see what you can do.'

My head swam with words. UK. Scotland. Truth Kills. Christmas single. Budget. Arrange tour. I nodded like a spaced out woodpecker. It was too surreal to be true. 'Thank you.'

'Can I get you a glass of chilled Sancerre or Meursault?' Robert asked.

Even though I didn't have the foggiest idea how either tasted, I thought about what Audrey Hepburn might choose. 'Masat.'

'Coming right up.' Robert stood, picked up an envelope and held it up. 'Look at the contract while I'm gone. The rehearsal studio is booked this week. I was thinking Streetcrash might want to use it next Wednesday?' As Robert bent over and passed me the envelope, I was enveloped in the smell of Sandalwood. I knew it was that because I once bought a bottle of Sandalwood bath oil from a shop called Floris in Jermyn Street. He talked about bringing in Max from Ginnie Linnie to play rhythm guitar, how I'd need a solid crew to carry equipment on tour. My head swam with more responsibilities I didn't know the first thing about. 'Are we on the same page?'

'Absolutely.' I sat up straight again.

'By the way, I'm preferring your Audrey Hepburn look to the other one, and it's good to see your eyes.' Robert sat back on the sofa again. 'Which side of your family did you get such exceptionally green ones from?'

I had no idea because my mother wasn't sure who fathered me. 'My dad.'

We chatted small stuff until the telephone rang and Robert reached out to answer it. 'Oh, hi Carol. Come up to my hotel suite at 8 tomorrow night. Haha. Yes, it has been too long. See you then.'

I wondered who Carol was and if his wife knew about her. Robert hadn't struck me as a Casanova type.

He replaced the phone on its stand and turned back to me. 'Let me go get that bottle of wine.'

I listened to him clatter down the iron staircase to the kitchen, glad he'd be gone for a while so I could relax my mind. Glancing around his living room which was grand, there was no doubt Robert had excellent taste, but I was struck by the precision of the layout of the furniture and the exact placing of every item. It looked like something you might see in House and Garden for a 'home of the month' feature and gave me the feeling nothing was ever ruffled or touched.

On top of the coffee table, sat a silver platter piled high with chocolates in Fortnum and Mason wrappers. My eyes were drawn to the rack underneath where trade music magazines were stacked on one side and a photo album on the other.

Downstairs in the kitchen, I heard Robert talking on the phone to a business associate in the USA. Curiosity getting the better of me, I reached under the coffee table. Normally I wouldn't have any interest in looking at someone's family photos, especially someone I'd only met twice but something urged me on. Quietly lifting the album onto my lap, I opened it. I wanted to see what his wife looked like since the only photograph on the mantelpiece was of an old lady.

On top of the first page was a crumpled ticket for an orchestra playing big band hits at the Astoria, Finsbury Park on May 11, 1936. I smiled at the ticket price of sixpence and glanced at the two photos underneath. They were grainy black and whites, both faded with age and showed an orchestra. The man in the middle held a trumpet and was surrounded by women in feathered hats, scanty dresses and tap shoes.

I listened. Robert was still talking and It sounded like the conversation wouldn't end for a while so I skipped a few pages until I came to some photos showing Robert as a toddler. In all he looked sullen but the picture that made me giggle was one of him angrily thumping a mug against his head. Behind him were a couple who beamed like rays of sunshine. The woman wore an apron and a hair net. The man was wearing a cap. They reminded me of the comic strip characters Andy Cap and his wife.

I strained my ears. I could tell by Robert's words that the call had reached its end and quickly turned to the last page. It was Robert, wearing a black tuxedo as he held up a music trophy – but still no wife. I put back the album and sat tapping my knee as though I hadn't moved an inch. 'Sorry about that. Business call.' Robert handed me a glass of wine and sat down. 'Now, back to where we were.' I could have watched the way his hands moved when he talked about music for hours and listened intently. It was similar to what Monster said about Inge. Robert had something I couldn't put my finger on, 'Have I lost you?' he smiled.

I took a long, deliberate sip of wine and made my face look ecstatic. 'No, I was just thinking how delicious Masat is.'

'A woman of taste,' Robert said, as someone honked a horn outside. 'Sorry, time's run out on us. Must be my date. Music convention at the Grosvenor House Hotel.'

*Another date? Robert was a dark horse.* 'Enjoy the music convention.'

He stood to show me out. 'We'll get back to where we were next Wednesday when Streetcrash come in to rehearse.'

# TWENTY-THREE

The following Wednesday, Robert called to say his flight was delayed and he wouldn't be in the office until late afternoon. His secretary had been given the day off since she'd gone to a wedding in Scotland but his accountant was there to let me in. I went in early to prove my worth by answering calls, following up on what I could and attending to my own work. The three boys came in together at noon. Tate and Charlie went into the rehearsal room to check it out. Monster came into the kitchenette. 'Guess who I just met?' He poured himself a mug of coffee. 'Fucking Rick Wakeman! He was coming in the building to see someone when we came in.' Monster heaped three big teaspoons of sugar in his mug whereas he normally had one. I let him get on with it thinking he needed a sugar fix. 'What a nice bloke. Right down to earth.'

I slapped cheese and pickle on another bread roll and added it to the pile so Streetcrash could snack on something during the day. 'Wakeman played keyboards on Bowie's Space Oddity didn't he?' I said. 'Wasn't it amazing that the record release coincided with the first man who walked on the moon?'

Monster bit into a roll and munched. 'Yeah, but it *was* coincidental. Bowie wrote the song as a tribute for Brian Jones of the Stones after he was found floating face down in his swimming pool.'

'You should have asked Rick to play keyboards on one of your tracks.' I joked.

'Yeah, I should of. Heart Trapped in a Jar would have been *right* up his street.' A bit of hot coffee slurped over Monster's mug, burned his wrist and snapped him out of his daydream. He put down the mug to rinse his hand. Charlie bounced in the kitchen in his usual ants in the pants way, snatched a roll and picked up Monster's mug. Monster grabbed it back, had a mouthful and spat it in the sink. 'You tipped half a pound of sugar in my mug when my back was turned, you moron!'

'It wasn't me. It had to be…' Charlie glanced about with wild black eyes. 'Look it was him, that big scary ghost. Whoooooo.' He jigged off to the tune playing in his head. 'See you in rehearsals, Diva.'

Monster was pouring a second mug of coffee when Tate came in and took a bottle of water out of the fridge. 'Ready Mons? We're set up.'

'Charlie's a fucking delinquent, Tate.' Monster complained.

I didn't put him straight. It was my way of paying him back because ever since I told him my dildo story, he teased me mercilessly.

Monster, Tate and Charlie had been rehearsing for about an hour when the doorbell rang. I opened the door to see Max Oliver from Ginnie Linnie. He looked as gaunt and anxious as the first time I saw him but didn't recognize me due to the fact I wore a big floppy hat and sunglasses on that occasion. 'Hi, Max, Monster's waiting for you in…' I didn't get to finish my sentence because Monster came out.

'Max old mate!' Monster said. 'It's been too fucking long.' They bonked foreheads and banged their fists together. 'Razzle dazzle,' they said in unison. 'Just like old times.' Monster slapped a hand on Max's shoulder. 'Great result you having a single at number 28 in the charts.'

'Dunno mate,' Max said. He puffed and blew, thinking about what to say next. 'I'm in a slump. Can't seem to write. My mind's fried.'

'Fucking slumps! Monster said. 'I hate it when that happens.' I thought that was generous of Monster to say considering he had enough material for his next three albums. 'Tell you what,' Monster said. 'When we finish recording, come over to my place and we'll see what we can come up with to rescue some of your songs.' He turned to me. 'Laura's our manager. 'She'll be looking after us on tour, so if you have any special requests, let her know.'

Max swung his ponytail at me. 'Thanks. I will.'

For the first time it stuck me that apart from looking after Streetcrash, there was Max, two crew members and a lighting technician to account for and that we'd be living squashed together on a tour bus for three weeks. Monster pinched my cheeks, something he never did. 'I fucking love this woman.' He put his arm around Max's shoulder. 'Just need to take a leak. See you in rehearsals.'

I was having a moment of panic thinking about what lay ahead, when the bell rang again. I opened the door to see an old woman shake rain out of her coat. Smiling, she handed me her dripping umbrella. 'Didn't like to leave this downstairs, the world's full of tea leaves isn't it, dear?' Although I had never heard the expression *tea leaves,* I guessed it was slang for thieves and laughed. 'Is Robert in?' she asked. 'I was just riding around on the buses to get myself out of the house and the bus stopped on the corner so I thought I'd pay him a visit.'

'Robert won't be back until later but if I can help in any way?' I said, wondering who she was.

'I'm Mrs. Pluckrose, Robert's foster mother,' she said in answer to the question in my mind.

'I'm very pleased to meet you Mrs. Pluckrose.' I gave her my hand to shake.

'I'm not one for airs and graces, dear.' She ignored my outstretched arm. 'Ah well, since Robert's not here, suppose I'd better get back home.'

'Why not stay for a cup of tea. It might not be raining so hard in half an hour or so?'

'Are you his secretary? Where's what's her name, the girl I saw last year? She seemed very efficient.'

'She took a day off to go to a wedding in Scotland.' I took Mrs. Pluckrose's umbrella back. 'Come in, let's get that wet coat off and give your hair a dry.'

'Went to Scotland with Mr. Pluckrose once. We didn't go away much but it was very nice. All mountains, lavender and sheep. And kilts of course.' Mrs. Pluckrose sneezed.

'Come in Mrs. Pluckrose, you don't want to catch a cold.

'Maud, dear.'

Mrs. Pluckrose hobbled in and struggled with arthritic fingers to unbutton the buttons on her coat. 'My hip's playing up today. Always does when it rains.'

'You'll be nice and warm here. I put the heater on in Robert's office this morning.'

'I'd rather sit in one of chairs outside the kitchen if you don't mind. His office gives me the colly wobbles. Always think I might drop or break something.' I smiled at the memory of me jumping about like a big bummed puppy retrieving pens for its master. Mrs. Pluckrose gave me her coat to hang up and sat down on a chair. What did you say your name was, dear?'

'Laura.' I fished a clean tea towel out of a drawer and dabbed her wet hair.

'Very kind, Laura.' She took the towel from my hands to dab her hair herself. 'What's that fashion called then? I can't keep up with the fashion of today.'

Mrs. Pluckrose flapped the towel at my pale blue trousers. I ran my hands down my legs. 'These are called gaucho pants.'

'They look like sailor trousers that got shrunk in the wash and with your hair in plaits, you look like a Dutch girl.' I had no idea why but I curtsied.

A look of nostalgia filled Mrs. Pluckrose's eyes. 'I used to dress Robert in sailor suits when he was little. He liked himself in sailor suits.'

I put an assortment of biscuits and two bits of sponge cake on a plate. 'Bet Robert was a lovely little boy?' I poured a cup of tea and placed it with the plate on the table beside her.

'Don't know about that, dear. He was very fussy. Wouldn't eat at the table unless I covered the plastic cloth with one made of material, had to have his own napkin – a cloth napkin not a paper one – and he would only drink out of his own special mug. When that got chipped, he wouldn't drink out of anything else until I could find exactly the same match.' Mrs. Pluckrose dunked a digestive biscuit in her tea. I sat down beside her and asked if the mug had a picture on it because of the photo I saw of Robert thumping his mug. 'A trumpet.' Mrs. Pluckrose took a sip of tea. 'I had to ask his father, who'd given him the original one, if it could be replaced. Fortunately. he had another in his house in Bournemouth and sent it in the post.' Putting two and two together I guessed the big band trumpet player I saw in the photograph was Robert's dad.

'Was Robert a happy child?'

Mrs. Pluckrose bit into a jelly wheel biscuit and chewed thoughtfully. 'Very quiet. Sat in his room a lot, but when it was bitterly cold and Mr. Pluckrose built a fire of a night, he'd come and sit with us while Mr. Pluckrose roasted marshmallows over the coals. Robert didn't say much, but he loved to listen to his stories of when he started out as a coalman. That was when coalmen still had horses. Mr. Pluckrose was a very good storyteller. Course he made a lot of things up to make Robert smile but it was hard to crack a smile out of him.' She took a sip of tea. Her hands shook so much she spilled some on her dress but didn't seem to notice. I lay a napkin on her lap as spillage protection and was just about to ask my next question when Monster wrapped an arm around my shoulder.

'Just came out to make Max some coffee.' He winked at Mrs. Pluckrose. 'And who's this sexy lady with the twinkling blue eyes?'

Mrs. Pluckrose gave her lilac tinted perm a pat. 'I used to be sexy once. Not that you'd think it looking at me today.'

'It's Robert's foster mother, Mrs. Pluckrose,' I said.

'Maud,' she said, and gave Monster a saucy smile.

'Well Maud, if I was a bit older, you'd be just my type.' I stood to go into the kitchen. Monster sat in my chair, reached out and kissed her hand.

'Your leather trousers look tight.' Mrs. Pluckrose tutted. 'You need to be careful they don't damage your ghoulies.'

'Phhahaha, haven't heard that word for a while.' He stroked her wrinkled hand as though it was a jewel. 'My gran calls testicles ghoulies.'

'Are you in one of the bands Robert looks after?' Mrs. Pluckrose asked. 'Your hair looks wild enough, although I think it could do with a wash to get those tangles out.'

'Phhaha. You're so f- fudging like my gran. That's another thing she says. Let me introduce myself Princess. I'm Monster from a band called Streetcrash.'

Mrs. Pluckrose nodded. 'Streetcrash is a good name. Have you got a record coming out?'

I brought back the mug of coffee I made for Max and lay it in front of Monster on the table. 'We have,' Monster said.

'What's it called?' Mrs. Pluckrose asked. 'I'll ask Robert to give me one.'

Monster beckoned her with his finger to come closer. 'Telling you the title might make you blush, Maud.' Mrs. Pluckrose looked Monster square in the eyes to show nothing unnerved her. 'It's called Everyone's a Mother Fucker.'

Mrs. Pluckrose tittered. 'Then I'll give one of your records to the man next door. He's a big one of those,' she offered Monster a custard cream biscuit.

Monster politely waved it away. 'Send Mr. Pluckrose to sort him out, Maud.' When Mrs. Pluckrose said her husband passed away five years earlier, I saw a light come on in his brain and knew what he was thinking. 'Must be hard when you've been with someone so many years?' He gently rubbed her hand between his.

'I'm over it now but the loneliness is dreadful. I rattle around all day talking to myself for company.' Mrs. Pluckrose shook her head at her sorry situation. Monster told her that he knew a man about her age who was rattling around in his flat on his own and would love to meet someone like her. Mrs. Pluckrose looked flabbergasted. 'Why would he be interested in me?'

'Do you like days out at the seaside, maybe a night out at the cinema and romantic meals from time to time?' Mrs. Pluckrose said she did but not on her own. 'That's the right answer, Maud. And do you enjoy a good kiss and cuddle?' Mrs. Pluckrose told him she thought cuddling kept couples young, at which point Monster mentioned Mr. Krakowski.

'Ooh, no. He sounds like a foreigner and foreigners have funny ways, dear.' Mrs. Pluckrose waved Mr. Krakowski off as if he was standing there. 'They eat smelly things like curries. There's a couple near my house who stink the street out.'

'Mr. Krakowski was born in London,' Monster said. 'He's lived in the flat above mine in Ladbroke Grove most his life and the smelliest thing he eats is fish 'n chips. You can come over for a cuppa and I'll call Mr. Krakowski down so you can have a chat?' Mrs. Pluckrose said she'd have to think about it. 'Well think hard, Maud, because men like Mr. Krakowski are as rare as diamonds.' Monster kissed her on top of her head and picked up Max's mug. 'As you are as rare as a diamond. So have a think, let Laura know and I'll sort something out.'

Mrs. Pluckrose and I started chatting again. She loved relating the memories in her head to someone who showed so much interest but everything about Robert fascinated me, so every time she took a sip of tea, I topped up her cup to keep her talking. 'Must have been strange after the war when everything was rationed?' I said.

'We had weekly coupons that allowed you this much sugar, bread, eggs and such. Robert was always first in queue to make sure he got his eggs 'cos he was worried there'd be none left on the shelves.' Mrs. Pluckrose waved the teapot away. 'Well, dear, I think I've taken up enough of your time. If you'd just get my coat, I'll be on my way before rush hour.' Yawning, she eased herself out of the chair. 'Don't know what's come over me. Our chat's worn me out, dear,' she said. I helped her on with her coat, feeling guilty that I was to blame for her tiredness and hoped she wouldn't mention our chat to Robert.

# TWENTY-FOUR

The scent of Sandalwood wafted over me as Robert took off his ankle length black leather coat and hung it on the stand. 'Sorry I was delayed.' He glanced at my gaucho outfit and plaited hair. 'Never the same look two days in a row.' I wasn't sure if he liked it until he said, 'Suits you.' Cocking an ear at the rehearsal studio door, he asked how it was going with Streetcrash. I told him pretty good from what I'd heard. 'Let's go in and see what they're up to?' As we walked down the hall, I realized that Robert not only had very long legs but that I had to take three steps for every one of his. I felt like a Geisha girl bobbing along beside him. When he opened the door to usher me in, I missed the step and tripped over my foot. I made it look like a dance step to match the rhythm of what Streetcrash played. I could sense Robert laugh behind my back and even thinking of him in a sailor suit didn't make me feel less stupid. I clapped my hands to draw attention to Mr. Bauman's presence.

None of the boys looked up. Charlie drummed double time, his arms conducting a one-man orchestra in organized pandemonium as his face contorted to suit the sound. Monster stood in the middle of Tate and Max, playing a new set of chords he'd come up with for Truth Kills. Tate filled in the gaps on base while Max kept the rhythm going. 'No. Stop,' Monster said. 'Listen again. Tate come in deeper. Max bring the sound…'

'Mr. Bauman's here,' I shouted.

Monster put his guitar down. Tate and Max followed suit. Charlie primitively attacked the cymbals, his eyes closed as he grinned to himself. 'Charlie,' Monster called out. 'Mr. Bauman's here.' Charlie looked around as if he didn't have a clue which day it was then jumped up to join the others. 'I can't tell you how fucking happy we are, excuse my French, that we're signed to Scorch'. Monster slapped Tate on the shoulder as if he was slapping Robert's shoulder, 'Thank you for having faith in us.' Tate and Charlie said a few words in a similar vein. Max stared at the ground.

'And you Max?' Robert asked. 'Is this working for you?'

'Yeah, it's working well,' Max mumbled. 'Just what I need to get back on track.'

Robert smiled. 'So, let's hear what you've done with Everyone's and Truth Kills?' He sat down in his canvas director's chair. I stood by his side while Streetcrash and Max sorted themselves out.

'Ready?' Monster checked Charlie was ready. 'OK, on a count of three.'

Both songs were brilliant and I could tell Robert enjoyed listening because he tapped his fingers on the arms of his chair and hummed bars here and there. When they finished, Robert told us he'd decided to push the boat out because he had a gut feeling Truth Kills would chart and Everyone would put them on the map as a heavy metal band. Excited, Monster told Robert he had tons of ideas to make the songs better.

'I'm sure you have,' Robert said, 'but I was thinking about record producers.' He strode across the room, tapping his thigh. 'There are two producers I had in mind. Jimmy Miller and...'

'Jimmy Fucking Miller, excuse my French again,' Monster said. 'He made Steve Winwood famous with Traffic and did Beggar's Banquet for the Stones.'

'Now he's working on their new album, Sticky Fingers, so isn't available,' Robert said. 'The other producer I have in mind is Bob Cramer. He'd get the right edge on your sound but he's in France working with the French equivalent of the Doors. That leaves us with…'

My mind started spinning. Bob – France. 'Excuse me,' I grabbed my handbag. 'Just need to go to the loo.'

Glancing at my bag, Monster winked. 'Don't be too long or we'll know what you're up.' Tate and Charlie caught on to what he meant and grinned like Cheshire cats. Monster turned to Robert. 'That leaves us with?'

I went in the bathroom and searched through my bag. With trembling fingers, I dared to look at the name on the card. Bob Cramer. Record Producer. It was the same Bob I talked to about my lurid sex life in Mortons! I went in the toilet and sat down to pee wondering where so much came from. On and on it went like a fountain until my nerves calmed down. Did I dare to call him? What was the worst that could happen? Recalling the scenarios I lived through those past months the answer was – Nothing. Since Robert's secretary was away, I crept into her office and dialed the London office number on the card.

'Bob Cramer's office,' a girl answered.

'I'm calling on behalf of Robert Bauman from Scorch Records. I know Bob's in France but Mr. Bauman needs to talk to him. Is it possible for you to give me his number?'

'Yes, of course. How is Robert?'

'Busy as usual.'

'Take this number down. It's the hotel Bob's staying at and I know he's there because I talked to him a minute ago.'

Bingo! I jotted it down. 'Thanks a lot,' I put the phone down and dialed the number.

Bob picked up. 'Bob Cramer.'

'Bob, you probably won't want to remember me but if on the off chance you do, it's Laura.'

'Laura?' I could feel Bob scraping his mind for clues. 'You mean Laura, fanny story?'

'That Laura.'

'You realise I'm in France? How did you get my number?'

'Your London office gave it to me.'

'Well, I'm surprised to hear from you. I mean I'm surprised you're calling me abroad – but I gave you my promise, so shoot – how can I help?'

'I'm at Scorch Records with Robert Bauman.'

'You know Robert?'

'Remember when I told you I'd started a new business, and that was the only good news in my miserable life at the time we met? Well, I manage a band called Streetcrash and Robert just signed them. Anyway, I know I've got a nerve, but Robert brought your name up in conversation as the producer he'd most want to produce Streetcrash's new songs so what I'm asking is if I can send you a demo tape by express courier so you have a listen?'

'If Robert thinks I'm the right man for the job count me in, he's done enough for me in the past but I'm here working right now. When was Robert thinking of hiring a studio?'

'We were literally just talking about it so nothing's booked yet.'

'Well the only time I can take off is next Friday. If you can sort something out, I'll be there.'

'Wow, I'm so grateful Bob.' I laughed. 'I mean Uncle Bob.'

'No gratitude necessary soul sister. You have no idea how you helped me that night.'

'You mean regarding the ballet dancer with a small dick who pranced around in a leotard?'

'Yes, that bitch!' Bob's voice rose shrilly. 'But mum's the word. Can't wait to see you again and as we've said, I prefer to keep my sexual preferences private.'

From the way Bob talked, I imagined the whole world knew about his sexual preferences. 'Mum's the word, soul sister.'

When I put down the phone, I belly danced around the room screaming 'Ya habibi yala yala,' then rehearsed how I was going to deliver the news in an offhand way to impress Mr. Bauman.

Back in the rehearsal room, Robert and Streetcrash still discussed producers.

'I just spoke to Bob Cramer,' I announced, as if I was saying I just spoke to Bob the window cleaner.

'Stop messing about Laura,' Monster said. 'We're having a serious conversation'.

'Give me the spare tape of Truth Kills and Everyone's. I need to send it by courier to France.' Monster gave me it and searched my eyes to see whether I'd laugh. I gave nothing away in my moment of triumph. 'Courier number?' I said to Robert.

'You'll find one in my secretary's office. There's a box with all the numbers on her desk.' Robert gave his head a puzzled shake. 'If this is a joke, I don't get it.'

'If we can find a recording studio for next Friday afternoon, Bob will be there to produce Streetcrash. If you want to give me a list of studios you've got in mind, I'll ring around and organize that too.'

'You called Bob where?' Robert asked.

'In France.'

Monster, Tate, Charlie, Max and Robert gathered around me in a tight circle. 'You are talking about BOB CRAMER?' Monster said.

'Yeah, we're friends,' I said. 'Go way back.'

'A woman of a hundred faces,' Robert laughed. 'You really do know Bob.'

'My hundred faces do a lot of socialising, Mr. Bauman – ooh and by the way, I forgot. Your foster mother popped in to see you.'

'I'll call her later,' Robert said. He looked at his watch. 'Want to call it a day, boys?

'Yeah,' Monster said, and turned to Tate, Charlie and Max. 'Let's go back to my place and do whatever?' They started packing up their stuff. 'Fucking Bob Cramer!' Monster called out. 'You're a star, Laura.'

While I was ringing around to sort out the fastest courier service, Robert came in. 'That's perfect, so you'll have someone here in the next half hour?' I said. 'Yes, no worries. I'll be waiting.'

'Both things done then,' Robert said. 'I've booked a studio called Trident not far from here.' He pinched his lower lip as though he was weighing something up. 'I was hoping we could grab a bite to eat but another meeting's just come up.'

Even though I felt disappointed since for once I felt calm and composed around him, I nonchalantly tossed my plaits. 'We'll grab a bite when you're under less pressure so we can make it a leisurely bite, Mr. Bauman.' I could still feel him smiling after he left the office and knew it had to be something I said. Then the words *leisurely bite* came back and I wanted to put my fingers down my throat.

# TWENTY-FIVE

'You know who put this studio on the map?' Monster nudged me and pointed to a photograph of Manfred Mann. 'They recorded *My Name's Jack* here a couple years back.' I felt like a kid on the first day of school - not on earth but in Narnia. The walls were lined with pictures of famous artists who recorded there. The Stones, Joe Cocker, Peter Gabriel... I could hear snippets of their songs in my head.

As I walked beside Monster, Tate and Charlie, through heavy soundproof double doors that took us into the live room, I felt supremely cat whiskered. My lipstick was burgundy red. My dress was by Ossie Clark. It was a fitted mid-calf black crepe wraparound dress slit to the thigh (which revealed nothing as long as I kept my legs shut), and high-heeled black suede peep toes.

'This is where we'll record later,' Monster said. 'As you see, it's also where we relax between sessions.' The live room had a stage and a lounge area with sofas and a coffee table. Soaking it in, I nodded with awe. Monster licked his lips at the tasty array of snacks. 'I could murder a couple of those rolls and a mug of coffee but since Laura loves learning stuff, let's show her what the control room looks like?' he said. Tate nodded, and carried on listening to Charlie who was back on a topic that troubled him lots. It had to do with his belief that humans were faulty robots and that God was deranged and should have issued humans with manuals so they didn't spend their lives blowing their brains out. A lot of what Charlie said needed much mind excavation. I was glad he had Tate to talk to since his topics were a bit like Debs. Endless. Monster took my hand and the four of us went in the control room. 'How's it going?' Monster asked the engineer. The engineer was sitting at the mixing desk reading The Rag, an American underground newspaper. He nodded without looking up. Monster pointed to the levers on the mixing desk. 'This is an eight track studio, Laura. That means eight tracks can be used to mix sound at different levels.'

Charlie leaped out in front of me. 'And this microphone,' He tapped one above the mixing desk, 'is what the engineer uses to talk to us in the live room when we're recording and he wants to tell us something.'

Tate put an arm around me. 'And everything that's recorded goes on that tape spool which is called a master tape, and when everyone's happy, it's used to cut singles.' He pointed to the spool.

By the time I stopped touching levers and making different sounds down the microphone to test it, Monster and Tate were in deep conversation with the engineer. Charlie sat at my feet, his big inquisitive eyes soaking up the print of the mag he pinched from the engineer as he snorted with childlike delight. I glanced over his shoulder. He was reading the Furry Freak Brothers comic strip. I glanced through a copy of The Rag someone left at the Speakeasy so knew the Furry Freaks were three characters whose lives revolved around marijuana, where to buy it cheap and not getting busted by the cops. Tears of laughter rolled down Charlie's cheeks as he rocked back and forth banging his feet. My urge to squish his chubby cheeks got sidetracked by someone hugging me from behind. 'Soul sister,' a screechy voice sang out.

When I turned, my face lit up. 'Bob!'

Rushing into each other's arms like long lost lovers we kept repeating each other's names. Bob dramatically pushed me away to critique my appearance. 'Your long wavy tresses, your red lips, that exquisite dress. You look ravishingly Hedy Lamarr,' he squealed. I had no idea who Hedy Lamarr was but since she was ravishing, I soaked up the compliment. Bob gave a flamboyant shake of his head, waiting for me to critique his appearance. He was wearing a peach coloured suit, a peach shirt with jumping monkeys and smelled like a peach tree. There was something about Bob's looks which reminded me of Ken - the man doll in the Barbie doll series.

'Divine,' I kissed Bob on the cheek, feeling certain males of his ilk would find him irresistible.

Monster and Tate watched us without interruption and carried on chatting to the engineer. I was about to introduce Bob when Robert appeared in a pristine grey T-shirt which brought out the grey in his eyes.

'Bob,' Robert slapped him on the shoulder. 'Really grateful to you for taking time out to produce Streetcrash.' Robert gave me a polite kiss on the cheek then pointed out each member of Streetcrash. 'Monster there writes the songs, sings and plays lead guitar. Tate plays bass and Charlie plays drums.' Charlie was still engrossed in the Furry Freaks and had tears of laughter dripping off his chin.

'Great honour.' Monster walked to Bob and warmly shook his hand. Tate stepped up to do the same. Monster tapped Charlie on the head. 'Say hello to Bob Cramer.'

Charlie wiped his face on the sleeve of his purple shirt. Leaping over, he shook Bob's hand. 'Having you produce us is huge, enormous, far out, cool.'

Pursing his lips theatrically, Bob looked at his watch. 'You won't have time for a break due to my tight schedule.' Bob waved us out of the recording studio like a herd of cattle. 'Follow on people.' We trooped behind him into the live room. 'Monster, Tate and Charlie, set yourselves up. The backing singers and crowd will be here shortly.'

Monster mouthed. *'The crowd?'* at Tate who shrugged because he didn't have a clue what Bob meant either. Monster took a longing look at the coffee, licked his lips at the snacks then followed Tate and Charlie to tune their instruments.

When Robert, Bob and I sat down on the sofa, Bob put his hand on my knee and told Robert he'd made an excellent choice signing Streetcrash since he felt Everyone's and Truth Kills had real chart potential. Robert patted my other knee in agreement. I was sitting in the middle. A haze of sandalwood wafting over me when I turned my head towards Robert and a haze of peaches wafting over me when I looked Bob's way. As they caught up on news, my mind wandered back to the first time I met them. If Chris hadn't come into my office and caused a brawl, I wouldn't have got the sack, would never have met Bob in Mortons and wouldn't be sitting between them on my way to fame with Robert's hand resting on my knee. Whether it was intentional I couldn't be sure, but he left it there until three Diana Ross lookalikes walked into the live room with some bikers and four men in builder's overalls. 'The crowd are here for Everyone's,' Bob announced, jumping to his feet. Robert stood up and left to go to a meeting, saying he would be back later. 'Crowd, gather round,' Bob grabbed a biker by the scruff of his shirt for attempting to make a cup of tea. 'When Streetcrash start playing Everyone's, I want you all head banging like....' Bob turned to the builders. 'You'd been out on a ledge in the freezing cold for a week and your boss gave you not a penny because his building project ran out of money.' The way he made faces to accompany his arm movements was like watching a Shakespearian actor. 'And you bikers are ready to kill because your motorbike's been carted off to the pound by the police. Feel the anger, fury and insult.' He swiped a hand over his forehead then clasped his hands. 'Give it your all.' I loved his passionate delivery especially when he flapped a hand at the Diana Ross lookalikes and said,

'You're furious because the man *you* thought was **he** was stolen from under your nose by a cheap, frivolous floozy.' I smiled, knowing Bob was talking from experience. Max had arrived by then and with numbers accounted for, Bob said it was time to make music.

I settled back on the sofa to watch as Monster, Tate and Max, tuned their guitars. Charlie adjusted his foot pedals. The backing singers took their positions behind microphones. They looked perfect for the set in their black shoulder length wigs and black sequin mini dresses.

Bob raised a hand to the engineer. Streetcrash started playing Everyone's. The singers started to sing and the crowd started to dance but they were nothing like the head bangers at Streetcrash gigs. The builders were messing about having a knees up. The bikers jumped up and down like lumps of wood and wore such pained expressions it looked as if they had nails in their boots. Streetcrash hardly got through the first verse when Bob, having a tantrum, crossed his arms and ordered the engineer to stop recording.

'What's the matter, Bob,' the engineer called out through his microphone.

'Everything's the matter,' Bob pranced on the tip of his toes as I imagined the ballet dancer who pranced off with his boyfriend did. 'You are offending my ears, my heart, my whole being!' Blowing and puffing, Bob held his head in his hands. 'Monster, more brute force, more passion. Tate. More bass. More bass. Max, distort and emphasize the rhythm, we didn't come here to fall asleep. Charlie, make the kick drum *cry* with rage. What I'm hearing is not music alchemy, its musical catastrophe.' His voice rose an octave. 'PLEASE, get it right!'

'OK Bob,' Monster said.

Since I had a tour to arrange, I went out into the street which had a public telephone box to continue my enquiries about the cost of tour buses. Thus far I'd found nothing suitable on my budget and the one within my price bracket conked out on its test drive. Getting nowhere as I phoned around, my coins ran out so I went to a nearby bank to get more, then decided to pop back into the live room to see how Streetcrash were doing.

'Stop, STOP,' Bob tugged at his hair. 'How many times do I have to say the same thing over and over and over!'

Monster loomed on the verge of jumping off stage and smashing his guitar over Bob's head. 'You missed five fucking *overs*, Bob. This is the eighth time you've stopped us. And get rid of that fucking dance crowd because they're doing my head in!'

Bob flapped a hand at them like a ballet choreographer. 'Head bangers, thank you, you can go back to Joe's Cafe.' I'd gone completely off Bob because his tactics were making Streetcrash worse instead of better. I made him a cup of tea hoping that might calm him down. 'Thank you darling.' Bob flopped down on one of the sofas, had a sip and was back on his feet. 'Monster, I have ears that hear the future and know Everyone's a hit so why don't you sing it like you mean it?'

'I am singing it like I mean it.' Monster shouted. 'It's your fucking ears that can't hear it.'

Bob rested his head against my shoulder. 'See what I mean? They all think they can do my job better than me!' Jumping to his feet, he took a deep breath. 'Forget I'm here,' he told Monster. 'You're playing in your living room with these other wonderful, talented musicians and those glorious soulful, backing singers. Your girlfriend thinks your penis isn't big enough and dumps you for someone who likes opera. You want to end it all because you're sick to your stomach with all the mother fuckers in this Godforsaken world.'

Monster eyes twitched as he struggled to keep composure. 'Bob, I know what the song's about.'

'Then can you lead the musicians so they know what the song is about?' Bob screamed.

'I will lead the musicians if you'd sit still for two minutes!' Monster's lips trembled with rage. 'Take a valium and chill!'

I fixed my eyes on Monster until he looked my way so I could try out a technique I'd seen on a TV programme aimed at calming down mental patients. Drawing my hand up from my stomach to my mouth I inhaled. Bringing my hand down from my mouth to my stomach I exhaled. Monster followed suit, glared at Bob then looked up at the ceiling and roared like a wild boar. Fingers back on his guitar, he nodded at Tate, then Max. 'On the count of three.'

Bob flopped down on the sofa again. 'Let's hope they get it right soon because I'm drop dead exhausted, darling.' I wanted to scream *they're all drop dead exhausted* but since Robert thought Bob was the best producer for the job, bit my tongue.

When Streetcrash started to play again, I was glad I hadn't made a fuss since Bob's tactics paid off. Monster played with such ferocity, I thought the strings of his guitar would snap. Tate used more pedal to amplify the sound of the bass, Charlie played drums off any scale I'd heard, Max's rhythm was three times faster and the backing singers sounded so aggressive I wholeheartedly believed they'd been dumped by the mother fucker they sang about. I gave Uncle Bob a hug. 'They sound *amazing.*'

Bob patted my thigh. 'Thanks for not doubting me. When you get back off tour, we'll go for dinner, soul sister.'

Truth Kills was a piece of cake after that. The way they played was astounding. When the backing singers joined in with the chorus, Bob and me sang some of the words to confirm our bond. We were gazing into each other's eyes as Bob acted out Romeo from Romeo and Juliet when Robert came back. He listened to the last part of the song and applauded. 'Great work Streetcrash.'

Monster mopped his forehead with his T shirt and smiled broadly. 'Whoever wants to come to the pub, I'm buying.'

# TWENTY-SIX

Having twirled me in the street amid a dozen get together promises, Bob jumped in a cab. That left Robert and me standing on the pavement. Bob's grand show of sisterly love made me feel bold so I reached up and kissed Robert on the cheek. 'Thank you for everything.'

'Where are you going? Robert asked.

'Just home,' I looked down the street. 'Think I'll get a taxi.'

'Where do you live?' Robert wrapped his blue scarf around my shoulders since he saw me shiver and thought it was because I was cold. The truth was I felt awkward due to the kiss.

'Queens Park,' I hailed a taxi with no lights on.

'I'll give you a lift,' he took my arm and led me to his car.

Robert's car, a convertible sports Mercedes model, was as pristine as his house. Even that smelled like a pine forest and matched the colour of his sofa. I was afraid to sit down in case I put a dent in the leather so sat on the edge until Robert said I didn't look comfortable, at which point I lounged back like the lady of the manor. After we pulled off, we talked about work related stuff. That I found easy but when those topics dried up, didn't know how to fill the gaps so looked idly out of the window as if I found something fascinating in every tree, traffic light and bus stop.

'Have you heard of Billy Holiday?' Robert said, after a while.

'The name rings a bell.'

'Let me play you one of her songs. 'It's been going around my head the past few days.' I got totally involved with the words which were something like, '*the very thought of you and I forget to do those very ordinary things that I'm supposed to do. I'm living in a daydream and see your face in every flower.*' I wondered if the song made him think of his wife or one of his girlfriends.

With Robert concentrating on the road, I glanced at him sideways. Why did he seem more fanciable every time I saw him? His sandy, shoulder length hair flicked out around his ears and the way it flopped over one side of his forehead make him look like Robert Redford with a beard. I liked his ponderous look, his frazzled look - and his deeply attentive look when I was lucky enough to get one. I glanced at his hands on the steering wheel. I even liked his artistic slender wrists, his neatly manicured nails, his…

'So where were you born?' Robert asked, turning to smile at me. I'd never sat that close to him before and felt naked.

I pulled Robert's scarf closer round my shoulders. It smelled of Sandalwood like him. 'Finsbury Park.'

'Finsbury Park?' I grew up there? Where did you live?'

'Riversdale Road,' I said.

Robert skidded. 'What a coincidence. I lived in Riversdale Road. What number?'

'Eighty two.'

'I lived at number nineteen,' Robert shook his head as if he couldn't believe his ears. 'How old are you?'

'Twenty three.'

'So, when you were born, I was ten.'

I did a quick count. That meant he was 33. I couldn't make up my mind if he looked older or younger because I never hung out with men his age. 'I bet you were the boy who kept stealing the rattle from my pram,' I laughed.

'It wasn't me. I know you'd have bashed me over the head with it!' He glanced at me. 'I bet you were a real tomboy when you were little – you still stomp about like you're ready to punch anyone with the gall to get in your way.'

I pointed to Robert that the next turning was where I lived. 'No-one's ever called me a stomper before,' I said, deciding it was something I needed to work on because it didn't sound feminine.

Robert turned into Fordingley Road. I waved him to a stop outside my flat. Instead of coming around to open my door which I expected a gentleman like he would do, he settled back in his seat. 'Tell me something about your childhood?'

I liked the fact he didn't want to say goodnight straight away and said the first thing that came into my head. 'I loved raw onions, including the skin and used to hide under the kitchen table so my mum didn't catch me and take it away.'

Robert turned to face me, his smile lighting up his face. 'What was it you liked so much about onions?'

Turning sideways so I could see him properly, I kicked off my peep toes, tucked my feet under my dress and made myself comfy. 'I liked it when the taste burned my tongue and my nose start running and made me cry. I have no idea why I wanted to cry because I did enough of that without onions.' I heard what I said in my mind and couldn't believe I told him something so stupid. 'What about you?'

Robert stroked the front of his scarf I wore as though it helped to jog his memory. 'I built fortresses with moats but no-one was allowed inside except me– and my horse of course.'

Normally hearing something like would have made me laugh, but Robert wasn't smiling. 'Weren't you lonely living in a fortress with just your horse?'

'Oh, I'd ride out in the day and allowed the King and Queen to visit me once a year.'

That time I couldn't help but smile. 'You were as strange as me.'

Robert rubbed the side of his nose. 'I'm sure my foster mother thought so.' He glanced at his watch.

Sensing my time was up, I wriggled back into my shoes, carefully making sure the slit in my dress didn't open. 'I should let you go – Thanks for bringing me home.'

'I wasn't looking at my watch because…'

'No. We've both had a long day and I'm sure you're looking forward to getting to bed as much as me,' I said.

Robert came around and opened my door. 'I'll wait until I see you safely inside.'

Concentrating on gliding, as opposed to stomping, I walked slowly down the steps to my flat. There were no lights on so I assumed Debs was in bed since it was past midnight. Fumbling in my bag for the door keys, I waved at Robert. 'Goodnight.'

He stood there while I carried on searching in my bag. *Where the hell where my keys?* I checked the iron shutter we fitted to our front window after a burglar got in. That was locked so I couldn't get in that way. Discreetly pressing the bell so that what I was doing wouldn't notice, I waited. No answer. I pressed again then remembered that Debs had gone to spend the night with Dave who had few days off from his work in Cardiff. 'It's OK,' I shouted. 'I forgot my keys but I can see Debs coming down the hall.' A minute later, Robert still stood on the pavement and I still stood at my door like a lemon. 'No actually, I just remembered, she's gone away somewhere.'

'Might that be Djerba to get some sun?' Robert teased.

Pretending I hadn't heard and wondering if he would ever let me live it down, I glided back up the stairs and pointed at a house on the other side of the street then a couple more a bit further down. 'Don't worry about me, I've got loads of friends who live round here.'

171

I could see the smile playing on his lips. 'I'll walk you there. Which house would you like to try first?'

'Well I...well...' He'd stumped me. What could I say next?

'Be a shame to go and wake your friends up at this time of the night. Come on. Get back in the car.'

'Why? Where are we going?'

'My house. We'll sort something out.' I don't think I said a word on the journey. Robert smiled at me from time to time which I think was to make me feel less awkward. He was playing the same song by Billy Holiday so didn't talk either. My question was - why of all the people in the world had fate thrown me with Robert Bauman, and more to the point, if his wife was at home, what would she think about me turning up like a stray?

# TWENTY-SEVEN

I took off my high heels before going up the steps of Robert's house. I didn't want to stomp and wake the neighbours because unlike Fordingley Road which could be rowdy, especially when people piled out of the pub on the corner, even the houses were asleep on Robert's street. Tiptoeing into the hall in case his wife was asleep upstairs, I crept into the living room and sat down on the green leather armchair.

'Can I ask why you're creeping about like a mouse who doesn't want the cat to know you're at home?' Robert said.

'Don't want to wake anyone up in case they're sleeping,' I whispered.

Robert pointed to nothing on the sofa. 'Don't worry about him. He can sleep through a hurricane, and he,' Robert pointed to the fireplace grate. 'Only comes alive when I put the fire on.'

I nodded at the ceiling. 'I meant your wife.'

'My wife? What wife?' Robert laughed. 'Why wasn't I there at my own wedding?'

'I thought you were married,' I said, in a normal voice.

'Why would you have thought that?' Robert said.

'You asked me where I might send you and your wife on that…'

'Oh, I see, on that exotic holiday you tried to bribe me with. No, I'm not married. It seems I have a fear of commitment.' Robert smiled. 'Call me a commitment-phobe.'

I wanted to say I was another commitment-phobe but it sounded too personal. 'And I thought you were carrying on with two girlfriends behind your wife's back,' I laughed.

'You've been here less than a minute and I've accumulated a wife and two girlfriends – are you sure there isn't a third girlfriend I should know about?'

'Ignore me,' I said, 'I'm the owner of a very fertile mind.'

'I'm feeling like a cup of cocoa,' Robert said. 'How about you? Come down to the kitchen. We can carry on talking.'

I followed him down the circular iron staircase that led into a huge combined breakfast room and kitchen. It was all marble, Italian tiles, shiny copper pans above the Aga stove and a mix of modern and antique furniture.

'Sit yourself down, I'll get some milk on the boil.' Robert pointed to a glassed topped circular table that had chairs around it.

As I pulled out a chair, the legs scratched against the stone tiles making an unholy racket. 'It was a mistake putting stone tiles down,' Robert said, as he watched me lift the chair off the floor. 'They magnify every sound. I used to be like you but now...' He pulled out another chair and purposely let the tiles screech as he moved it around. 'I couldn't care less. Relax Laura. You'll give me a complex.'

I put my chair down and stood beside it. 'Guess I'm not used to being around men like you.'

'Don't be fooled by my working persona. I'm not as conservative as you might think. In fact, I dance a mean tango.' Robert waved me over. 'Would you like to?'

'What here?' I looked around like a twat. 'You mean now?'

Robert strolled over to a tape player on top of an antique bureau, selected a tape and pressed play. 'This was composed by Piazzolla,' he said, as a tune began. For all I knew about tango music, Robert could have said the pizza man composed it. 'Could I interest you in a tango m'lady?' Robert bowed.

'I've never danced tango.'

'Leave it to me.' Robert took hold of my left hand and placed his right hand between my shoulder blades. 'Now, place your hand firmly on the centre of my back.'

Shuddering with shyness I tried to hold his look, more aware of the antique grandfather clocking ticking in the background than the music.

'Just follow my lead,' Robert gripped my hand. 'I'll walk you through the steps.' He moved back on his left foot. 'Move back on your right, move back on your left, move back on your right again'. I followed him trying not to tread on his toes. 'Now go to the left with your left foot,' he said, 'bring your feet together by moving your right foot to meet the left and we're back at the beginning.' Robert stopped dancing. 'How was that?'

I'd never seen his lips as such close quarters before and couldn't stop staring at them. What we were doing felt dangerous and Pizza man's music wasn't helping.

'Dancing the tango is a collaborative process.' Robert said. 'It's aimed at developing trust and respect between partners.'

'That's very good for our business relationship,' I said.

Laughing, Robert pulled me close. 'The object is for us to maintain harmonious connection and allow our bodies to speak through the steps.'

I wished we could dance with our eyes closed because my body already spoke volumes.

'You're a natural,' Robert said, as he led me through the steps. 'Now we'll do the same in a counter clockwise circle, then we do the same steps to the side.'

I took to the steps like a woman born to tango, imagining Robert with a rose between his teeth to help me concentrate.

Robert pulled me closer, lifted one of my legs and wrapped it around his waist. The slit in my Ozzie Clark dress opened which meant my thigh was bare. Robert seemed unaware of that or the fact his dick made contact with my vagina as he bent me backwards.

My hair whirled as he whirled me, my body orgasmed when our private parts touched but it was nothing like the feeling I got when I shagged. We were like seahorses performing an intimate mating dance that developed the trust Robert spoke about.

When he picked up my leg again, I clung on tight because the feeling gave me tingles like none I'd known. Robert's lips were so close, I had an urge to suck them.

'Cocoa time.' He pulled away and glanced at the pan of boiling milk. 'We'll drink it in the living room.'

# TWENTY-EIGHT

Wearing pyjamas like kids at a sleepover party, we lounged together on the sofa. I smiled at Robert's stories of when he started out in the music business but rattling around my brain was the near suck incident. I had the cringeworthy feeling I danced with too much abandon and brought out feelings Mr. Bauman didn't want. I didn't want them either. They made me feel unnerved.

'Tell me more about your childhood,' Robert said, his grey eyes steadily holding mine. 'The only thing I really know is that you liked raw onions. Tell me about your mother?'

Cupping my cocoa mug with both hands, I took a sip. 'Truth, or what I tell everyone else?'

Robert patted my knee. 'Go for truth.'

I thought about it. For once, I wanted to say it how it was and not feel shame. 'My mother was an alcoholic – always popping pills for depression and anxiety. She didn't know I was there half the time.' Robert nodded to show he was listening. 'Her big dream was to get married, but it never happened because she kept choosing losers. She was dumped at the eleventh hour twice,' I said, feeling a knot of emotion in my chest. 'The last time I was thirteen. She turned into Miss Haversham – you know from Great Expectations- curtains drawn, living with her memories, never going out.' I could see myself twiddle with my pyjama leg.

'How did you deal with it?' Robert's eyes moved through me, peeling off layer after layer of the crust I'd built around myself. I wondered if he'd take me out of my depth and I wouldn't be able to swim back to shore. I could feel my breath coming fast. 'Don't tell me if it's painful,' he said.

'I want to tell you. Call it part of my recovery process.' I didn't say my recovery process had to do with going from a slapper to a woman who didn't use sex as some sort of revenge, because he didn't need to know that. 'I was a teenager trying to deal with my own problems, that even the best psychiatrist couldn't have solved. Hanging out with bikers helped but I counted down the days until I was sixteen and could leave home. Since then my mum never tried to find me and I'm happier without her.'

Robert looked inside my mug. It was empty. 'Want a cocoa refill?'

'I'm fine thanks,' I put the mug down on his coffee table. 'Don't know where I found the courage to get that off my chest! What about your childhood?'

'My father was a philanderer,' Robert ran a finger down the stripes on his pyjamas. 'He had five children with three different women before he married my mother. My mother didn't want children so when she fell pregnant with me her first thought was to abort, but she was too far into the pregnancy.'

I moved closer to absorb the details. 'So, she found Mrs. Pluckrose?'

'Mrs. Pluckrose was a cleaner at the Astoria in Finsbury Park, a venue my father was working at for a season. My father was a big band leader. My mother was one of the dancers who came on to warm up the audience.' Robert twirled a strand of my hair in his fingers. 'From what I gather, you eked my life history out of my foster mother over copious amounts of tea and jelly wheel biscuits, so I'm guessing you know the rest?'

I had the confidence to laugh. 'We left the story at you having to be first in the queue to make sure you got your eggs before there were none left on the shelves after the war. Then the rain stopped and Mrs. Pluckrose wanted to catch the bus before rush hour in case there weren't any seats left, so I was left on a cliff-hanger – and when I went to the kid's cinema club in Kentish Town on Saturday mornings those cliff hangers *really* got on my nerves.'

Robert laughed. 'Ah, so you were a child who read the last page of a book so you knew the ending beforehand?'

'Except in the case of the Lion, the Witch and the Wardrobe, which I can still recite most of because I read it that many times. Did you see your real parents much?'

Robert stared into the distance at something only he could see. 'I went to visit them once a year during the summer holidays in Bournemouth where they went to live.'

'Ah, the King and Queen in your fortress scenario?'

'What an astute young lady you are, I don't think I realized that before.' Robert put his hand to his mouth and yawned. 'Sorry, think it's time to get some sleep?' He stood up.

I jumped up off the sofa. 'Yes, of course. Where are you sending me?'

'The guest bedroom's being redecorated so you can have my bed and I'll sleep here.'

'Oh no,' I couldn't do that,' I said, thumping the hard leather Chesterfield sofa. 'This looks very comfortable.'

'Wouldn't hear of it,' Robert said. 'Let me show you to my bedroom. I'll be fine down here.'

'No,' I insisted with more force. 'I won't be able to sleep if I think I've taken your bed.'

Robert smiled. 'In which case, since neither of us are sex offenders, let's both sleep in it?'

*Little did he know he was talking straight at a major offender*, I thought. 'I'm not sure how I feel about that Mr. Bauman. I've never slept with a man before.'

'Don't worry, I have no intention of trying to deflower a virgin,' he laughed.

*BUGGER, I'd made him think I was a virgin.* 'No, I meant...'

'Let's just get to bed and get some sleep?'

What we were about to do felt more dangerous than the tango. 'Of course. We're both grownups who can get in the same bed and go to sleep.' I wanted to stuff my hand in my mouth for saying something so pathetic. I followed him up the stairs. Him all elegant in his pyjamas, and me looking like a shrunken dwarf because the sleeves came down to my knees and the legs trailed around my feet.

'Bathroom in there,' Robert said. 'You go first. I'll read until you come out. Take as long as you like.'

I didn't know what Robert thought I'd do in the bathroom but in case he thought I'd be getting up to something funny, I decided to get in and out fast as I could. I was hit by the smell of sandalwood. Rows of sandalwood products stood lined up on the end of his bath. Bath oil, bath foam, bath salts, a whole basketful of sandalwood soaps and by the side of the sink was a huge earthenware pot full of sandalwood pot pourri. I brushed my teeth, washed my face, left my false eyelashes on and was in his bedroom in a flash.

Robert sat up in bed with a book in his hands. 'So fast?' I didn't even get to read one page.' He pulled the bedcover back. 'Get yourself settled. Doubt I'll be as fast as speedy Gonzales but won't be long.'

I settled myself in Robert's bed by fluffing up the pillows, pulled the maroon satin sheet over me and sat up straight. Apart from the false eyelashes it was the first time a man had seen me without makeup and I was glad the only light came from a fancy glass lampshade on Robert's side of the bed. Giving myself a pep talk about how normal what I was doing was, I looked around the room. Although it was three times the size of the bedroom I shared with Debs, it was sparsely furnished. The king size bed was the main feature with a heavy oak headboard engraved with a leaf pattern. Apart from that there was just an antique wooden trunk at the bottom of the bed and a small circular table with ornate chairs by the window. I could hear the shower running in the bathroom. It seemed to take ages before Robert came back. When he did his hair was wet and he'd combed it back from his face looking like a model for a shampoo advert. For something to do I twiddled my thumbs until Robert climbed into bed smelling so delicious, I wanted to lick him. 'Ready for me to switch the light off?' he said.

I pretended to yawn even though I felt as wide awake as if I'd had four coffees. 'More than ready.' The room fell into darkness apart from a faint light coming in from a lamppost outside in the street. We lay down and turned our backs to each other. 'Goodnight,' I said.

Robert reached a hand over his back to pat my hip. 'Sweet dreams.'

I don't remember falling asleep but lulled by Robert's gentle snore, I took off for dreamland where our dance continued on an Argentinian beach. It changed from a tango to the flamenco, Robert wearing black satin breeches as I moved around him stamping my feet and clacking castanets. Every time I woke, I was aware that some part of our bodies touched or his arm was flung over me. Disturbed by the sound of rubbish trucks emptying dustbins along the street, I semi woke again to find his body pressed into mine, dick erect against my back. His breath came light and even so I knew it wasn't intentional. Imagining his dick nestled cozily between my thighs, I nodded back off to sleep.

When I woke for the last time our positions were reversed. I was snuggled into his back, one leg stretched out over his thigh, my foot grasped in his hand. I sniffed his pyjama jacket. It still smelled of sandalwood from his shower. Kissing his neck like a mother might kiss a son, I carefully reclaimed my

181

leg, removed my hand from his stomach and turned on my back. As I did, Robert stirred in his sleep. So, we're both awake?' he said. 'Tea or coffee?'

'Tea,' I said, wondering if he felt my kiss and thought I was coming onto him again.

By the time Robert came back I was washed, dressed and made up, although I left off red lipstick since I still wore my Ozzie Clark dress and didn't want to overdo it. He was still in his pyjamas. 'I really am going to call you Speedy Gonzales.' Robert laughed and put two cups of tea on the table by the window. He seemed different to the Robert who'd gone down to the kitchen. That one seemed aloof. The one who came back seemed at ease as he sat down in one of chairs. 'Sit here a minute.' He patted his knee.

'OK boss,' I perched on it lightly, wondering if he was going to tell me not to get the wrong idea about the near suck incident or sleeping together in the same bed.

Robert moved the hair away from my face and kept his hand on my cheek. 'What a funny one you are,' he said, searching my eyes. 'Where did your dreams take you last night?'

'Flamenco dancing on a beach in Argentina,' I said.

'Oh, so that's what all the *Viva la Riva* shouting was about. Was anyone with you?'

I thought on my feet, wondering what else I might have shouted. 'Just a passing holidaymaker.'

'A passing holidaymaker who became your slave?'

I started to feel nervous. 'Why? What was I saying?'

'Something about he'd better keep licking or you'd horse whip him,' Robert laughed.

'Oh yeah, I remember now. He didn't want to lick my ice cream,' I said, making the story up as I went along because my dream was a blur. It suddenly struck me that if I'd been shouting all night, Robert probably hadn't got much sleep. 'I'm really sorry if my shouting kept you awake.'

'That didn't keep me awake but having my willie trapped between your legs did.'

I had the feeling the look on my face was similar to the bit in horror films when a woman's taking a shower and the curtains open to reveal a man with an axe and would have slid off Robert's knee if he hadn't supported my back with his hand. 'What?' I squeaked.

'You had it wedged between your thighs along with my pyjama trousers and growled viciously when I attempted to take it away. I actually thought you might bite me.'

'I didn't? I...I...Bugger!' I went to stand up.

Robert pulled me back down and laughed. 'Laura, I have no idea how you wormed your way into my mind but I find myself thinking about you a lot.' I could feel myself holding my breath, could feel the tightness in my chest and my whole heavy weight pressing on his thighs but was incapable of moving. Robert tapped my leg, 'You look like you've stopped breathing. Breathe.'

My breath came out in a whoosh. *What had happened overnight?* 'But,' Robert said, continuing where he left off, 'I'm not looking to complicate my life right now so let's agree to....'

I put my finger over his lips. 'I'm not looking to complicate my life either. I'm on a journey to find out who I am underneath who I thought I...'

Robert waved my words to a stop and picked up the ringing telephone. 'Let me just...Yes, it is Robert Bauman, and good morning to you Debs. Aha, you want to speak to Laura. Yes, she's here, let me pass you over.'

'Debs?' I said.

'I put two and two together and took a wild guess you might be at Robert's when I found your keys this morning'. Debs said, rushing her words.

'What's wrong?' I asked.

183

'Tate called. He said Monster's behaving like a lunatic and he can't get him in from the window ledge. He asked if you'd go over and calm him down before he jumps?'

The whirlwind of scrambled thoughts in my head multiplied. 'On my way.' I jumped off Robert's lap.

'Trouble?' Robert asked.

'Nothing serious.' I grabbed my handbag, no intention of getting Robert involved in Monster's lunacy. 'Just need to get somewhere,' I pretended to laugh. 'A woman's thing.'

Robert walked me down the stairs to the front door. 'See you when you get back from tour.' He chuckled. 'You might find you have your work cut out with Monster and Charlie.'

I gave another false laugh then raced down his street like a pumpkin on fire, caught a cab and told the driver to put his foot down on the pedal.

# TWENTY-NINE

Monster's legs dangled over the ledge of his window when I arrived. A small crowd were gathered on the pavement and looked up as though they expected him to jump. I urgently pressed the bell for Tate to let me in wondering what had possessed Monster. I took off my shoes so I could climb the stairs two at a time. When Tate opened the door to Monster's flat, his hands trembled. 'I came over around noon to see if he wanted to go out for a bite. He was so far gone I couldn't get a word of sense out of him.'

I stopped to catch my breath. 'What's he been taking?'

'Booze, pills, weed, coke.'

I flew at the window ledge and grabbed the back of Monster's T shirt. 'Monster, come in. Let's talk about this.'

'Get your hand off my fucking T shirt,' Monster shrilled. He picked up a glass of Jack and swallowed the contents. The bottle beside the glass on the ledge was half empty. The bottle on the table had nothing left. I looked around for his packet of Marlborough's, lit a cigarette and offered it. Monster waved it away. 'Those things can kill you.'

'As can sitting on a window ledge on the third floor,' I said.

'I am not sitting here thinking of killing myself,' Monster slurred. 'I've drunk myself sober.'

'Don't jump Monster, *please* don't jump.' Mr. Krakowski appeared in the growing crowd of onlookers and pleaded with his hands. 'I live my life through you Monster. The sunshine would go out of my life without you.'

'As I was telling Laura here, Mr. Krakowski,' Monster waved his empty glass at me. 'I am not going to jump.' The gory monger onlookers who hoped he would, lost interest and moved away. 'I am sitting here contemplating the pointlessness of life and how some die tragically before their time.' A bus rattled past so I was the only one who heard what Monster said.

'Who died Monster?' I asked.

'Jimi fucking died that's who.'

I made a face at Tate. 'Jimi Hendrix,' Tate mouthed.

I was in as much shock as Monster because I hadn't heard the news or read a paper since the day before. I wanted to cry my eyes out but that wasn't the time or place. 'Was it an accident?

'Nothin' is an accident. Everything's pre-ordained by whoever it is sitting in the sky calling himself God.'

'Was it an overdose?'

'Who the fuck knows. The point is that Jimi was only 27 – the best fucking guitar player in the world and by this time next year he'll be forgotten.

'Jimi will never be forgotten Monster. You know that.'

'Everything gets forgotten,' Monster looked at me, tears in his eyes. 'You know where Jimi was last night?' I shook my head. 'Well I do. I was up all night working on a song and it was announced on the radio. Jimi was in the Lansdowne Hotel just around the corner from here. Just around the fucking corner. If I'd have known I could have been there. Maybe I could have saved him. My biggest dream was to play with Jimi…and now…' Monster couldn't go on.

I turned to Tate and mouthed, 'Play Watch Tower.'

I lit another Marlborough and passed it to Monster. 'Still not smoking?'

Monster snatched it. 'Who said I wasn't smoking?' Monster looked down at Mr. Krakowski. 'Go and do your shopping you silly old sod.'

Relieved, Mr. Krakowski gave Monster a thumbs up sign and trundled off.

Watchtower started to play. Monster's head whirled around. 'You're a moron Tate. Take that off.'

'It was my idea,' I said. 'I thought we should give Jimi a proper send off.'

Monster glared at me, face red and bloated, arms shaking as he gripped the window ledge. 'I said, fucking take it off! Or do you want me to bawl my eyes out?' I looked across at Tate who turned the record off.

'Take his mind off Jimi by asking him about Inge,' Tate mouthed.

'How's Inge?' I said.

'INGE? INGE! How the fuck would I know. She's on honeymoon in Jamaica.'

The penny dropped. Monster suffered with a double dose of sorrow. 'She didn't waste time,' I said.

'She married her childhood sweetheart. He should have fucking stayed in South Africa or wherever he went,' Monster refilled his glass of Jack. 'A mate of mine phoned to give me the news – five fucking minutes after I heard the news about Jimi.'

'You're much better off without Inge. I bet she was screwing loads of men behind your back, not just the ones you knew of.'

'She could have screwed the whole of fucking London. Who gives a shit about that, but now she's married! MARRIED.'

I decided to play a long shot to turn his grief to anger. 'That first day I came over, she told me you didn't satisfy her and she had to fake orgasms when you shagged her.'

'Bollocks, and where was I?'

'You'd passed out.'

'The lying cow!' Monster pushed his uncombed shaggy mane back from his face. 'I only had to touch her and she came all over the place like a burst water pipe!'

'Well, that's what she told me,' I rested my hand gently on his back. 'Come on in Monster, you nearly slid off the ledge. Let me make some coffee?'

'Fuck off and leave me alone,' Monster said.

'Fine!' I said. 'Kill yourself for all I care.'

I walked over to Tate. 'Let's do a war dance,' I whispered. Tate screwed up his face. 'Just follow me. We'll need some stuff from the kitchen.' I picked up my bag and we went to prepare ourselves.

'What are we going to do?' Tate asked, once we were in the kitchen.

I took his hands in mine to stop his tremble. 'We're going to do a tribal dance wearing war paint and annoy Monster until he gets so furious, he'll have to come in to stop us.'

Tate smiled. 'Liking the idea.' I took out different coloured eye shadows from my makeup purse and smudged blue, green and purple streaks on his cheeks then Tate took over and did the same to me.

'We'll need three big saucepans and something to bang them with.

Tate found saucepans while I found metal spoons and once back in the front room, Tate and I faced each other, weapons in hand. 'WA WA WA,' I chanted banging my saucepan and dancing around what I imagined was a blazing bonfire. 'WA WA WA,' Tate joined in, stamping his feet. 'DEATH, DEATH,' I chanted and banged the saucepan harder. Pumping my hand in and out over my mouth. I chanted, 'WAWAWA'. Tate and I faced each other stomping like gorillas, and chanted, 'DEATH, DEATH. WAWAWA.'

Monster turned to glare and screamed. 'What kind of sendoff is this for Jimi. Show some fucking respect.'

Tate and I took no notice and danced with frenzy. 'DEATH, DEATH, WAWAWA.'

'If you don't stop, I'll bang your heads together with those fucking saucepans!'

On we went. 'DEATH, DEATH, WAWAWA.'

Monster threw his legs around the ledge and rushed at us. 'Jimi just died. STOP!'

I jumped about in front of Monster and banged my saucepan. 'This isn't about Jimi, it's about Inge. DEATH, DEATH, WAWAWA.'

Tate banged his saucepan on top of Monster's head. 'Fucking stop Tate!'

'This second do you love or hate Inge?' I asked.

'I used to spend hours licking her cunt and the fucking cow told you I couldn't satisfy her,' Monster shook his head. 'I used to *more* than satisfy her!'

Tate kept up the tribal dance, while I got the third saucepan and metal spoon for Monster. 'Say with me, I HATE INGE'S GUTS.'

Monster grabbed them. 'I do hate Inge's guts for talking bollocks.'

Tate and I danced around Monster. 'Inge's a bitch. WAWAWA'.

Monster stood there and banged his saucepan without moving. 'Inge's a bitch. WAWAWA.'

'KILL INGE,' Tate chanted.

'DEATH TO INGE,' I screamed.

Monster banged his saucepan harder. 'Where's my war paint?'

I grabbed my makeup bag and streaked Monster's cheeks like a warrior, Tate chanted, 'Inge said you were useless in bed,' as he banged his saucepan in Monster's ear.'

Looking as though he hated Inge's guts, Monster joined in with our tribal dance and screamed 'Death to Inge.'

'I am going to take revenge by smashing up Inge's painting to show what a cow she was. REVENGE,' I shouted in Monster's face.

Monster closed his eyes and banged his saucepan so hard he dented it. 'REVENGE, REVENGE.'

Still dancing, I turned to Tate. 'Get me hammers, knives, chisels and anything you can find so I can smash Inge's painting to smithereens.'

Smiling, Tate went off to gather the tools.

Monster stopped banging and opened his eyes. 'You're not doing that on your own. I wanted to destroy it the minute I saw it.'

I didn't know what to expect but Inge's painting took up half of one wall and looked like it belonged in a horror film. The background had terrifying creatures carrying bloody limbed babies in their beaks. It was a resurrection scene and the man hanging upside down on the cross was made of plaster cast. Its face was grotesque. Its mouth wide open in a silent scream as tears of blood ran down its cheeks. Its arms flayed into the room grabbing at something or someone to save it.

Tate put a box of tools down on the floor. 'I'll make some coffee for when you've finished,' he said, leaving us to it.

Monster grabbed a hammer from the tool box and rushed at the painting. 'Grrrrrh, WAWA.' He broke off one of the arms, threw it to the floor and started bashing it with the hammer. One of its fingers nearly poked me in the eye as it flew by. I copied what Monster did with the other arm, making my own sounds as I bashed away. Monster ripped off the man's plaster cast head and stuck a knife through both eyes. 'You've been scaring me to death for months you bastard!' He stabbed the man's mouth. 'Shut your fucking mouth and die.'

I took a rolling pin from the box and bashed at the man's body until he was body less and I was covered in dust. 'Death to the cow,' I shouted, spurring Monster on as he hacked off

190

the man's ears. Deciding I had done enough, I threw myself down on his mattress. 'I feel great'.

Monster delivered a blow to the man's head. It split in half. 'Tell Tate to bring me a saw.'

I sat up. 'Why do you want that?'

'To demolish the frame.' I stood up and walked to the door, feeling the worst had passed. 'And tell Tate to put Watchtower on. I want to give Jimi a proper send off and let him know how missed he'll be,' Monster said.

# THIRTY

The tour bus I rented for eight people looked huge when I saw it empty because it didn't have as much as a pair of socks on view. Overnight it looked like a refuse dump. The six coat pegs were burdened with so much outerwear, I had to fight my way through coats to get on or off the bus. The formica topped table on which I envisioned fresh flowers and fruit, housed stands with Diana Ross wigs, music mags, boxed games, cartons of cigarettes, half-eaten packs of biscuits, bags of sweets and chewy bars.

The benches on either side of the table sat six at a squeeze and apart from the eight of us, was the lighting engineer, Seedcake, and Big Pete and Titch, the crew. They slept in Monster's van but used the tour bus to eat, ablute and shower which meant a constant flow of bodies pushing and jostling – and nowhere to fix my makeup in peace.

The four bunks on the male side were occupied by Monster, Tate, Charlie and Max. On my side, were Marilou, Celeste and Desiree, the backing singers. Marilou and Celeste were lesbians who I called the kissy or hissy girls because their relationship blew hot and cold. Kissy mode meant the bedframe above mine not only squeaked incessantly, I had to put up with earsplitting climaxes. Tate and Max were gone to the world by midnight. Little woke them, whereas my eyes shot open at the slightest snore or bum missile and I had delinquents Monster and Charlie to contend with.

One night when I thought we were all asleep, I heard someone throw a stone. Being sleep deprived, my nerves were such that even a feather woke me up. I fell out of bed and was at the window in a flash. Monster stood on the back of a motorbike screaming, '*I got off when the driver stopped to refuel. I was just having a burger and the bus took off without me*'. He'd been on a booze binge, and almost toppled off. I felt furious he could have killed himself. Charlie, thought Monster's escapade was hilarious. They kept me awake until 6a.m when it was time for me to face another grueling day.

Outside of the tour bus, my learn as you go strategy paid dividends. I bluffed when I didn't know something and came up gold, struck better deals with venues as I got the hang of it and ensured Streetcrash were at sound checks, rehearsals and nearly everything else on my list. The Streetcrash gigs in Brighton, Birmingham, Manchester and Leeds went down a storm, not that I saw one gig from start to finish because there was so much work to do behind the scenes and my heart was always in my mouth due to Seedcake, the lighting technician. Monster recommended him because his lighting method was unique and he thought he was on the verge of new discovery. Seedcake's services came free because he wanted the Streetcrash tour on his CV, so I agreed, and at pinch, was able to hire the singers.

Big Pete and Titch didn't get on with Seedcake who spoke in riddles, spaced out on LSD and kept them awake reading Henry stories by torchlight about the exploits of Trurl and Klapaucius, the robot geniuses of The Cyberiad – a book Seedcake carried everywhere as if it was a sacred edition of the robot bible. 'We didn't bloody well expect to be sleeping squashed between boxes of Streetcrash merchandise, a rack full of stage outfits, nutty Seedcake and a one ton Dalek,' Big Pete complained. I wanted to sack Seedcake but my hands were tied due to diminishing funds.

Seedcake didn't have a lighting box as was customary but a metal Dalek called Henry to do the job. Henry's eyes flashed red, orange and green like traffic lights, produced psychedelic displays of colour from his fingers and emitted triangle and star shapes from his stomach. At first sight, for a one ton Dalek, he looked impressive. In reality he was a pathetic creation who needed Seedcake to pull levers, press buttons and move him around on wheels. The audience loved his authenticity but Henry was so temperamental, one of his eyes blew out at the first gig, he broke down at the second and electrocuted himself at the fourth.

When I asked Monster to have a word with Seedcake, he told me to stop being so uptight and assured me Seedcake was an experimental scientist on the verge of doing great things. I begrudgingly came to terms with that. What I couldn't stand was the way Monster expected me to do his dirty work and pass on messages to our driver, who started out a passive, turban wearing Seik. I found ways to change, *'Tell the driver not to play his radio so loud, or fucking tune it to a decent station,'* and *'Tell him his fucking snoring keeps me awake'* so they sounded like polite requests but the driver swore at me as though I was to blame.

There were pleasant interludes as we journeyed from city to city. I particularly liked it when Monster, Tate and Max took out guitars and strummed melodious harmonies which took away the tediousness of endless highways, but being cooped up with so many people started to wear me down.

Another night, having sat up until 2a.m. to organize everything for the following day, I'd just got into bed and put my nose and ear plugs in place, when I felt something tickle my neck. I touched it. It moved. I sat up to see the shadow of a huge daddy long legs run across my chest and shrieked my head off.

Night lights came on. The lookalikes screamed, assuming I'd seen a ghost as I pointed to a spider which had since vanished. Charlie bounced on his bunk delighted with himself.

I threw my can of Lavender spray at him. 'That was Not funny!'

Monster, shocked awake, jumped down from his bunk, grabbed Charlie by the neck and shook. Charlie was wrapped like an Egyptian mummy to protect himself. 'It was a joke,' he protested.

Irritated by Charlie's behavior, Tate turned over in his bunk without a word. Monster carried on shaking, the lookalikes reigned blows on his head and I battered his thighs with my fists. 'Stop,' Charlie screamed. 'You'll damage my equipment. If you want to punish me, hit my bum.' Monster kicked the blanket in which Charlie was embedded. 'Say sorry.' Charlie made a muffled apology to me. My heart softened towards Monster for coming to my aid. 'Not her. Say sorry for waking me up you prat.'

Next morning, I trudged through a blizzard to call Robert as promised and let him know how things were going on tour. It was a long trek due to the fact our driver parked in the middle of nowhere after Monster and Charlie had an all night party in a truck driver's layby and caused a riot. Wind howled in my ears as I stood outside the phone box, thinking about Monster and Charlie's selfishness and listened to a pointless conversation about the price of pork. The slow dripping tap of frustration built into rage as the pork conversation carried on. I banged on the window and played a shocked woman who saw someone murdered and needed to call the police.

How I managed to convince Robert everything was under control was a miracle. 'Yes, no probs so far. All is calm.' I was ready to pat myself on the back when the man I sent on a wild goose chase, thumped on the window. 'Get out, you scheming little liar.'

Backside pressed against the door to stop him getting in, I shouted 'Just a mo,' and tried to bring my conversation with

Robert to a close as the man outside threw his weight at the door from the other side.

'What's that racket?' Robert laughed.

'Two truck drivers having a fight,' The man's arm came around the door and punched me in the back. Vulgar language echoed around the phone box as he pushed in and tried to grab the phone. 'One of the drivers needs to call the police.' I slammed the phone down, dodged his fist, exited and trudged back up the highway wishing I was at home with Debs eating spaghetti boloneska in our meticulously clean flat instead of heading back to a mad house.

# THIRTY-ONE

Next day in Newcastle, Monster was afflicted with a dark dog depression which grew on the hour like a brooding cloud. He managed to get through his radio interviews and some of the other things on my list but by evening, the most I could get was a grunt. Tate told me Monster's dark dog days didn't come often but when they did, he plunged into death thoughts. Part of the reason was that Janis Joplin died that day – a couple of weeks after Hendrix. Monster went so deeply into gloom, I was a bag of nerves.

Tate stayed close in case Monster needed him. Max sang My Old Man's a Dustman which Monster loved because his grandfather sang it to him. I tried to bring Monster around by using breathing techniques created for the mentally disturbed and profoundly confused. Neither made a scrap of difference. I encouraged Monster to remember Tarzan. Head slumped between his arms he said Tarzan wasn't real.

Marilou and Celeste were having a hissy-fit cat fight that had to do with Janis Joplin. Marilou had a crush on Janis and felt if Janis had been with her, she could have stopped her overdosing on heroine. It was the Jimi Hendrix saga in reverse. To make matters worse Marilou kept singing, *Who to believe in when your heart's trapped in a jar, bleeding,* which was the chorus from Monster's song, Heart trapped in a jar.

Celeste poked Marilou in the chest. 'What d'ya mean you scraggy bitch?' 'What am I? Shit?'

'Janis was an icon,' Marilou sobbed. She tugged Celeste's wig. 'I hate you for not feeling me, you butch dyke.'

Worn out with their outbursts, I marched over. 'From the first night you've kept me awake with your fiddling, diddling and fights,' I shouted. 'Which one of you is to blame this time?' Lips trembling, Marilou pointed at Celeste. Fury in her eyes, Celeste hissed at Marilou. I slapped them both across the cheek. 'Another word and I'll tape your mouths shut!'

Charlie who stood next to them, and chatted to Desiree, chuckled. 'Glad I'm not in trouble tonight, Melons.' His hair had grown so long at the front, I blew it out of his eyes and squished his ear lobe until he winced.

'There are eight hundred people waiting for tonight's show and look at the state of Monster.'

Charlie bunched his lips, then wiggled them in contemplation. 'He'll just say he wants to slit his throat. He'll be fine when he gets on stage.'

'Say something that makes Monster want to pelt you with something. Do what you're good at.'

Charlie leaped over and flung his arms around Monster. 'Come on Diva. Where's the Monster we know and love? Have a line of coke. Have a glug of Jack. Pelt me with…'

'I want to die,' Monster croaked.

The crowd started to cheer. 'Go ahead,' I ordered. 'I'll sort Monster out.' Tate hesitated. 'Go.'

Not knowing what I'd got or how I was going to persuade Monster out of his dark dog depression, I slid my arms under his armpits. He was made up and ready to go complete with a blue highwayman shirt and a blue bandana because I'd already taken care of that. I pressed my weight against his back. 'Up we get.'

'I'm going to fuck up and forget the words,' Monster mumbled.

'You never forget.' I linked my leg around his and moved it forwards. 'You are the one and only, amazing, incredible, talented Monster. Listen to the crowd scream your name.'

With a pathetic shake of his head, Monster whispered. 'What if I die tonight?' I decided that as soon as the tour was over, I was going to get a degree in psychology because his manager needed one. I pulled him to his feet, held his waist from behind and levered his legs forward by pushing against them with my knees. He was like a horse that refused to go into the starting box and shook violently as he walked forwards in sleepwalk mode. 'You'll be amazing. Go kill 'em tiger.'

Monster took a timid step. I gave his bum a hard pinch. 'I said a tiger not a mouse.'

Monster walked on stage like a blind man. He picked up his guitar and stared unseeing at the audience. My heart raced as I wondered if he'd turn back and how I'd handle it. Tate strummed the chords of their first song. Monster's freeze thawed. The blind man blinked. 'Fucking great to be here. Are you ready to rock?'

# THIRTY-TWO

Physically and mentally exhausted, I couldn't wait to pull off my boots, leather trousers and Everyone's T shirt, which was my standard outfit for gigs, and crawl into bed like a dying slug. When Tate and I climbed back on the bus, it was obvious that option was a no go because the heater broke down and it was ice cold. Since my fake fur coat was buried under the rest on the pegs and my boots couldn't be found, I resorted to wearing someone's tacky fleeced jacket and a pair of ugly fleeced boots. In the background, the Seik driver, cursed in Hindi and hammered on the heater to force it back to life.

Outside, the scene was like something from a surreal Fellini film. Beside Monster's van, Seedcake gave Henry an overhaul and sat cross-legged behind him wearing a toggle pegged duffle coat as he fiddled with wires that stuck out of Henry's back compartment. Deep in conversation with Henry who wore a cap and woolly scarf as if he was made of flesh, Seedcake giggled at what I imagined to be Henry's sense of humour and continued knotting wires with the dedication of a nuclear scientist.

From throwing up behind a tree, Max ducked out of sight to poo since he had a stomach bug.

Monster sat in the middle of the field, with a blanket wrapped around his shoulders. When he wasn't having a one-sided conversation with an owl that alighted in a nearby oak tree, he gazed into the fire he built with twigs playing death march tunes on his harmonica.

Tate and I played Scrabble to pass the time. I won the last game with the word *SHAGGING*. What a joke? Not a sniff of a shag in eight weeks and I was so numb with weariness, didn't have strength to open my legs.

'Bet you weren't expecting all this when you signed up as manager?' Tate said, glancing out of the window. Putting the scrabble pieces back in the box, he looked at me with concern. 'You need to get more rest, Laura. You look exhausted.'

My answer was a shrug. 'Think I'll take Monster a sandwich. He hasn't eaten all day.' Pulling myself up from the bench, I walked to the sink, splashed cold water on my face, wiped a blob of ketchup off the sideboard and made him a ham and pickle sandwich and a cup of tea.

Tate moved deftly around me picking up stray footwear and tucked them under bunk beds. 'I know this tour can't be easy but since Robert sent those sneak previews out, Radio Luxembourg and Radio Caroline are playing Everyone's on the hour and BBC radio says Truth Kills could chart on the first day of release.'

I squeezed my buttocks together to stop wind escaping. I wanted to feel excited but Monster's misery wouldn't let me. 'It'll sink it soon,' I said.

I sat down on the grass beside Monster, and lay the plate and cup at his feet. 'How's it going?'

'Jimi and Janis were only 27. Twenty fucking seven. 'Monster stared into the glowing flames. 'What does God want to do? Open a 27 club!'

I pulled a wisp of hair out of his mouth and tucked it behind his ear. 'Life's a bitch.'

A twig crackled. Monster poked the fire with a stick. I put the cup in his hands. He took a sip of tea. 'Life *is* a bitch.' He turned with a pained expression. 'You know you gave up sex on a voluntary basis?'

'Yes.'

'What if it's not voluntary – like in my case?'

'What's your case?' I was so worn out, my voice sounded like an irritated psychologist probing an irritating patient. I sweetened my tone. 'Tell Aunty Laura. Take all the time you need.'

Monster pulled the blanket around his face as though he didn't want anyone to see or hear. 'Do not mention what I'm going to tell you to anyone.' I crossed my heart. Monster blew out a long stream of breath. It was so bitter cold, his breath hung in the air forming the shape of a question mark. 'Since Inge, I can't get it up and it's because the lying cow said I couldn't satisfy her.' Nerves made me want to spurt with laughter since it was me who planted that seed in his mind. Monster whispered as though the owl had ears. 'If Inge was faking it, all the others could have been. The other day I ran through a list in my mind of the women I screwed over the past year. I could hear them say "No-one's ever licked me like you, Monster." I could hear them scream, "I'm coming, you're the best." I've read the Kama Sutra. I pride myself on my sexual prowess – so tell me, were those women fucking liars?'

I faked orgasms when a shag wasn't up to par because who wanted someone thrusting away when they weren't hitting the mark, but that was the last thing Monster needed to hear right then. 'I lied about Inge. I never even spoke to her. When the meeting with Tate and Charlie finished, we looked in on you and you were both dead to the world.'

'WHAT?' Monster pulled the blanket off his face. 'Then why the fuck did you lie?'

'To make you angry so you could deal with Jimi's death and get Inge out of your system.'

'What, banging saucepans and shouting WAWA?' I nodded. 'So, all that, '*Inge said you were rubbish in bed*', was a load of cobblers?'

'Cobblers.'

'You cow!' Monster banged an imaginary saucepan. 'Wawa, death to Inge. Inge said you couldn't satisfy her. Hahaha.'

I glanced back at the tour bus to see Tate standing at the window. He made a 'what's up' gesture with his hand. I gave him a thumbs up to let him know I had everything under control.

Monster nudged me. 'Thanks for letting me know that. I get a lot of pleasure out of pleasing women.' His hair, parted in the middle, had grown longer. His face, no longer covered in acne, had a marble sheen. Framed by the moon, he looked like a male Mona Lisa as he smiled peacefully. Putting a hand to his mouth, he yawned. 'I'm so fucking tired.'

Monster's yawn made me yawn. 'Me too. Let's go in.' I held my hands over the fire to bring warmth into them. 'In the morning you've got a radio show talk, an autograph signing at the city centre, a press conference at 4 pm, our daily meeting at five, the sound check at six, rehearsals, and a TV channel who want to interview you after the gig.'

Monster shook his head. 'I want to stay here until that owl flies off. It's been keeping me company. I know it hasn't understood a word, but before you came out, I unburdened my heart to it.' He bit hungrily into his sandwich. 'This is tasty – what's in it?'

'Ham and pickle.' A wave of motherly love came over me. Underneath the neurotic tyrant was a little boy lost. 'When I was a kid, I was convinced the same robin came back every year.' I brushed bodies with Monster in affection. 'I used to talk to it for hours.'

From the corner of my eye I saw Charlie, Desiree, Marilou and Celeste zigzag towards the tour bus. Charlie, a bottle of tequila in his hand, took a slug, passed it to Desiree and performed a wobbly cartwheel.

Monster watched the owl flap its wings, mirrored against the moon as it flew high into the sky. 'Owl's gone home. Guess we should.' As Monster helped me to my feet, I felt proud I handled him so well.

'Let's have a sing-song around your camp fire, Mons.' Charlie called out. 'Let's have an all-night party?'

Monster waved at Charlie. 'Bring me my bottle of Jack and my cigarettes and some cheese and onion crisps. And make a pile of ham and pickle sandwiches – and bring a few chewy bars. The strawberry ones.'

I shook out my feet which felt like blocks of ice and glanced at my night glow watch – twenty hours I'd gone without sleep.

'Stay,' Monster said. 'It'll be a laugh.'

I wanted to hit him over the head with a twig, set his hair alight and stuff his chewy bars down his throat. 'Some of us take our responsibilities seriously,' I snapped, stomping off in the humiliating fleecy lined boots I wouldn't have been seen dead in before the selfish, self- obsessed, sod took over my life.

# THIRTY-THREE

Pressure built as the size of the venues increased, together with more responsibility for me. By day nineteen, by which time Streetcrash performed in Portsmouth and Sheffield, I felt like a sleepwalking juggler who sat for hours with Seedcake to analyse Henry's malfunctions, tried to keep law and order on the tour bus and herded Streetcrash to autograph signings, press events, radio and TV interviews. I'd lost an eyelash down the plughole, my hair was dirty because there was never time to wash it and I felt close to collapse.

Tate and Charlie were in the Blackpool venue at 3 pm sharp to talk to Blackpool newspapers. Monster was missing but I knew where he was. Sleeping off a hangover. Furious, I stomped back to the parking lot where Big Pete and Titch unloaded equipment from the tour bus. They nodded that Monster was inside. I marched up the steps and fought through the coats. From behind Marilou's curtain came kissy sounds. I yanked Monster's curtain open and blew my army whistle. 'Get out of bed. Now!'

'I was having a wank listening to them. 'Monster tugged the curtain back. 'Now you've made me go soft.'

I marched to the sink, filled a cup with cold water and tipped it over his head. 'Soft problem solved. Get out of bed.'

'Alright, keep your hair on,' Monster begrudgingly threw his legs over the bunk. 'I'll just have a few lines of coke to…'

Hating Monster with a vengeance for choosing a wank over his career, I shoved his jeans and a T shirt in his arms. 'You'll do nothing of the sort. Put these on!'

Back on the tour bus from 4pm till 4.55pm, I ignored Monster's insults about me dragging him out of bed, ignored his complaints about Seedcake who he since decided was a deranged psycho, and made him two coffees as requested.

Sat around the table at 5pm for our regular agenda run through, my patience reached frazzle point. My stomach was a constipated mess because someone always banged on the toilet door before I was ready to excrete. It was the shipwreck sideboard and dirty plates, coffee mugs with dogends floating on the top, the pimples on my chin, my tired looking eyes and the way my hands shook due to stress.

I pushed Monster's junk off the table onto his lap so I had space to lay out my notes. 'Clean your rubbish up, please.' Monster shifted his cigarette cartons, music mags and bag of chewy bars in a pile beside him on the bench. 'Someone needs to sit there. Throw them on your bunk.' I blew my whistle. 'Time for today's run through.' Max emerged from his bunk and joined Tate at the bench.

'Fuck me, it's like being in the army,' Monster moaned.

I showed Monster, Tate and Max the madness in my eyes. 'Things need to change.' I pointed at a mound of wet towels on the floor, men's socks that stank like ripe Camembert and ropes attached to the framework of upper bunks that hung with jeans and T shirts.

'This is like being in prison,' Monster grunted. 'Say something Tate.'

Tate smiled. 'You try the patience of a saint, Mons.'

'A manager is not supposed to make the band tense,' Monster said.

Noting Charlie was missing, I looked out of the window. 'Charlie, I can see you and Desiree behind that parked van.' Charlie put up a hand to signal he needed more time. 'You have one minute to finish off.'

Monster laughed so hard he was doubled over. 'Fuck me Laura, we'll all end up with erectile dysfunction.'

Tate and Max smiled. I growled to show there was nothing humorous about Monster's wit, poked my head out of the window and blew my whistle until Charlie climbed off Desiree. She hid behind him as he stood to zip his trousers. 'And *you* Desiree are not to entice Charlie during office hours!'

As soon as Charlie squashed in beside Monster, I resumed where I left off. 'Don't you *see* how we're living?

'She's right,' Tate said. 'It's a pig sty.'

Max nodded. He was neat like Tate. Charlie blew the hair out of his eyes. glanced around and said, 'Pigs.' He was one of the main culprits but looked innocent of all charges.

'It's not my fucking fault it rained for five days and it's not my fault we live in a pig sty.' Monster said. I glared at the second culprit. 'And why haven't you sacked Seedcake? Henry was a fucking lunatic last night,' he said. The fuse inside me sizzled. 'By the way, the driver still looks at me funny. Did you ask him why he doesn't fucking like me?'

I could feel words forming in my mouth I never used before the tour since I saw myself above the likes of Brassy but was too far gone to restrain myself. 'I'm not your fucking skivvy, Monster!' Charlie chuckled. I silenced him with my murderess look and cast it on Monster. 'Wanna know whether the driver likes you? Ask him your fucking self!'

'Laura's started swearing,' Monster said to Tate.

'It's the strain of being with us 24 hours every day,' Tate said. 'It's a wonder Laura hasn't had a breakdown.'

I blew my whistle. 'Since tomorrow is a free day, we are going to work together to do something about the state of this shit hole. I've suffered this for nineteen days. Enough is enough.'

'You're like some mad witch,' Monster said. 'Put your fucking whistle down. You've been blowing it so much, it's covered in spit.'

Charlie spluttered into his hand. 'She's even got frizzy hair like a witch.'

Wanting to strangle them, I looked at my spit covered whistle, touched my hair which felt like a nettle bush and screamed.

'Laura's doing everything singlehandedly. It can't be easy taking care of us, the crew, the lighting technician and all she does in between. Haven't you noticed how tired she looks? When did you ever see Laura with chipped nail polish?'

I looked down at my jagged slutty nails, patted my puffy eyes, smacked my swollen belly and glared at Monster and Charlie. 'If I'm a mad witch, you two turned me into one.' Cackling, I grabbed a broom, rammed it between my legs, marched to the toilet and slammed the door shut.

Shaking with rage, I gripped the sink and gasped in shock. I did look like a mad witch. My hair *was* frizzy, I had bushy eyebrows and apart from the two pimples on my chin, had a red blobby one on my nose. That ugly cow wasn't wearing false eyelashes and looked like an Albino. That ugly cow had black rings under her eyes. My lips wobbled like jelly.

'I think Laura's losing it,' I heard Monster say. The wobble in my lips moved up my face. How and when did I transform from a fresh skinned fashionista into a battered old hag? I heard a tap on the door. 'Laura,' Monster said, 'I've been a prat – but I honestly fucking love you.'

'Fuck off prat,' I shouted.

# THIRTY-FOUR

'I've decided,' I announced to Monster the following morning, 'that since we have free time until Friday, I'm going to explore Blackpool and unwind.'

'You never take time off to unwind,' Monster said. 'What am I supposed to do without you here ordering me about?'

'I couldn't care less,' I said. 'The mad witch is taking off on her broomstick to remember what life's like as a human!'

How I loved the feel of the therapist's fingers kneading and pinching the tight knots from my neck all the way down to my coccyx. Even my vagina came back to life after its long draught. I promised myself a self-pleasuring session at the earliest opportunity to make up for the two failed attempts due to finger and mind fatigue. Oh, the feel of the therapist's fingers shaping my eyebrows, extracting pus from my pimples, ironing the lines out around my eyes and plumping my cheeks with a serum meant for women of forty plus since I knew drastic measures were needed.

When she finished scrubbing my feet with a pumice stone and applied neutral coloured nail polish (to match whatever outfit I'd buy later), she asked if I wanted caterpillar or giraffe style false eyelashes to complete my make-up look. The giraffe style eyelashes were thicker and furrier so I opted for them and when I saw myself in the mirror wanted to kiss myself because I never realized how seductively flirty-eyed giraffes were. When I was whisked off to the hair salon and asked which hairdresser I wanted, I chose a gay one because I always found they tuned into women who weren't afraid to stand out. When I said I wanted to look like a mermaid with big hair, he flapped his hands in delight. 'Dahling, I shall create the most divine mermaid ever.' Having backcombed the top part of my hair, he swept my fringe to one side then primped and curled the ends of my hair into tumbling snakes. The hairdresser was so excited by his creation he covered me in pursed lipped kisses like the happiest fish in the sea.

Remembering to glide as though Robert could see, I wandered from boutique to boutique. In Adelaide's Fashions a model in the window wore a dusky pink boucle swing coat with a matching pencil skirt. It even had high heels in pink. The outfit wasn't an original but who could afford couture when my worldly possessions amounted to a measly three hundred pounds?

The salesgirl in the shop wasn't sure what to make of me. I looked like two different women pasted together. The top half a big haired mermaid. The lower part a scruffy rocker because I still wore my Everyone's a Mother Fucker T shirt and black leather trousers.

'I'd like to try that outfit on,' I pointed to it in the window. 'Complete with shoes.'

'It costs one hundred and twenty pounds,' she said, hesitantly.

'Compared to the money I've spent recently, that's a drop in the ocean,' I sniffed.

The assistant looked me up and down sizing me for size. I prompted her in my mind to bring me a size fourteen because surely with all the stress, strain and dieting, I'd lost weight? She brought back a sixteen which fit perfectly. Conclusion: No point going on diets due to unshrinkable assets.

Back out in the high street, I knew my hair was so full that ten white doves could set up home in my tresses but I didn't just get wolf whistles. A motorbike crashed into the back of a car because the mesmerized rider couldn't take his eyes off me. Fortunately, apart from falling off, no damage was done to either bike or car.

Giving the biker a wave for his troubles I went into a posh restaurant and ordered steak, petit pois and potatoes dauphinoise, washed down with a glass of red wine. Studying the menu, I saw that what I called Masat was spelled Meursault and practiced saying it until I sounded like Edith Piaf.

When I woke up next morning in my B&B at 10am between fresh sheets, in a room with rose patterned wallpaper and rose patterned china beside the Teas Maid on the table, the image of me on a broom made me giggle. With the mad witch liberated and confidence restored, I was ready to face the hell hole again.

The tour bus was parked in a layby on the outskirts of Blackpool. When I got out of the cab, Marilou, Celeste and Desiree talked to Big Pete and Titch outside Monster's van.

Big Pete and Titch's mouths fell open as if a Hollywood star had arrived to pay Streetcrash a visit. Marilou, Celeste and Desiree blew me a kiss, put their hands on their hearts and mouthed 'We're sorry.'

I knew it was rehearsed but I gave them a regal nod, clattered up the steps and opened the door expecting the usual fight through twenty coats. There was just one on each of the six pegs, including my fake suede beige coat that I hadn't seen for weeks.

The tour bus was so neat, it looked as if a professional cleaning company went through every nook and cranny with magical cleaning tools. The smell of sweaty socks was replaced by rose air spray. On the table was a bowl of fruit and bunch of flowers.

Monster and Charlie were sitting on a bench. Tate and Max sat on Tate's bunk.

I blinked at them and they blinked back until the mutual shock wore off. Monster stood up. 'I have no words to say how sorry I am – and by the way you look *fucking* hot.'

I could never look at Monster and not see his raw handsomeness. My heart melted in a pool of love as his sultry hazel eyes begged for forgiveness but he wasn't getting it that easily. He placed a black velvet box in my hand. 'I know I don't show it but I do fucking love you, Laura.' Monster glanced down at the box. 'Go on, open it.'

Inside the box was a gold bracelet. On the top side the gold tab had Laura inscribed on it. On the other side it said "Thanks for believing in us. Love always. Monster.'

'Put it on,' I offered Monster my wrist.

'Do you like it? Monster asked, as he snapped the clasp shut.

'It's beautiful. Thank you,' I waved Monster away. He was so dumbfounded he stood there staring. I could see Tate smile and knew he'd tumbled my game.

Charlie approached with a bouquet of red roses. 'Monster's the biggest prat, but I know I'm as bad sometimes.' He curled my arms around the roses and waited for my reaction. Charlie was wearing the brown and orange T-shirt and orange jeans he wore at the Rat gig. His big, round eyes were like a repentant schoolboy's trying to get back in his teacher's good books. I wanted to laugh but kept my face stern as I read the note attached to the bouquet. 'To my special Melons. You were the best free gift that ever came into our lives. Sorry. Charlie.'

'I thought a bottle of Moet was in order to toast Laura's monumental feat in getting us this far,' Tate said, twisting the cork on a bottle of champagne.

Max produced five glasses that were hidden behind his back.

Monster looked so dejected I put the roses on the table and tickled him under the arms. 'Come on you big diva –tonight's our last night and you've got two thousand people to entertain.'

'Do you really like the bracelet?' he asked.

'I'll never take it off, Montague.'

Monster sighed with relief. 'That's alright then -but don't ever fucking call me Montague in public or I'll call you Melons.'

'If Mons is forgiven why can't I have a tickle?' Charlie simpered.

I gave Charlie one so he didn't feel left out, kicked off my shoes and sat next to Tate. 'Serve the champagne.'

'Yes madam,' he winked.

# THIRTY-FIVE

That morning on the tour bus felt as if we'd signed a silent bond to come together as a loving family. Marilou, Celeste and Desiree sang Marvin Gaye and Tammi Terrill's, *Ain't no mountain high enough, ain't no valley low enough.* Their voices, which rang out like gospel singers were joined by Monster, Tate and Max singing harmonies on the lines, *No matter how far, call my name and I'll be there.* Charlie sat cross legged on the floor with an upside down saucepan between his knees and played it like a tom-tom. On the bus steps, Big Pete, Titch and Seedcake ate bowls of corn flakes and chatted with the driver whose passiveness had been restored due to the fact his heavy metal tour sentence neared its end. I knew the moment was as rare as finding a pearl inside a rhinoceros and felt so uplifted, went around kissing everyone.

The driver pulled off and headed for Glasgow. I pulled out my schedule for the day and called a meeting. Max nodded as Tate offered his usual helpful comments. Monster saluted as I flew through items on my list and Charlie listened without cracking jokes. I finished talking at the exact moment the driver parked in a Glasgow layby. The taxi driver honked his horn to let us know he was there. Monster, Tate, Charlie and I jumped in and he took us to the Grand Central Hotel where we had a suite to do an interview with BBC TV about Streetcrash's surprise overnight rise to fame.

'I would hardly call it overnight,' Monster said, when asked that question. 'Tate and me have been going at it since age eleven so fame's been a long time coming. For a while we thought we might end up wrinkly, arthritic, old rockers playing at working men's clubs and go on stage clacking false teeth with dribble coming out of our mouths.' Monster pretended to catch a dribble.

Whether it was because I survived 21 days on tour without committing suicide, I had no idea, but when Monster said that, I couldn't stop laughing. A reporter from Glasgow Music News asked if I'd taken a dose of laughing salts – inferring drugs. Holding a pen between my fingers as though holding a fat Columbian cigar, I said. 'Take this down to write in your newspaper. Our tour could be described as that depicted in the Cliff Richard's film Summer Holidays. Song, dance and laughter all the way.' I was so on form I believed every word.

Monster, Tate and Charlie sat on a plush sofa wearing yellow T shirts and black trousers as the cameraman zoomed in and out with his lens. Charlie never talked much at interviews. He said cameras made him tongue tied but it didn't stop him from being a silent clown. Every time the camera turned his way, he wiggled his eyebrows, stuck his tongue out, made squinchy shapes with his lips or pointed to his purple streaks. Tate, who sat in the middle, occasionally nudged Charlie in good spirit but kept up banter with Monster, who made sure Tate was included at every juncture of the interview.

Reporters from the Scottish Chronicle, Glasgow Hound, Glasgow Express, Glasgow Weekly News and Glasgow Insider's Gossip mag, scribbled furiously or took photographs as the interviewer went through the questions on his sheet. I sat behind a desk going meticulously through contracts for Streetcrash's upcoming performances on a German rock TV show called Beat Club and Top of the Pops as I worked out ways to get us more money without me being the main investor and prove I was the toughest heavy metal manager in the music business.

'What I'm seeing here is a rock-solid relationship between you and Tate, Monster,' the interviewer said. 'Is that the case behind closed doors?'

'That's a good question,' Monster said. 'But you know what, we haven't had a serious fall out in eighteen years.' The camera zoomed in to get a close up of his eyes. I made them up to look like a cheetah and imagined girls panting in front of TV screens. 'I wouldn't describe myself as an easy character.' *No flaming kidding*, I thought. 'But thank f-fudge, Tate's like f-fudging Buddha. Nothing rattles him.'

'If Buddha was around to see me, he might not have agreed,' Tate smiled. 'But no long term partnership is smooth sailing, so all in all, we've been lucky.'

I glanced at my watch and caught the interviewer's eye. 'We need to get going,' I mouthed.

'We look forward to seeing you in two weeks on Top of the Pops when you'll be performing your new single Truth Kills,' the interviewer said. 'Any last words, Monster?'

'Yeah,' Monster said. 'Gran, Grandad. I know you'll be watching, so Gran, I just want to say thanks for buying me my first electric guitar and being there for me when I was a snotty nosed kid. And Grandad, it's time we changed that broken down jalopy you've been driving around in for the past ten years. We'll talk about it over our next pie 'n mash night when I get off tour.'

The cameraman turned to a reporter from the Glasgow Hound who blew into her hankie overcome with emotion. He held it on her face for five seconds before clicking the camera off. Without realizing Monster was about to make Streetcrash headline news, and for the first time it wouldn't be for chucking a manager out of the window, trashing a hotel room or a drug binge.

When we got to the Glasgow venue, there was a queue of fans all the way around the building holding up *Love you*

*Streetcrash* banners. I gaggle of girls ran towards the tour bus screaming Monster's name. 'Stay here,' I told Streetcrash. 'I'll fob off the girls and get the driver to take you around the back.' The backing singers jiggled to get off the bus because they needed a pee. 'Say Streetcrash are following on in a separate car and you know where it's headed.' As soon as they were out, hundreds of fans turned on their heels to follow their lead. 'I'd say you've made it, Streetcrash,' I said, as they laughed among themselves.

The contrast between Streetcrash's gig at the Rat and Parrot and the one in Glasgow was as different as pork scratchings to lobster tails. The venue was huge, had plush green seats and green carpet down the aisles. Seedcake, who stood behind Henry on the other side of stage, flashed lights at the Streetcrash banner through Henry's fingers and made stars dance across it. I gave Seedcake a thumbs up sign to spur him on. There had been three gigs in all without mishaps and having spent so much time with Henry, I'd grow fond of him. In the background Truth Kills played to familiarise the audience with the song. The backing singers came on, waved at the cheering crowd and boogied their way to microphones. As they stood swaying, Henry's eyes crisscrossed their sequin dresses with orange and green lights. The two thousand strong audience clapped steadily in anticipation, electrifying the static in the air.

Max walked on in his red T-shirt, turned on the spot, waved at the crowd and picked up his rhythm guitar. The tour had transformed him beyond recognision. His slump was well and truly over. Charlie came on saluting and hopscotched to the drums. Picking up a stick, he pointed it to the edge of the stage to announce Tate. Henry shot out flashes of gold from his stomach. Tate came on in his red T-shirt, bowed at the crowd, strolled to his bass guitar and slung it over his shoulder. In the background, Charlie clashed cymbals while the lookalikes clicked their fingers and sang, '*Have the courage to listen. Listen and learn,*' a line from Truth Kills that would be sung in its entirety at the end of the show.

I told Monster to wait for thirty seconds to create as much tension as possible. The crowd chanted MONSTER, MONSTER, although it sounded more like MONSTA, MONSTA, because we were in Scotland. Monster swaggered on wearing his red highwayman shirt and red bandana, placed his hands on his heart to thank fans for their support, picked up his guitar and brought his mouth to the microphone. 'Fucking good to be here. Are you ready to rock?'

'AYE,' the crowd screamed.

A dazzle of coloured shapes bounced off stage and transformed into a red spiral as Charlie played a fanfare on the drums. Seedcake held up his fingers in the peace sign. I crossed my fingers and smiled back.

'What d'you want to hear first?' Monster shouted.

'EVERYONE'S A MOTHA FUCKA,' the crowd screamed.

'Glad you agree,' Monster laughed. Henry shone a silver spotlight on Monster's face. He looked so raunchily sexy with his theatrically made up eyes, one girl fainted. 'I'll just wait until someone revives her,' Monster joked. Someone dribbled water on her face. As soon as she came around, Monster turned to Tate and strummed the first chord on his guitar.

What to say? How to describe the way the three guitars bounced off each other like synchronized catapults as they progressed through their set? The sound escalated to fever pitch as Charlie kept a solid anchor with his kick drum. The backing singers soared like a celestial choir against the backdrop of raw guitar chords. When Monster twanged his strings to make them scream, it was as though his idol, Jimi Hendrix played through him. I was as mesmerized as the audience. It was the first time I'd seen a gig from start to finish.

'And that's about your lot,' Monster said. 'Except for one more song which is called Truth Kills - the A side of our single. You'll be able to buy it on...' he looked at Tate to give him the answer even though he knew the release date. 'When can they get their hands on a copy, Tate?'

Tate smiled warmly at the audience. 'Two days time.'

'Remember to fucking buy it,' Monster said. He was about to start playing but stopped, looked over to where I stood and called me on. 'Before we play the last song, I want you to meet our manager.' Pointing at myself, I looked around, not sure I heard correctly. 'Come out Laura,' Monster shouted. Max, Tate, Charlie and the backing singers clapped me on. The crowd joined in chanting LAURA. I walked over to Monster, nearly sliding on a pair of panties because the stage was littered with them. 'This woman believed in us when no other mother fucker wanted anything to do with us and singlehandedly steered us to what you're seeing tonight. She's the one who saw the potential in the song we're about to sing.' Monster kissed me on the cheek. 'Thanks from all of us.' He nodded for me to say a few words.

Tears welled in my chest. I fought them down before they reached my eyes, a dozen replies flashed through my head before the one that felt right forged through. I put my mouth to Monster's microphone. 'All I would like to say, apart from that Streetcrash are awesomely talented.' I raised my arms. The audience whooped in agreement. 'Is that if you believe in something, don't give up on your dream until you get there.'

The audience applauded. 'WOO HOO.'

Monster winked at me. 'Well said.'

219

# THIRTY-SIX

As the taxi rushed towards Julie's restaurant in Holland Park, I felt sick with nerves because I hadn't seen Robert since the night I trapped his dick between my legs. Every time I spotted a girl stomp along the pavement, I saw myself through his eyes, a backstreet girl who didn't know the difference between a glass of plonk or expensive wine. When we passed record shops, I heard Pizza man's tango music in my head and had visions of when I nearly sucked Robert's lips. Every time the taxi passed a phone box, I saw my backside pressed against the door, fighting off an outraged man I lied to about a murder then slamming down the phone on Robert amidst swearing and thumps.

I straightened my shoulders and concentrated on being Hedy Lamarr. Since Bob mentioned her name, I read up and wanted to model myself on her description, 'a ravishing understated beauty.'

My red crepe Biba jumpsuit and matching jacket with a single black button on the front, was accompanied by black suede high heels with bows at the back. To me that summed up ravishing. To comply with 'understated' I left my hair down to tumble naturally over my shoulders. As a fashionista, my outfit, with matching makeup, deserved to be in Vogue magazine. Spoiling the image was a cold sore the size of a fat marrow pea which sat on my lip like a crusty dead wasp.

When the taxi dropped me at Julie's my excitement was so mixed with nerves, I gave myself a breathing session and must have really got carried away because a passerby asked if I needed assistance. I waved her off explaining Streetcrash went straight into the charts at 17 and we were having a celebration lunch but I had a bad stomach and was trying to settle it. Instead of going straight in, I peered through the window to see who was at the bar and spotted Robert. As though he sensed my presence, he caught my eye and smiled.

My reflex reaction was to duck. Pretending I dropped something, I stood up again and waved my purse which made Robert laugh. As if that wasn't enough, when I plucked up courage to go in, I tripped over the step and would have knocked the man in front on me flying, if I hadn't caught his trouser leg in time. I apologized by whispering I needed new glasses and crouched behind a woman wondering why Robert brought out such strange behavior in me.

Monster sat at the corner of the bar talking to Keith Richards, (the musician he most wanted to bump into again), so I guessed he was on cloud nine. They could have been twins since they both wore black T shirts, black bandanas and had similar unruly hair. Monster spotted me and winked. I straightened up, concentrated on gliding and continued smiling at Monster even though he'd gone back to his conversation with Keith.

I was vaguely aware of high-pitched Sunday lunchtime chatter, the guffaws, laughter, the sound of champagne corks popping, the smell of cigars, pipe tobacco and the scent of Chanel No. 5 that a nearby woman wore. Only at the last second when I couldn't go a step further without bumping into Robert, did I dare to look up. All sounds faded. My confusion was such I didn't know whether to shriek or wag my tail.

Robert stepped forward and kissed my cheek. 'Congratulations.'

With one hand covering my cold sore, I nodded like a twat and would have kept going if Robert didn't turn to the man he'd been talking to. 'Mick, this is Laura, Streetcrash's manager.'

I did a double take, my eyes widened as Mick Jagger swung around on his stool. Grinning his trademark boyish cheeky grin, as charismatic in real life as he was on stage, he extended a hand for me to shake. In my mind I saw him chicken strut across stage, feet moving to a crazy samba-cha cha rhythm, the midair splits, his sensual rubber lips. Before I changed my ways, Mick was number two on my must shag list, I was awe smitten. 'Good job,' he said.

'Coming from you that's the highest compliment anyone could get.' I let go of Mick's hand before I shook off his wrist and cringed with more embarrassment than when I snatched Aretha Franklyn's banana.

Mick brushed off my compliment with a shrug. 'Anyone who makes it in the music business deserves success.'

Keeping my cold sore covered so Mick wouldn't remember it, I told him I owned every one of their records and hoped they never broke up like the Beatles. It was a pathetic thing to say but having Mick and Robert to deal with in one dose, knocked me off balance.

Laughing, Robert rested his hand on my back. 'Seems Laura's a fan of yours.' He stroked me with the lightest touch. I sensed there was more to it but what did I know in my confused state?

'Me and that fart over there,' Mick nodded at Keith. 'Are in for the long run assuming he manages to live through his excesses.'

'Excuse me Mr. Bauman,' a waiter in a bow tie said, interrupting our conversation. 'Nearly everyone else is waiting at the table downstairs. Would you like to join them now or…'

'We'll join them.' Robert patted Mick on the shoulder. 'Good to see you, Mick.'

'Likewise,' Mick grinned and stood up. 'Better see if I can drag Keith away from his meaning of life conversation, before he drinks the bar dry.'

Robert waved at Monster to get his attention. 'We're going downstairs.

'Be there in a mo.' Monster laughed his head off at something Keith said.

Robert took my arm. He looked so sweepingly elegant in his pale grey suit and grey cotton shirt, I felt proud to be at his side. 'Shall we?' he said, and lead me down the staircase.

Downstairs had a different feel to the bar. There was a honeycomb of dimly lit alcoves that looked like mini Victorian parlours with assorted antique lampshades, a mishmash of furniture in dark oak and overstuffed leather armchairs where people enjoyed pre-lunch nibbles. 'To your liking?' Robert asked as he watched me suck it all in. 'It's considered the *in place* for people in the music industry.'

'I can see why,' I said, correcting my stomp as Robert escorted me down a hall which had a labyrinth of dining rooms. The first one reminded me of a masonic funeral temple because of its gothic windows and mosaic tiled floor. I couldn't see into some of the other private dining rooms because the doors were closed.

'This is ours,' Robert said. He stopped at an airy conservatory feel dining room with intricately patterned church windows. I took in the faces sitting around the oval table as Robert pulled out a chair and I sat down. Everyone other than Debs (who sat opposite me and smiled), were engaged in an activity or chatted.

Robert bent over and whispered in my ear. 'Just need to make a quick phone call. Back in a jiff.' He went off leaving me with the hint of peppermint from his breath.

Debs put a hand around her mouth. 'I feel like a celebrity. Isn't this restaurant swish?'

I nodded, wanting to tell her I'd met Mick Jagger but decided to save it for later when we were back at the flat. Dave (Debs fiancé) chatted to Tate, next to whom was a girl I guessed was Kate. She was exactly as I imagined. Shoulder length fringed brown hair, simply dressed in a cotton dress and with the look of a wholesome farm girl who collected fresh eggs for breakfast. On my side of the table to the right, was an empty chair where Monster would sit when he came down. The chair next to that was occupied by Charlie who made a fleet of boats out of linen napkins. Next to him was Charlotte, her lips bunched together as she copied him with hers.

'Love your outfit,' Debs said. 'And your hair.'

'Love yours too,' I said, meaning every word. Dave bought her a velvet boho dress with puffed sleeves from Portobello market and since her hair had grown, she'd pinned it with a velvet rose. 'Everything alright with Dave?' I mouthed, because I'd seen neither for days.

'We're more in love than ever.' Debs rubbed her shoulder against Dave's, who stopped talking to Tate, kissed her on the nose and went back to his conversation.

Debs nodded at the empty chair on my left where Robert would sit when he came back. 'He looks right for you,' she whispered.

The hint of sandalwood told me Robert was close. 'Monster's sitting at the Stones dining table having a chat,' he said, and sat down in the chair next to mine.

'I think Monster's more excited at seeing Keith than having Truth Kills in the charts.' I laughed. 'We'd better order without him. He could be hours.'

Using his hand to express agreement, as Robert said 'Good thinking', he knocked over his water glass. It toppled on its side then crashed against the starched white tablecloth. 'I've done that twice this week.' Robert wiped his fingers with a napkin as the waiter mopped up water blobs. Seeing how unperturbed he was by his clumsiness, made me understand something important. Even if I was clumsy and not as ladylike as I wished, Robert never made me feel stupid. It was only me making me feel inadequate.

'I know that look in your eyes,' Robert said. 'Where have your thoughts taken you – hopefully not back to the holidaymaker you whiplashed because he wouldn't lick your ice cream?'

Laughing, I kicked his shoe. 'I guess I'd better get used to being teased by you, but no, I wasn't thinking of the holidaymaker, I wanted to thank you.'

'Thank me?' His eyes were pure bright grey as he smiled the smile guaranteed to light up any room he graced.

'For taking a chance on Streetcrash. And taking a chance on me.'

'You, beautiful lady, have a bright future ahead – and according to that piece I read in the Glasgow Music News, your first tour didn't faze you in the least.' He pressed his finger over his lips to stifle a laugh. 'I believe you said it was all song, dance and laughter?'

I held my hands to the sides of my head to depict someone trying to keep their brain from spilling out of their ears. 'You and I both know the tour was so *not* like that depicted in Summer Holidays.' Robert bit his lip trying not to laugh. 'What did I know?' I said. 'I'm glad their next tour isn't until Spring so I can get my strength back!'

Robert giggled like a girl. The sound was so real I wanted to make him giggle like that every day. He dabbed a tear in his eyes. 'In the process, did you find out who you are? I remember that was your goal last time we spoke.' Turning to face me, Robert rested his elbow on the table, propped his chin up with his thumb and gazed into my eyes.

My hand instinctively flew to my mouth to cover the cold sore. Robert tapped it away. I let it drop to my lap. 'Sort of,' I said. 'An hour ago, I was worried sick about you seeing that monstrosity and now I'm uncomfortably coming to terms with it.'

'You're beautiful, Laura.' Robert tickled my cold sore. 'I hadn't even noticed until you started doing strange things with your hands.' He patted my thigh. 'I meant at a deeper level.'

I thought about it. I wanted to be honest. 'Due to my mum, I was left with a lot of emotional debris. I can't explain why, but living with Monster and Charlie helped a lot. They were so infuriating, frustrating and exasperating, they brought out all the pent up feelings I carried from my childhood. I almost feel exorcised,' I laughed.

'While you were away, I also made progress.' Robert smiled. 'So, what I wanted to ask was...'

Whatever he wanted to ask was left there because Charlotte, who'd proudly added her boat to Charlie's fleet, noticed me.

'Laura, Laura,' she screamed. Running at me like a wild baby bear, she tugged at my trouser leg as if she had a hundred thoughts but didn't know which one to share. Still tugging, she pointed to her red dungarees. 'Look we're both like twins again except you're wearing black shoes and I'm wearing blue ones.'

'We're just like twins,' I laughed, as without asking, Charlotte wiggled in front of me and scrambled onto my knee forcing me closer to Robert so our bodies touched. 'I've got a *big* secret to tell you,' Charlotte whispered, glancing at Robert.

'You know who that is don't you?' I said to her.

Charlotte shook her head. 'No.'

'His name is Robert Bauman, he's the man who helped to make Streetcrash and your daddy famous.'

Charlotte looked shyly at Robert then back at me. 'Does he like Everyone's a you know what?'

Robert laughed. 'I love it.' He looked at me for confirmation of who Charlotte was.

'Tate's daughter,' I said, stroking Charlotte's ringlets.

Charlotte looked around as though there might be a secret spy lurking in the room then cupped her hand around my ear. 'We're having another happy accident.'

'That's fantastic news.' I looked across at Tate and Kate who watched us and had obviously guessed what Charlotte said, since they smiled.

'It was confirmed yesterday.' Tate put his arm round Kate's shoulder then looked at Charlotte. 'Want to come and choose what you want for lunch Lotte, or shall I choose?'

Charlotte shook her ringlets at Tate. 'I have to go to make sure they don't put any green things – except peas - on my plate, Laura.' She jumped off my knee and raced off.

I looked around the table with love in my heart. Debs was happier than I'd ever seen her. Monster's momentum returned to his dick in Glasgow so he was OK. Charlie was a mad hatter who took things as they came so he'd always be fine. My mind drifted to Mr. Krakowski and Robert's foster mother. A meeting had been arranged for the following week and if Mrs. Pluckrose could overcome her bias of foreigners, perhaps they would share cuddles on cold nights.

Robert slid his arm discreetly around my back and stroked my spine. 'So, back to what I wanted to ask. What are your plans for Christmas?'

'Haven't made any,' I shrugged.

'I know a hotel in Acapulco that has bungalows set in a mountain – each one has a private swimming pool so it's a great place to relax.'

My heart skipped a beat. *I knew he was inviting me but what if it all went pear shaped?'* I swallowed. I'd bribed him, nearly sucked his lips, trapped his dick and shown him every facet of the strange woman I was. 'Sounds very relaxing,' I smiled.

'On arrival,' Robert said, 'there's a very nice touch. The hotel issues guests with pink and white candy-striped jeeps.'

'Ah, but do they issue guests with lock proof pyjamas because I don't want you moaning all night,' I joked.

'I didn't ask.' Robert found my hand under the table and held it. It felt comfortable.